The Epic Of Ryn

I: The Arvaita Emerges

S.L. BURKHART

T0204675

ISBN: 978-1-68524-664-8
Editing contribution by Eric Holmes
Cover Art by Richard Birdsong

DEDICATION

This work is dedicated to our God in Heaven, out of Whom comes the Holy Spirit, the Great Wind, that spoke to me as a child and changed the course of my life forever.

CONTENTS

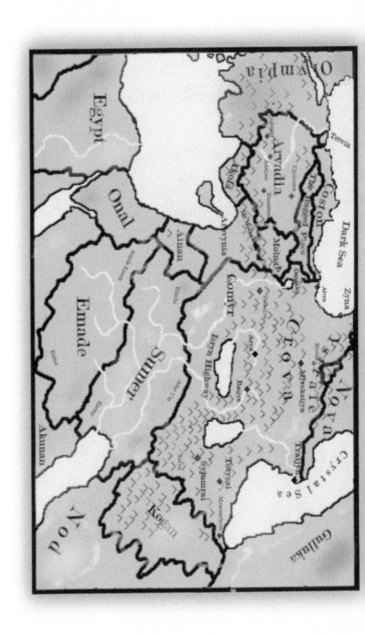

The one he'd been in service to until just a few weeks ago, until the day he'd been released to attend to his father's house. Now it seemed irrelevant. Still, he thought about that man. Could that man, all that he was, all that he is, with the Wind at his back, do anything for the world now? Or would it continue to be like a beautiful field of wheat left to be slowly burned by a raging fire that knew no value other than domination? He hoped, no, he prayed, he would see him again and that the world would be a different place than where it seemed destined to go.

Turning the horse around, he kicked it and raced on westward, towards the hills and to the mountains.□

*   *   *

The cool and crisp air of the night began fading, along with the mist. In its place came the vibrant movement and stimulus of the new day. As the mist receded and the landscape got its effervescent glow that pushed back the darkness, the eater of innovation and strength. High on the slope of a golden field mountainside, soldiers were up—their powerful forms preparing for the day's journey. A somber intent was in each of their feline eyes.

Behind them was a strongly built manor of log and mud, made of humble pieces, fused tightly by an unseen magnetism. The auburn colored wood stacked perfectly and symmetrically into a square structure, alluding to the character of the beings of the land. They glanced at the building as they finished preparations. It was near time, but they did not think to approach those within. There was no need. They knew--the King and Queen.

In the single upstairs room, soft but heavy footsteps moved back and forth across the building's cedarwood floor; light like a butterfly but heavy like a mountain. A powerful entity, whose presence commanded the attention of all matter around it, was within. He moved from spot to spot like a smoothly shifting boulder. The flow of energy in the air ran through him, pulsating to the beating of his heart. The cabin's organic wooden walls vibrated with every splash of life that emanated from his pounding veins.

He was an imposing figure, standing about six cubits high. His dark hair medium hair was thrown back. He had olive-yellow skin and a trimmed dark beard. His stance was strong, and the rawhide pants and jacket over his body seemed to be a formality as his presence exuded to fill the whole space.

He took a deep breath and seized the wind. As he inhaled, all substance came to him, and the walls contracted around him with creaks and moans, bending the moist wood to the point of cracking. Then as soon as he had wrought the walls full of tension, he exhaled, and the wood bounced back into place. He was a master of *ryajakapai* or *windscaping*, even more so than most of his kind. He could feel the wood on the tip of his fingers as though they were in his hands.

Despite the surge of power at his fingertips, he was sad and humble in fear of some anxious event far off. In the air hung the winds of battle and the odor of doom. The stench of their enemy filled the air with its spirit. Every man, woman, and child could see the teeth of savage souls tearing apart flesh every time they closed their eyes. The foul odor permeated every soul as it saturated everything. The land was repulsed

5

by it. Every rock and tree, every blade of grass, cried for him and his kind to alleviate it of that rotten aura.

"Ryn," he heard the land cry, "where are the stewards going?"

They had been welcomed there. Long ago, when his ancestors settled the land, it welcomed them everywhere they went. They took it captive and made it their own, watching over it, and by their will and their might, they pushed back against the forces of those who did evil. They pushed back with the strength of their own hand and fused with the power of the Wind.

He looked down at his hands. He was no coward, and he did not concede. He was not a reed swaying in the wind, but a tree that did not move, ever channeling the force of life. He clenched his hands and curled his panther-like claws. He was a Crovan. They were powerful and noble. Many said they were the most powerful race, right behind the dragons.

He saw the Empire, grand as it was, as high as it was, seem to fall through his fingers like sand. He remembered the armies, the ranks of men marching, and charging in unison. They were like masters, all of them. Wherever they tread, the earth feared them. Now, where had they come? What could he do?

Looking to the side, he extended his spirit. He felt. Reaching out and touching the wind, he tried to read it; tried to understand it. Before he was made king, back when he was a monk, he learned to listen and understand first. He acted second. With all the plans of the generals spoiled, there was no more council. There was no more grand army. There was only what was left.

Sighing deeply, he remembered where he came

from and how it shaped who he was. Devoted, spiritual, disciplined, and high-minded. He was skilled in combat yet devoted to enlightenment and the way of love and life. It was the way of the Source. They were not the holy men of the gods. But were people of the Source. They did things differently than the gods. They rejected the gods. Some said that was their undoing. That was why they were where they were. How could he think that, though?

Their enemy of the last 50 years was the epitome of the order of the gods. It was one of the gods, a proud god. Crovans rejected the gods, just as their national father had. The holy men of the gods had their divination. To pull their answers and power from the forces that resided in the darkness; in the mist. The Crovans had the Great Wind. The Wind was life and light; to be without it was to be dead. It was the very force behind all space, all substance, and all things living. The Great Wind was the very breath of the Source, filling all creation. All wind came from the Great Wind, and it was sacred. That sacredness was who they were as a people.

He was still listening. A good monk listened long, and as the time drew nearer and nearer, he felt the insatiable desire to hear deeper. Anything at all would be satisfactory. Was there an answer in the Wind regarding the battle today? He'd prayed. Oh, how he had prayed. But all he heard, again and again, was what to do, not how it would turn out.

It was the barrier. The separation that every holy man had admitted. Oh, how the holy men of his people had studied it, how they longed to break through it. Whole lives were devoted to it, devoted to the quest, in the teachings of Ano, the great prophet.

*   *   *

She rose with a gasp. Not too strongly, he would sense it and worry. Cold sweat was on her brow. She wiped it. She saw it again. No matter how many times she prayed, no matter how many times she was asked to dream again, it did not change. It was the same every time. She stood slowly. There was no denying it now, and they were out of time. With soft and steadfast steps, she made her way upstairs.

Ryn felt the land cry out to him. Oh, how he wished he had guidance at this moment. Still nothing. What was it? Was it that he was not able to hear? Was he not good enough yet? Just like he'd feared he'd not been good enough these past 50 years? Was that really it? Or was it that he simply did not like the answer? He heard her coming.

Ryn's pacing ceased as he sensed her presence and smelt her fragrance whisk by his nostrils on its way out the window. He loved her scent, and he could feel her tenderness and love approach him. He quickly began to soak up as much as he could, for there seemed no better remedy to his anxiety. When he turned to her, the warmth coming off her spirit overcame him. It guided him to her image as a beacon guides weary travelers to rest.

Though he had seen her a thousand times, he was shocked at her beauty still. She was his closest friend and confidant in all times of trouble. Juya, daughter of Yoshyr, stood just over four and a half cubits, about a cubit shorter than Ryn. She was unusually strong physically and had a firm frame but with delicate and crafted beauty. She had dark hair with auburn highlights streaking through it. She wore it in a long fishtail that kept her hair from interfering with day-to-day activities. For the unusual life of one such as Juya, these activities had always included combat. Her bangs stretched down just past her ears, were parted in the front, and a bright yellow. Crovans could always tell the sex of one another from the color of their bangs. Women were born with yellow bangs, while men were born with red ones. It had been that way from the beginning, told in a powerful tale about their national father and how he'd received the Great Wind by a touch on the forehead.

Juya was dressed for combat. She had a long leather vest, the front of which was covered in hundreds of small square iron plates and strung with beads and leather ties. Her similarly armored skirt ended about her knees where her shin guards began. Upon each arm was an armguard and all her armor bore runes so she could spiritually empower it, lest they serve to protect little more than a dead leaf can guard a tree from the ax. A dagger was on her hip, and a quiver of arrows was strapped onto her back. Her bow was slung over her right shoulder. Her skin was a bright yellow apricot, more gold, and bolder than that of most Crovans.

She approached him slowly. Her eyes were externally cold and calculating, but with a window into her soul only he had. As always, she was an open door for him and him alone. She graciously stopped in front of him and spoke with concern on her voice, "do you doubt this?"

She was asking him? That was unusual; she was the one gifted with dreams. She had always been the one to see the conclusion if there was one to see. What coming from a long way away.

The thoughts of earlier suddenly clouded him again. Were they good enough? Was this the reason they had fallen? Was all the praise and comparison within his own people like comparing hand shovels to ox plows? Were they just that much inferior as if this whole quest to reconcile with the Wind was so difficult it had stifled them and made them weak compared to their heartier neighbors? Something in him struck back with passion against that. Not only did it not matter, but there was no way that was true. They had bested foe and after foe, endured so much internal and external strife to create the empire they had. No one else had also created almost a century of peace by the sheer fear of their force. And on top of all of that, reconciliation and the Great Wind were who they were. If you took that out, they were no longer Crovan. They no longer had the heart of their national leader.

It didn't matter who was left, ten million, or ten hundred. He would be there for his people, and he would be there for her, both then and now. The "now" caught him. Knowing that this would be their last battle, he embraced her and enjoyed her presence for what may be the last time.

She rested in his strength, and her beauty brought harmony to his heart.

Feeling power come from a call to arms deep in his spirit, he spoke with the authority of a lion and the power of a dragon. "Death will befall me before it comes to you."

She felt his power and let it cover her. She sighed deeply, pulled herself away, and looked up at his eyes.

Straightening up, he launched a spirit of defiance

against the enemy and confidently stood before her as king one last time. Juya reached up and tugging on his vest, made it straight and rigid. Nodding her head strongly, she affirmed him and turned around. They descended the stairs with the bold confidence expected of their royalty.

Twelve men and two women mounted on seven *felycars* waited for them at the bottom. With the exception of the two women, who were Juya's, these were the western scouts and village watchmen, pulled by Ryn himself for this encounter. At this point in time, there was not a single Crovan soldier, conscript, or able-bodied person anywhere in their remaining territory other than right there at the battlefront ahead. Ryn mounted the eighth felycar, and Juya climbed up behind him. She reached around him and tightly held him while they began their descent down the mountain.

The mountain was covered in yellow grass, and sparse patches of evergreen trees covered its slope. They rode down the decline at a quickening speed the felycars were good for. Soon they came on a trail and raced along its path.

The smooth and worn trail they rode brought back memories. Ryn still remembered going to the school and monastery to teach a *sasyrat*. He still saw with vivid memories of the monks and monkesses walking the trail up to the school one day from an activity. He closed his eyes; ghosts they were now. An eerie feeling of lostness overcame him. He shook it from his mind.

The trail shot the riders out on the east edge of a monotonous country of evergreens, rocks of milky white, and short olive tipped maidaja grass. After ascending one last yellow hill, they saw the wide-open expanse of the Aryn highway, a long stretch of smooth trail, a trade route that shot down the open coast of the Takyn Sea.

Ryn breathed in every bit of the countryside, for he knew he might never see it again. Before him was an enormous smooth maidaja coated decline. It melted out of the rolling hills on his left and glided into the sea on his right. The Takyn Sea stretched east to west almost a hundred alans where its shores hit the rolling cliffs of mountains. To the north, it crashed upon a long sandy beach, while to the south, it pressed against the violent rock and sand of the desert.

Rolling olive-green hills to their left faded north into the Aryn Mountains. To the far west sat the town of Aryn from which they had departed. Over grassy slopes far ahead of them, the two forces were already staring each other down at opposite ends of a grand expanse. Their enemy's innumerable sea of treacherous Nephilian creatures was spread out in front of the entrance to the deep and lush Isryn river valley.

Their enemy had come straight down the Crovan Empire's southern life-line, the Isryn highway, bypassing the Najyn Desert, one, among a number, of harsh terrains that had helped their nation survive this long. The land had helped them greatly. It didn't want anyone else there. It hated their god. It did everything it could to hinder him. Perhaps that was one of the reasons they had held on so long.

To the west, it gave them the Yzke, mountains, and highlands that ran along their western frontier from the Dark Sea's southern coast, all the way down till they wrapped around Aryn, the Takyn Sea, and the Najyn Desert. No army would dare attack even a human nation on the slopes of its very mountains without having certainty in a superior force. They stood proud and protective, charging their stewards with stalwart strength. But their enemy had found their way in. Ryn recollected the events.

Fifty years prior, his vast army exploded into Nova, Crova's sister nation to the north. Crova reacted quickly along with their brothers to the north. But they were stunned. They cut down three for every one of their own, only to face a never-ending sea of armies. That and the gods were very active back then. Every battle they fought, they sought merely to contain them. It was a war they had won in front of them but lost after the numbers were calculated. In hindsight, despite their enemies well trained and equipped professional army at the time, they would have still won had it not been for the gods. They were very difficult to overcome and required dedicated teams to match them or disqualify them from battles. They had built many teams just for that purpose.

Within only several years, they had taken every Novan city. Rather than use the mist to hide warbands, the Novans used much of it to move their people north, to be out of the path of the enemy advance. They did exactly what Ryn expected and soon crashed upon the mountains in the south.

But the plains of Nova were not the mountains and valleys of Crova. The jagged, un-scalable mountains of the Ystrafe, which divided the sister nations, befuddled their progress. His Crovan strategy had been dependent on his western army, which had attacked along the southern coast of the Dark Sea at the exact time he'd attacked Nova. It failed. Ryn still recalled the horror and trembling that befell the first enemy armies as they experienced the Crescendo for the first time. This story would have been duplicated in Nova had it not been for the work of the gods.

After Nova fell, they consolidated the professional army and came again along the coast of the Dark Sea. Again, they were routed, but the gods kept them from being overwhelmed. They pushed on despite heavy losses and moved forward with numbers. Having gained a foothold, they had paved a way to launch another campaign. They took great casualties while still forging ahead. They finally lost their advantage in the wooded foothills of Mokaijyn, where they learned the frustration of fighting the Crovan Gauntlet, a complex rotation of troops networked by spiritual intuition and communication they could never seem to figure out. Olympia was thwarted, and what remained of the Novan forces in the north fell back into northern Crova and helped them fortify.

For thirty-six years thereafter was a stalemate of conquest and re-conquest with occasional times of inactivity. The far better warriors of Crova, blessed by their native land, amassed huge victories over their enemy's greater numbers, but could never muster enough strength to re-conquer Nova or press past the Yzke to the eastern lands of the Arvadian Peninsula. There was then a period of peace and inactivity. At that time, Ryn started to think that his enemy had finally given up. He was wrong.

After a two-year period where no major army moved, he came back with a new method of war. First, he rebuilt his army to the ghastly thing it had become. Then he looked east of Nova and acquired the alliance of the *Gullukans*. This alliance allowed him to march around the Crystal Sea and into Crova's eastern expanse, bypassing the Ystrafe. In the East, the Highlands of Syjomrai proved a softer barrier. They were lands once tainted by wickedness and rebellion; the spirit of the land was not faithful.

Attacking along the fertile coast of the Crystal Sea, he made short work of the highland and lowland defenses in the east. He was rebuffed strongly, but he seemed to have a never-ending supply of monsters in his horde. Their armies were overwhelmed. Within a month, the floodgate had been opened, and Zeus' armies poured into the fertile grasslands and woodlands of Crova's heart. The Empire was suddenly split in two as Zeus drove Crova out of its most fruitful land from the Dark Sea to the Crystal Sea. Most went north, but Ryn stayed south, behind the Aryn Mountains with the thought that the mountains were the greatest ally of those in the north. But those in the south would need him the most.

It was there that Ryn finally felt like they had truly lost something. He also began to look for reasons at the time. All it would have taken was a single threat from Sumer, Egypt, or even Kogana to divide Zeus enough to give them the foothold they needed. The reasons came riling up even now.

"The sheer cowardice of…" he had to stop. It was long past now. They held for three years until his foe recruited the Arovynians to their west. Launching an invasion from Arovynia, he took Comyr, the highlands, then on through the southern frontier along the Najyn Desert to finally access the Isryn Highway. And of course, now they were here.

The Plain of Raijyn was at the inner gate of the Isryn River Valley and was snuggled west of its vast arm of the Aryn Mountains. The river valley was the only access point to the pocket of fertile plains that they now possessed, and Raijyn was the first piece of it. Every able-bodied soul, he'd commanded to make a stand there. If the plains fell, the Takyn Highway fell, and it would be over. Their only hope was the drive the army back into the valley. But he didn't know what he would continue with. He didn't even have enough troops to form teams against the gods anymore. Fortunately, the rest of the pantheon seemed aloof in the south. Still, numbers made their task daunting.

A few days ago, he had a Western Battalion and an Eastern Battalion with a scarcely fortified northern frontier. The Eastern, of course, had most of the seasoned forces due to its position at the River Valley. He'd sent word for his Eastern Battalion to retreat to meet the Western for this battle, but the messenger either never arrived, or General Alaivan had decided to try and hold the valley. Either way, the Eastern Battalion was wiped out, and his numbers were a third what they should have been. But it was too late to ponder such things; this was the time for action.

As they soared down the highway at incredible speeds, Ryn watched the sea to his right in one last moment of mesmerizing thought. Its white sandy shore sunk into the deep and was visible for some way down. The Takyn Sea was crystal clear. Ryn could envision seeing for alans under the clear water. It was truly a blessed land, a faithful land that had loved them, and he was sad for it.

His deep thoughts were soon interrupted. Suddenly the shout of a comrade drew his attention to the road in front of them. Ryn's troops spotted a patrol of several hundred *uressines* approaching them from the northeast. They had no doubt inserted themselves behind the Crovan army to pick off reinforcements that did not have the benefit of protection in numbers. They had dark gray bodies that resembled those of plump men. Their hands and feet were rigged with long talons that were primed for tearing flesh. Their faces were like pigs, and they were less intelligent creatures. Despite this, each one had a wingspan of six to eight cubits and could stand six cubits. Although a single uressine was not possibly a threat to a Crovan, a horde of them was. The diaspora of their kind had planted them everywhere, and they were always ready to be paid mercenaries.

Ryn saw Juya reach her right hand out and open her palm to receive the air ahead of them. He waited on her assessment.

"The aura is strong. They are well armored. But it's a waste to use such equipment on uressines."

Ryn smirked, "That's our enemy's problem."

She gave him the important part, "The aura is interlocking, but a single break in the chain, and I will tear the defense to shreds."

Ryn nodded. "Ride through, attack to break the aura," he ordered his troops.

Tactically speaking, they would do better to circle up, forcing the creatures into favorable melee combat. If the enemy's auras were interlocking, they would find it hard to break through their formation. If they couldn't forge an opening, it would require a sacrificial rider to spearhead the attack to break the aura. Doing such would leave one behind to be encircled by the overwhelming horde. But Ryn could not afford delays. He would have to risk it and blast through them. He had to trust their strength.

Juya took one of three belts cast around her hip and strapped herself to her husband so as to free both arms. She then loaded her bow. She would get, but one shot, only as they approached the envoy, and it would have to be endowed with a significant amount of energy to supersede their great speed sufficiently. To someone who airscaped like Juya, that would be the easy part. The difficult part would be doing enough to make a difference. For that reason, she focused her effort on a single shot. Ryn extended his Yncucyn and prepared to blast his targets with it. The rest of the party braced themselves for the impact and moved into a 'V' formation around Ryn and Juya's felycar. The rider out front was Enraijan, his faithful armor-bearer who was offering himself up as the spearhead.

The uressines formed a tight-knit blob and lowered their altitude in their approach. Whether it was out of fear or strategy was unimportant, but the mob of on-comers approached in close proximity to each other. To do this, they had to come at a mild velocity. This proved to be a tactical error, and Ryn knew it. The whole group was little more than thirty strides high and offered little oncoming force. The catlike felycar could probably bound over the uressines without meeting enough resistance if the pack's aura could be dispersed over the top.

The two parties approached quickly. When the gap closed to about 300 strides, it was time to fire. Juya's arrow sliced through the wind at twice their speed, whistling loudly as she began to form a vacuum ahead of it. The arrow flew straight and powerful, illuminated with warm white runes. As the vacuum took hold of it, it became a blur. Almost evaporating forward, it struck the leading challenger who instantly dropped underneath the parade of his compatriots, tumbling into several more along the way. The aura fell underneath, but it was not the desired effect. They couldn't make a move there.

The second arrow, fired by another to Ryn's left, traveled in an arch and collided with its target, bursting it into flames. The beast drifted upwards and sadly missed the bulk of the horde.

A small throwing hammer was released before the others and at a far slower speed. It began at an angle above the approaching enemy. Well after the other projectiles had hit their targets, it slowed down and seemed to be coming back. But the hammer had been endowed with great heaviness and dropped straight into the middle of the approaching mob, thrusting a larger uressine to its left. Like an out of control leaf fluttering in the wind, the beast soared sporadically into the path of its companions. The result was a tumbling of the entire left rear of the mob.

Juya seized on the opportunity. Before the gap could close, she gripped the air with her hand and brought down a ferocious channel of wind that pushed the Uressines out from the impact point, creating a large gap. The leader did not need to have the gap pointed out for him. He shifted, and the envoy veered into the mob's left-center and bounded just as it arrived. While in the air, they seemed to pass between two dark clouds. The path in the middle drew little resistance. The blades of Crovan weapons tore and scattered the uressines like sand. The immense energy shielding the bounding warriors was not met with nearly enough resistance to stop them, and they went clean through.

When his felycar had softly landed in stride, Ryn turned to see that he had not lost a single rider. Now focused on the dark sky in front of him, Ryn noticed that the air began to teem with energy. Lots of power would be thrown around at the front, and as they approached the last set of hills marking the end of the highway, Ryn could sense the cold hatred of the enemy as a foul odor, perverting their gracious and beautiful land.

2 THE BATTLE OF RAIJYN

The pulses of negative energy began to grow more frequent as they rode into the hills where their army would be lined up. The sky grew darker, and thick storm clouds covered the land. Surely the golden yellow fields of the plain now looked white. Blue and purple flashes of light ascended into the sky from the mountains surrounding the river valley far ahead of them and then descending upon the hills around them.

What they saw were enemy artillery bombardments. Windscapers stood across the battlefield, firing blasts of exclusively negative energy at the Crovan line using their innate ability or the assistance of energy fusing armor or weapons that utilized sutras or runes. The Crovans had numbers of worriers and monks projecting shields over the army to protect the troops from taking pre-engagement casualties. Shielding was the most common and basic pre-battle military technique. Ryn also saw Crovan counter bombardments: balls of fire, lightning, water, and ice, being hurled from the hills across the plains into the valley opening.

The party finally cleared the last hill and found their troops lined up on the slopes looking over the plains. The hills were grassy green, although their color was tainted dark and blue by the sky. As he suspected, the plains below were pale white as opposed to the golden yellow that Ryn remembered. The flat plains stretch out for ten and a half alans before turning into a high cliff strewn mountain range that split wide in the middle with a lush river valley in-between. The river, which was called the Tigris, ran from the mountains of Aryn in the north and wrapped around the massive northern mountain that was part of the gate to the valley. It wound through the valley and eventually ran all the way south through the entire land of Sumer. The horde of monsters that consisted of the enemy army stood out front of it in mass. On top of the cliffs were the windscapers, bombarding from their positions.

From the high cliff that jettisoned out in front of the north gate, to the valley opening, stood the god of this horde. The one who had begun this war in his own pride. The symbol of evil for Crovans and Novans for a whole generation. His name was Zeus, the father of the Olympian pantheon, son of the great dragon of darkness himself. Accompanying him was his intimidation force. It consisted of two enormous dragons and heavily armored *dunataso* from his very blood-line.

The horde of monsters looked about 100,000 strong and consisted of trolls, imps, uressines, ogres, cyclopses, dragons, Gullukans , *Semaltars* , and all sorts of other monstrous and majestic beings from faraway lands that could hardly be described. There was little organization to the enemy ranks; they simply stood in mass. The only pattern Ryn saw was that the larger creatures, such as the giants, the dragons, the ogres, and the trolls, congregated towards the front. The more intelligent of them, the Gullukans and the Semaltars congregated towards the back. They were lightly armored and poorly armed. Most of these creatures did not need any sort of weapon to be a threat; their shear strength and spiritual power made them formidable foes. But the Gullukans and the Semaltars, which were more humanoid in physique, were heavily armored and armed with spears or swords.

The entire enemy army was chanting in unison. It was not an organized, musical, or rhythmic chant. Carnal beings of appetite did not synchronize well. Every two to four seconds, they roared across the field. Their hollers consisted of a conglomerate of high pitch screeches, loud hisses, and thunderous bellows. Every scream was filled with hate and a lust for blood, and the Crovan troops felt every wave of it.

Ryn had certainly been tracking the evolution of Zeus' army from when their engagement began and now. The god's first armies were made of extremely well organized and equipped Olympians. There were many noble races in his ranks, and they had an illustrious warrior culture that valued the valiant and brave. Ryn recalled capturing many of those early officers and, though disrespecting their allegiance, found them rational and capable of civility. Not so with his later armies. Perhaps the wearing thin of his army had forced him to rely on less noble facets to achieve his goal. As it was now, the noblest of the bunch, such as the Semaltars, were irritated mercenary participants who clung to the army for their several years of service only for gold. Everyone could tell that Zeus' rabble had devolved into a mess of toxic aggression that had forgotten nobility for bloodlust a long time ago.

Ryn dismounted his ride and walked across the ridge of the hills surveying his army. The infantry knelt on the slopes of the hills facing the field. The line stretched about 300 strides spread across two hills that ascended into each other. The line of infantry was about three persons deep and appeared to be around 1200 strong. Behind them were the archers, spread out evenly. They stood about three to four strides apart and numbered around two hundred. Behind them on the hill's ridges overlooking the battlefield, around one hundred fifty monks and monkesses returned bombardments of energy at the enemy lines. Out in front of the infantry stood thirty-five monks and about twenty-five monkesses, projecting the shield that warded off the bombardments of the enemy. The shield was only visible when an enemy projection collided with it and spread out across its surface, but it arced over the Crovan line. It went from the front to the back and stopped just above them, so bombardments could be unleashed from behind it over the top. Ryn took notice that over half of the infantry were women and entirely composed the line of archers. The men in the ranks of infantry were scattered throughout the front two lines of the three.

As Ryn approached, the hill's eyes began to watch him. General Calvyn came running up to Ryn, stern and professional. Calvyn was a shorter and fuller man than Ryn physically. He had puffy cheeks and a wider body frame that made him look tender and gentle, but his spiritual presence was authoritative and strong. Calvyn added a presence of structure to a place. He made things organized and demanded respect in that manner.

"*Kyfka*," he said. "I am glad you are here, unharmed."

Turning to Juya, he bowed shortly, "My lady, it is my pleasure to serve you." The three turned to the line and began walking together in discussion.

Calvyn's face was expressionless, and began relating the conditions of the battle thus far. "Kyfka, this is a very untested group. Every able-bodied adult from the cities and the heights is here. Most of the soldiers are women. Too many have soft nerves and little combat experience. There is an unusual amount of fear in the ranks. Not only this, but the spirit of the men is low. As you can imagine, a sense of failure is upon them for not being able to protect our sisters. Indeed, there are the young women who have been conscripted for a while, but there are others that have, until this point, served mainly in minor combat roles. They should not have been made to do so, and should have left this place long ago."

He spoke of things wished, not things as they should be done. He knew very well that for their beloved sisters, death on the battlefield was a grace compared to capture. "I understand, of course, at this point, we shall need anyone who can use a weapon. Only the children, weak, and elderly remain in Raijyn—we fight for them. They all know about the fate of Alaivan's battalion. How not a soul survived, how they were surrounded, and given no quarter.

Most feel the battle is hopeless. If there were any place to go, we might even see desertion."

Ryn looked at the faces of his brothers and sisters. Each one lowered their eyes in respect but made no motion of pride or valor. Indeed, Calvyn was right; the spirit among them was desperately low. There were no cheers and no joyous shouts as the king and queen arrived. His heart sinking, the king began to think desperately about how he could shift their fighting spirit. Finding their eyes, he saw that in the expressions of his experienced troops was gratitude that their king had not abandoned them. On the faces of the less experienced was the awe of being in his presence and the chill of battle.

"It pains me," Calvyn said softly in private. "A young girl among the archers, Adaira, no more than thirty, was terrified when they began chanting. She became ill and vomited—she tried to leave when an older woman—one of the few who was a state soldier, Kostnara, the one with a scar over her face, told her to stop. 'Let me go,' the girl said. I see my death." Calvyn's eyes showed a welling of emotion though his face was hard, displaying familiar Crovan sentiment. "The elder grabbed her and shook her, 'if you leave, your death will be gruesome,' she said. 'You can die by the blade, or by rape and devour.' The girl sat and sobbed, then suddenly stopped, realizing how she was hurting the others, she said weakly, 'I choose the blade.'" The general nearly wept, not making a scene, but his heart broke in front of the king, and the king's broke with it.

Calvyn stopped and directed their attention to the battlefield. "You must rally the troops, Kyfka," he said with unusual emotion. "I know as well as you that this may well be the end for all of us, but only your inspiration can make it such an end." Calvyn's lip quivered, and he had to bring his gaze to the ground to control himself. His look was that of a man who'd allowed war to harden him, only to wake up and re-grasp his heart, knowing the end was likely near.

As Ryn saw the horde across from them, he began to tap fully into the spirit of his people. Desperately tired of fighting, tired of losing, tired of watching family and friends butchered, they were at the end. Even Calvyn was sunk in despair as they lined up against the monstrous army.

Ryn glanced over at Juya and saw her wipe tears away from her eyes. Lowering her eyes, she tried to keep her feelings from the view of the troops. Watching the line closely, the king remembered every battle he had fought. He had not been a spectator; he had nearly fought every battle. He had known for a long time that this one might be his last. There were numerous battles in the empire's existence where Crovans overcame adversaries that outnumbered them ten or twenty to one, but this force outsized them fifty-to-one. Ryn looked at the faces of his brethren, who stared down the field in a daze. Everyone knew that this battle was lost, and even their best warriors stared silently at the overwhelming opponent, many of them gleaning the glassy-eyed expression of one destined for the afterlife.

He left Calvyn and Juya and began to make his way across the line. As he did, he met with the eyes of his brothers and sisters. He saw intense anger suppressed by a feeling of powerlessness. Some seemed in a trance, simply staring across the field at the massive opponent, while many began to follow the three leaders with their eyes, hoping that Ryn, the mightiest warrior king they had ever known, could lift them out of despair and give them hope. Ryn passed along the front of the line, where most of the men congregated. He moved from one to the other and locked eyes with them. Everyone in the front was a veteran warrior, and Ryn was glad to see their brazen and un-intimidated expressions form as he passed by them.

He came about a third of the way down the line and came to a thin and delicate looking young woman staring straight ahead in the front. Her hair was black with several thin braids in it, and her skin was paler than most Crovans. Though she had the catlike Crovan ears, she had a button dog-like nose characteristic of Novans. Her top was a brown leather vest adorned with beads and ribbons. She had arm and wrist bracelets on both arms and wore a long brown, beaded skirt. The colorful adornments and the spiritual aura coming from her made Ryn sure that she was the daughter of a banker or some other wealthy man. Her delicate skin showed little sun ware, and he could see that she was afraid. In her right hand, she held an Yncucyn, and though Ryn could tell she was well trained by how her spirit encompassed the weapon, the hand holding it was trembling.

She stared down the field with a frightful open-eyed expression, and when Ryn approached her, she did not return his gaze. So Ryn came to her and stopped. He stared into her bright green eyes, waiting for her gaze. Ryn wanted to look her straight in the eyes. The eyes would reveal much about her soul. It was not common for men and women to lock eyes if they were not related or wed, but Ryn had his reasons.

It would be unwise to have her in the front if she was unable to charge aggressively or offer front-line support. If the men were to spread amongst the women, then invariably, some women would be in front, but there must have been a reason the men let her, in particular, stay where she was, and he wanted to know it.

She knew that he was staring at her, but she feared to look back at him. It soon became apparent that she was more afraid of the king's gaze than fighting. She did not want him to find the fear inside her, the untested skills she had, for she was unfamiliar with combat, and he would see that. She feared he would remove her from the front where she wanted to be. The king stared back at her intently without changing his expression. He said nothing, and neither did anyone else. She realized that he was going to see her soul sooner or later, so she closed her eyes and redirected her gaze below his face and then opened them to ascend her gaze to his slowly.

When Ryn saw her eyes, he knew who she was. This woman was young, maybe forty or fifty, and in her, he saw the spirit of her father and mother. Her father, he recognized instantly as the long celebrated and successful general Raikan. Raikan was indeed wealthy, but his entire estate was obliterated when the invasion came into the east and took Kogybyrn. Ryn was unaware that anyone had lived. Raikan was dead now, a casualty of the war, but somehow one of his daughters found her way out of death. It could be assumed that she had avoided fighting for some time due to her greenness. She was here now at the last battle, and inside her, Ryn saw a burning spirit that desperately longed to battle valiantly in retribution for all the battles she had fearfully avoided. Her face stared right back at his, and eventually, she stopped trembling, and her posture straightened up.

Gauging her battle-worthiness, he saw that her spirit was strong, and most importantly, she had the gift of the White Flame. No doubt passed down from her father, he saw it inside her, ready to burn at disintegrating temperature. It bolstered her value as a warrior and made her unusually comparable to some of the male warriors around her. Being a special case, perhaps like Juya, he had no fear of letting her occupy the front line. She would no doubt be slower than those around her, but alongside aggressive and seasoned warriors, she would be good support. He was pleased with her.

He lowered his eyes for a second in an unimaginable gesture of respect and then returned to the rest of the troops. Alyra was the woman's name, and she stared across the field in shock, utterly amazed that the king had seen in her what she saw in herself. As queen Juya passed her, she saw the general give her the slightest of nods. Alyra intensified her gaze as encouragement and affirmation came from soldiers around her. Her hand steadied and wrapped itself tensely around the hilt of her weapon.

Ryn steadily continued down the line until he came to another young warrior. This young man's name was Eljaryn, and he was renowned throughout the army as being extremely fast in a sprint and very quick in combat. He would instantly appear from angle to angle in a fight as though he need only think he was there, and he was. The young man had trimmed golden brown hair and light bronze skin. His smooth face and gray eyes stared down the field without expression but soon lifted with pride and courage as Ryn met his gaze. The young man thankfully bowed his eyes in respect. They'd done many battles together.

Ryn looked back at his army and into every face. Every eye was now trained on him. Not even the most fearful of them looked elsewhere. The archers stood still and silent in the back, and even the monks and monkesses behind them bombarding the enemy stopped to listen to him. Only those in front, projecting the massive shield, still labored. The rest of them, including the infantry still kneeling in their ranks, focused their eyes on the king, waiting desperately for his powerful leadership to inspire them.

Queen Juya, standing silently next to him, was just as inspiring. She was a symbol of beauty, and all that was good about the nation. What came to mind was everything that was worth saving in their people. Her symbol was different now, having become the nation's first warrior Queen. Perhaps telling Crovan's their beauty was like a rose, gorgeous but with thorns, much like Juya's namesake. Having her there, as always, bolstered the confidence of the women in the ranks, letting them know that this was a task they could do. She had always had the effect of helping the men accept the help of the woman as well. Rather than see their assistance as their failure, they could look at her competence at combat and feel comfortable in fighting side by side when necessary.

Ryn humbly closed his eyes and lowered his head, then resigned himself to his knees and clenched his fists at his stomach and prepared to pray for their victory. They all did the same. In the face of such a trial, he found it hard to muster the faith to believe a victory was on the horizon, but Ryn began where he was at, not where he should have been. He started in his humility, in the hope he'd rally his faith and courage as he prayed. He lifted up his strife and his fear. In a voice searching for strength, he prayed fervently.

"Teoti, my master, our father... I do not understand why this is happening to us. I know that my kin are sons and daughters of heaven's black holes, but we have always glorified you as a nation. I humbly come before you, not knowing your plans, but in my limited understanding, I request our victory today. I do not want to die. Please forgive my forefathers and even myself for all of our wickedness. For all that we have done, we lament and stand before you as subjects of your desire. Ymaiyel abañad, Saiyan ala ja."

That phrase was the embodiment of the Crovan warrior. It meant, even unto death, I stand for you. And that was it. Ryn stood from his prayer and turned his gaze towards the heavens. He waited until he sensed that every Crovan had risen to his feet and had finished his prayer with that powerful promise on their lips. Then he brought his face back down to the troops, gave them a quick look, and then turned to look at the enemy.

He abandoned the outcome for his identity as a child of the Wind. As he did, he felt the surge of strength release from within him. He stared expressionless across the field until his face finally turned to peace, then confidently looked thoughtfully back at his army. No circumstance could change who he was, and who he was, was what mattered.

The air became intense, and his spirit sang a war song they could hear in the back of their minds. His aura told them they were invincible. The identity of a child of the Wind and a warrior of the Crovan nation was felt purely in those moments. Win or lose, live or die, forgotten or remembered, fight anyway.

The waves of cold energy had been colliding with his troops like a cold wind—one that penetrated the skin. But it now felt deflected, as though he'd put on a cloak. With eyes closed, he began to sing a slow yet powerful Crovan hymn called *Mayaje Tantajai Yantaj Aya*. He began it but soon the officers, and then the men, and finally the women, began to sing as well. It was a song of Teoti and how all darkness was chaffe before his might. Sung many times as a battle hymn, it was often chanted toward the end of a battle when it was obvious Crova was going to win. In the hearts of the opponents, it was heard as the dirge for their own funerals. Never had it failed to crush the last vestiges of resolve in their enemy. Sung now, it sent waves of positive power that doubled down on the enemy with the sense of impending judgment. It was light shattering the exposed darkness.

Ryn stepped out and confidently began to stare down the grassy plain at the cliffs where Zeus stood high above his force. Juya came up behind him and proceeded to calmly pull a short arrow from her quiver and arm it; the weapon meant for signaling rather than combat. The song of the brothers and sisters behind them was elevating. She remembered her unique calling, and her heart went out in front of her, eager to engage the enemy. Filled with passions, she felt very righteous anger towards the evil that resided within the hearts of the enemy, as well as fierce loyalty to those around her.

Looking down, she felt the itch in her hand, like every part of her had come alive for this moment. Though calm and composed, she swelled with a desire for war. She used to ask herself why she was like this. She had stopped. She had just come to terms with the fact that Crova's first warrior Queen was always meant to be someone different than other women. It rarely bothered her anymore. Still, the eagerness was a cause for question because of how it came. War was not noble in her heart; it was a carnal expression of something important. What was important was noble, but what moved her was questionable. The shrill cries for blood carried up and down her spine and ignited a desire to engage the enemy. She had not once backed down from this challenge. It was as if she had become made for this role. She shifted her fierce gaze from the opponent to her husband and back to the opponent again in anticipation of his orders.

The hymn of the Crovan army pounded waves of positive energy across the plains at the enemy and carried with it such an exposing presence the main army was pierced with the sensation of their own weakness and smallness as though a light had caught them and revealed their true might, exposing their deluded self-image. It was the essence of truth. It seemed to carry the spirit of the Source itself, as it ricocheted off of every rock, every crag, and through the air itself. Off the valley walls behind them, it only amplified, and it began to sound as though it were a chorus descending from the heavens.

Ryn stared toward Zeus and over the expanse of alans that separated them. He could sense the Half Star's eyes across even that large an expanse. No ordinary being could meet Zeus' eyes. The god's gaze was something to be feared, and mortal men were so frightful of the power behind his gaze that they would submit without Zeus having to look at them. But Ryn stared back without fear confident and tranquil as if to tell the god that he could do nothing to harm him.

The fearlessness of Ryn was disgusting to Zeus, and it spurred his rage. He hated Ryn. So long as one being in the whole world looked at him like that, he would not rest. Certainly not Ryn, the one who'd resisted crumbling under him and his majesty. It was this idea that he, a god, could not break his spirit, that he despised. Whatever it was that was in Ryn, it had to be stamped out for good. It was Ryn's fault that he'd stalled for over 30 years in his plan to sweep across the cradle of life. Ryn was the reason he'd not entered Egypt and Sumer. Ryn was the reason he could not enter the courts of the gods of the East and demand their allegiance. This one being and his people had been the unending obstacle that defied reality by not going away. He became angrier and angrier, thinking about all that Ryn had cost him. Every failure, every delay; how much had he lost because of this *Touka*?

It would not be enough for Zeus to defeat Ryn in the flesh, no, this Touka had to be taught that Zeus was above him. He had to be beaten spiritually, subjugated, and freed of hope altogether. At this point, he had to. Ryn had to be an example. It had cost him too much.

Zeus knew who he was, and because of Ryn, that had not been known. Who could not respect the sky and thunder god of Olympia? The highest of all the gods, he was. Wiser, more innovative, and superior in every way. He was a sight to behold; his arms and legs were sturdy and hard like pillars of granite. His skin was a glowing golden yellow, and his hair was white like a blue-sky cloud. His facial features were sharp and handsome, and his face shone with a glorious beauty that made him irresistible to mankind. His eyes were cloudy white, and inside they were like great gongs of thunder emanating from somewhere within his powerful being. He did not have to work to subjugate humans, for his physical handsomeness and power were enough to command worship.

All these outward signs of his actual majesty should have let Ryn know who he was and not to defy him. But he did, and at first, it was something he respected but knew he could snuff out. But after so much time, it was something agonizingly frustrating. The fatigue of the other gods had set in, just because of Ryn. He'd lost decades of worship, all because of Ryn. Ryn alone was the reason…

Zeus stopped getting baited into that thought. It was pointless. This struggle was at its end. This was the last of it. He was moments from victory, and he could tell it was going to go quickly as he lined up the battle's possibilities in his mind.

Resting his hands to his sides, Zeus stood expressionless on top of the cliff. He had the look of confidence, a sureness that what was happening was to be expected, and his counteraction was already calculated.

He turned his head towards his windscapers and lifted up his left hand, then formed a tight fist. He clenched it and brought it back down to his side. Olympian bombardments came to a halt. The windscapers, who were spread out on top of twenty or thirty high cliffs, immediately uncovered hundreds of large drums. These drums stood on their sides about nine cubits tall, and their tan skins faced the plain. Etched onto the skins were runes, each one glowing with a purple light.

Ryn knew what these were and snuffed air from his nostrils, beset with calculation. He had hoped Zeus' army would not have enough time to set up such tools for combat, or perhaps that the faithful mountains would stifle their progress or at least their power. But somehow, they had them, and they were prepared. Almost every windscaper was on a drum and held a six to seven cubit staff in their hands. Zeus lifted his left hand up again, and this time snapped his fingers.

The windscapers quickly began pounding the drums. Some frantically and some methodically in hypnotic dance with ritual attached. Each time they did, massive amounts of negative energy poured out from the runes like splashes of water. The dark purple light began to move over the opposing army and move across the field like a toxin. Whatever it overtook became covered in darkness. The drums were struck in no particular melody or in any organized pattern, but randomly all at different times. The resulting sound was a cracking of powerful booms that resounded quickly and without pattern. The purple mist clashed with the positive waves of energy emanating from the hymn over the plains. When a positive wave struck, the mist came to a halt but continued to advance between intervals.

Zeus stood unmoved, staring at Ryn to see what he would do next. He was almost amused to see what strategy this fallen king had for him today. He had matched against Ryn's strategy for thirty years. Unfortunately, Crova rarely had the numbers to route his armies. Thinking without attachment as his victory was nigh, Zeus could admit that the Touka's strategy was impressive and heaped massive damages on his forces. However, Zeus had never organized his army so as to route Crovan forces. His goal was merely to win. To do that, he needed to wipe them out, not push them back. Pulling them back into the meat grinder in the feign effort to save their 'homeland' was what he'd used for that. Thus, his strategy was simply to make his army fight and keep a constant flood of troops engaged with his opponents. Besides, he liked being dealt casualties. Long experienced soldiers made poor subjects who had either too much pride, war-weariness, a bland taste for blood, or even an uncontrollable passion for having gorged themselves on it. Thus, he preferred a high turnover rate in his armies.

Ryn faced the plains, but his eyes looked back at Zeus. Zeus' surprise weapons could be easily extinguished, but it meant that his troops would now have to expend extra energy and resources. He also knew that this would prompt the central engagement. Though optimistic, Ryn knew inside that they would need nothing less than a miracle to win now.

The king tilted his head towards Juya and calmly signaled for a full bombardment, including archers. Juya touched her arrow so that it glowed brown for full bombardment and shot it high into the air out in front of them. The monks in the back intensified their bombardments, and the monks in front of the line projecting their shields stopped and began unloading bombardments as well. The archers also began firing waves of glowing arrows across the plains.

This move did not surprise Zeus, for it was one of Ryn's possible counters. But this particular counter meant that Zeus would have to respond in a frontal assault, as Ryn was probably expecting him to. Zeus was unsure why Ryn wanted to meet them head-on so outnumbered, and for a moment, he wondered what Ryn could have up his sleeve. But it concerned him little. This last sniveling batch of Crovans would fall the same way so many had before them. Besides, the faster the battle was over, the sooner he could enact his judgment of Ryn.

Zeus looked around to see heavy Crovan bombardments descend upon his windscapers and his main army. Focusing on a high outcrop on the mountains behind him, he saw a smoking fireball came down upon a cliff of windscapers, burning them all to a crisp. His face was cold. Casualties did not concern him. Winning worship was his sole focus. Being the greatest was his focus. There would be no one higher.

The sounding of the drums had reinvigorated his army. They once again gnashed their teeth and howled across the plain. The negative energy billowing behind them did its work and raised the carnal hearts within them, offering a blood-boiling appetite that hollowed out the soul to organize the life of each spirit into a hardened and chaotic vessel, the aura of which was bursting with aggression. Officers came out in front of the army and awaited the order to charge. No one had relayed any intentions to them, but every soul on the plain could tell that the charge was coming.

Lifting his left hand up again, Zeus made a

pointer out of his two forefingers and set them against the faraway hills. Immediately a trumpet was sounded from behind him, and his horde thunderously began accelerating towards the hills across the plain. The earth began to rumble underneath the weight of their bodies. The aura of cold energy moved in force along with them. As they charged, the larger creatures began to disperse throughout the mass for lack of better speed evenly.

The bombardments from the Crovans continued as the sea of troops hastened across the plain. Zeus' windscapers were gone, and bombardments began focusing intensely on the fast advancing army. Lines and balls of fire, lightning, water, and ice struck down patches of them as they advanced but seemed to do little. Small gaps were created only to be filled by a never-ending flood of soldiers. Ryn signaled for Juya to prepare the infantry, and she fired a yellow arrow into the air. In unison, the army, still singing the hymn, stepped ten strides forward and prepared to burst from the hillside.

Juya and Calvyn quickly moved behind the line and up onto a rock. A commander gave the order, and the line of monks out in front of the infantry turned and weaved through the army, moving their way towards the back. They joined the line of monks in front of the archers and rejoined bombarding efforts.

Ryn remained in front. The hymn calmed as the soldiers eyed him with intensity. The enemy was coming in numbers far greater than their own, and if there was any remaining power, he could give them now was the time.

Ryn looked down at the earth and closed his eyes.

He stared at the ground for a minute as the battle hymn rang in his ears. The troops watched him as his body became spiritually more intense. A warm wind came up behind them and filled them with tranquility and courage. Ryn lifted his eyes and thrusting his weapon toward the sky; he shouted with the voice of a dragon-lion, "SAIYAMALA TEOTI!" As he shouted across the plain, the army responded with an enormous roar that made the air tremble. The faithful earth itself shouted with them, and its vibration was felt throughout the region. The faces of the soldiers went skyward in a verbal and physical expression of worship that defied their opponent, a glorious expression of their unbeatenness. They could not rattle the foundation of their great nation; their faith, and their god, the true God; not one who sat on a throne in the sky or on earth but THE throne from where all creation was governed. It was voiced with all their passion and heart as though it were the last act of freedom by a hero who makes a willing sacrifice.

The roar was so vivid, so shocking, so unforeseen, that the enemy ranks jumped with startling surprise at the immense power emanating from the Crovan army. The initial wave instantly dispersed the purple mist and staggered the assault to the point where they were tumbling over one another. The shouts intensified until Ryn brought his arms and gaze down to the earth in force, and the seasoned soldiers changed their roar into a powerful and melodic chant.

Zeus' eyes narrowed. His mind went to an image of a cornered cat, now at its most ferocious. This could be interesting. The Olympians, now clumping tightly together out of a need for security, began their shallow upward approach on the plain with about two alans to go.

The massive army shook the earth with its size, but the Crovans shook their spirits with their resolve. The Crovans were un-intimidated. The chant had changed to a strong one, a string of grunts. Their toes dug into the earth, and their eyes narrowed on their targets.

Ryn gauged the approach of the enemy with precision and, glancing at Juya, nodded his head. She immediately fired a red arrow high into the air. No sooner had the arrow sprung from her bow than did the infantry explode from the hills with overwhelming energy. Though they were outnumbered fifty-to-one, the energy with which they poured forth would make anyone who did not know better think the two sides were equally conscripted.

The monstrous horde charged relentlessly up the slope. The Crovans charged down it in a furious typhoon. They were swift and light but heavy and powerful, gliding across the grassy terrain like a sliding mountain. Ryn felt the confidence brimming in them. The Crescendo would be intense. Despite the inexperienced people in the ranks, they would fight expecting to cover their angles. They would still fan out in melee combat and set up the network. That was good. Even after more than thirty years, Zeus had done less and less to counter Crova's superior battle mechanics. This group was ripe for the picking. With every soldier flying down the hills, a few of the fastest began to move out from the rest, racing ahead of the Crescendo. Eljaryn, in particular, charged well out in front.

As they approached the base of the hill and the descending plain, the armies were no more than four hundred strides till impact. The bombardments had already shifted to the back of the oncoming force. Ryn eyed Eljaryn, as he would be the first to make contact with the enemy. The first impact would have psychological effects on the troops watching from the hills. The young man was lined up head to head with a giant ogre that must have stood about twenty-five cubits tall, and their distance was closing fast. The young Crovan would cover the distance between them in less than eight seconds.

Eljaryn pulled an Yncucyn from his back holster and held it out in his right hand over his head like a javelin. He took three bounds and then leapt high into the air, some eight cubits above the ogre's eye-line. Eljaryn came down with all his momentum and energy focused into the weapon's head, and it glowed yellow. As he descended, he accelerated his fall and fell underneath the ogre's high swinging ax. He buried the Yncucyn deep into the creature's chest, immediately halting its forward progress. The beast instantly dropped to its back under Eljaryn's momentum, and the young Crovan came down forcefully on top of the gray behemoth.

No sooner had the massive body struck the ground did the rest of the line begin to collide with the Crovans amassing a wall of power that slammed into the enemy. The Crovans instantly tore through the first hundred strides of opponents like bales of hay. The collision point became littered with blasts of energy in vast arrays of ice, water, bright and darker lights, fire, dust, sparks, and weapons as soldiers of the Olympian army were tossed about like rustled leaves. Even Ryn was awestruck by the power behind his army. In the first ten seconds of clashing steel alone, Zeus' army must have taken some two thousand casualties, but Ryn could only count a few of his own injured or already brought down, probably less than a dozen.

The charge eventually slowed down, and the armies began engaging in furious and disorganized melee combat. The Crovan ranks were spread far apart to keep the enemy from wrapping around them, so hundreds of enemy warriors had bled through the lines and engaged the mostly female force at the back. Eljaryn leapt from area to area, dealing lethal blows. Alyra and two other ladies had formed a loose triangle for cover as they downed oncoming opponents. Another Crovan named Raiyokyn seemed to be doing fine on his own. He was a large Crovan with plenty of girth.

He swung a *comtyr* at his fearful opponents. The enemy had formed a circle around him, for they were slow to meet with his weapon. It had already dashed several of them to countless pieces. The Crovan regulars fought with near godlike strength and ferociousness. The spiritual intensity of one's last stand filled them all. But after some time, overwhelming numbers began to pressure them. They fought with full knowledge that there wasn't a retreat, so they all fought to the last, and Ryn began seeing more and more drop in the field, despite taking more numbers of opponents before them.

After ten minutes of intense fighting, the horde began pressing the Crovans back as the network became too scattered to head off their advances. The sea of dead, which had been created since the first collision, was overtaken by the oncoming army as the line was pressed into a series of defensive withdrawals. As the horde pushed through the center, the line went into a rolling withdrawal as their footing was now backing up the hill.

Ryn felt the aura of the battlefield and looked to Juya. She confirmed it was time. Raising his weapon, he signaled for a second wave of attack to form. The bombardments came to a halt. Zeus looked out with a nod and a smirk. He'd drawn out the reserves and done nothing special to do it. Ryn and Calvyn jumped down off the rock and needed to make no gesture at all to have the others primed and ready to charge down the hill. Two hundred monks and monkesses moved together in a jog, armed with *Yncucyns* and *Dycucyns*.

The regulars went into full retreat at a rapid pace, like the sweeping undertow of an incoming wave. The Olympians began to chase but were pelted with an assault of elements dropping the front liners. The regulars swam around the monks, and the line was in the clear. The monks came together, and their interlocking aura began to rise frantically, stunning the advancing army.

The befuddled Olympians knew their obligation to run down the retreat but were stopped by the sight of the approaching line. There would soon be no room to charge uphill, and most of them stood stiff unknowing what to do. The spiritual energy coming off the monks was tremendous, and it struck fear into the hearts of the opposing side. The weapons of the advancing monks began glowing with energy as they prepared to roll over their opponents like a thunderous wave.

As Ryn and his monks closed in on the enemy line, the Olympians began scurrying with activity.

Some charged up the hill while some stood frozen. Others began falling back, suddenly realizing the impending doom awaiting those close to the front. They crashed into those behind them, stationary with the allusion of security being surrounded by numbers of their own.

Zeus looked frustrated at his army. How many times had they faced the Crescendo and still won the day? They had such overwhelming numbers yet had been scared into retreat by this latest charge. The irritating negative to his evolved military philosophy was its decrepit quality. But it wasn't an issue of functionality, only of unsightliness.

Fear is easy to control, he thought to himself. I would have hoped, however, that with enough bloodlust, they'd have forgotten it. Even after this long war, they are struck with fear for them.

He shook his head and gave orders to his black dragons. Fear was, indeed, the most practical way to turn a savage heart, and fear was something Zeus could do. He had to admire himself for being so prepared for this.

The line of screaming panthers slammed into the confused army with the sound of thunder. The full front of the army was quickly trampled under their advance, and, at the sight of it, the horde went into full retreat. Their fear was no longer centered in reverence to Zeus; it was centered upon the swift and powerful Nephilim behind them. Thousands of Olympian troops disappeared under the feet of the monks as they fled frantically. Wave after wave went down as the Crovans eliminated them like a fast-moving grass fire flooding a dry field.

The two dragons arose from behind Zeus and

swept toward the valley walls. In-flight, they gave out an enormous roar. The stones of the valley floor began to rattle as monstrous footsteps were heard.

From behind the rocks and crevices in the valley came several hundred large beings. Juya took note immediately and relayed the information to Ryn as he was still in stride. The dragons were coming forth, joined by giants, mostly from the line of Enlil's brothers, perhaps local mercenaries. They had been dormant and hidden in the valley's cliffs, specifically ready for a moment such as this. The efforts of a powerful network of runestones had hidden their presence. Another secret weapon Zeus had prepared for his final push just to turn the tables of a spiritual retreat back in his favor. The new wave came down onto the plains and formed a completely new line of a thousand or so that began to advance from the river valley as it gathered slowly.

Ryn and the monks halted their pursuit and regrouped with the regulars at the base of the hill. Calvyn took his cue and quickly ordered the withdrawal so they might reset their position on the hills.

Ryn reached out to Juya. "Continue bombardments," he said. The archers immediately began firing again. Ryn would now wait for another charge. He quickly looked over his army. The casualties had been incredibly high. He supposed it was about what he'd expect from a battle of annihilation. No one was retreating; they all fought to the death.

He figured he had about 600 regulars to add to his monks and monkesses. On the hill, he still had 200 archers. Looking across the plain, he figured the enemy to have around 70,000 still, but the dragons added a lot of firepower. There were thousands of family lines of dragons, but some of the fiercest were those of the line of Sed. These made up most of Zeus' line. He had not bothered to recruit the smaller kinds. What made Sed dragons so difficult to defeat was their sheer size and mass along with their robust hides.

These were still small in comparison to the dragons flanking Zeus on the cliff. They were natives of Emade and descended from Ezo, brother of Sed. Those of the line of Sed typically stood about thirty cubits on two legs and had a dark red, almost impervious skin, but these two stood well over forty cubits and had black, steel-like, armored scales. Though few in number, the Ezo dragons were well known across the world for their influence and were well known as vicious brutes of an un-negotiable type. Every major nation employed some of them. Some were quite intelligent and served in command, such as Zuze-Ozko, Zeus' celebrated general. But then again, that dragon was only half Ezo. Perhaps, like these two, all of the dragons of Ezo's line were witless brutes, a far cry from another dragon they all admired, the tribal father of the Crovan people.

As his first horde began to slow to a halt in front of the new line, Zeus surveyed the number of fallen. As far as casualties went, this battle had gone terribly thus far. His army was taking casualties around fifty times the rate of his opponent. He had no windscapers left to put bombarding pressure on the enemy and no further reserves. There were no more hidden cards to play, and no more surprise tactics. Still, Zeus did not look worried; he remained confident that this fight was going to be his. The Dragons and giants would tilt the fight favorably in his direction at the perfect time when his opponent was surprised and weary. Surly, all he had to do was wait.

The bombardments faded as the horde came to a stop. Juya spoke to Ryn. "Arrows are low," she said. "Most of the women have 3 or 4 remaining."

"Use discretion," he responded. "Spare them for when they will be most needed."

She received his instruction and relayed the orders.

Void of bombardments, the battlefield went silent. Scattered flesh lay across the field as only the stampede of troops could be heard coming to a stop. The Crovans saw their enemy stop their retreat and turn around. A loud rumble began again as the large horde approached. Exhausted, the Crovans stood willing yet weak with their weapons armed in front of them. Eljaryn, fearless as he was, rested leaning on his Yncucyn, catching his breath. Alyra too, who had suffered several injuries, found it difficult to stand and waited on one knee. Even Raiyokyn stared blankly down the plains at the oncoming horde without any energy left to calculate the situation. It was obvious that this group would perish in the next wave. That was hard to accept. No matter how hard his decisions had to be as their leader in this time, if he took even a moment to receive them in his heart there, he would break with sorrow.

He looked out at the fallen. Even on the plain in front of him, between the bodies of two ogres, was a young monkess taking her last few breaths as she bled out. Looking to the sky, her eyes desperately tried to understand why this had happened; how had she ended up here, and what was she to do in her last moments of life.

There was an old warrior of many years who stumbled on his feet back toward the line, knowing he might not even make it back before he went unconscious and fell to the grass. He had the look of a man of many honorable years of life, raising his children, mentoring his family, comforting those who mourned, living a full and sacrificial life in service to others. His dying here was a tragic affront to the honorable life he'd lived. As it was now, he wobbled back toward the line, refusing to die in the grass, having ever stopped for even a moment. Already dead, no one could help him, and he would be furious if any wasted their energy trying. He simply went on, his wind pouring out because he would do no other.

Ryn looked back at the hills and felt what any king should feel. No awareness of reality could overshadow how he felt for them. He began to imagine and wondered if, at that moment, they could make a successful retreat into the mountains. Defending from the mountains would be easier, and at least they were still going. Then he caught himself. Space and resources were the biggest issues. With the Raijyn plain overrun, their dominion was *Tyrakuma* , completely porous, unescapable, and indefensible. Even if Ryn handed himself over and Zeus left them to the reserve to turn on Sumer, they would suffer an agonizing and undignified death. Bottled up in the mountains, they would be hopeless to survive against their unceasing windscaping as they cursed the land from afar: tornados, hurricanes, hail, and ice storms. The food and the warmth would go quickly with no time to protect or preserve any of it.

No, this was the only place to stand. He knew that coming into the battle. This was where they could have the most impact, where they could hurt Zeus the most. In the back of Ryn's mind, when he knew one day that survival could no longer be achieved, his goal had been to set back Zeus' forces enough that he could not think of pursuing the remnant without being done in by the likes of Enki and Osiris.

Still in good health, the monks and monkesses moved to the front while the regulars filed in behind. The enemy was charging back across the plains, and Ryn, stepping out front, held up his weapon, readying them for the next charge. He knew what they needed, and he could only hope that in his state, he was good enough to give it to them. He had to inspire; he had to lead. He resolved that he would tear through them like papyrus, and if he could cut through the whole army, he would.

He took a breath and started the approach, the others faithfully following him down the hill. The line slowly began to pick up speed, and soon the weariness was forgotten as their hearts went in front of them. Every man and woman started locking into synchronization with one another like neatly-fitting bricks. He felt the rising surge of power in the line. Their greatest hope now was to inflict enough casualties, especially on some of the dragons, using their key weapon, the Crescendo, to force a withdrawal so they could charge again. That would be a challenge as the dragons and giants were deep in the line. They would simply have to cut the line deep to succeed. More power, they needed more power.

The Crescendo rose in power exponentially as it

often did, each Crovan throwing their very last into it, knowing it was their best hope. Despite their fatigue, they charged their weapons and let their bodies go numb to suffering this last outpouring.

As they drew near, back on the hills, Juya saw them, and suddenly she saw it. For decades, every battle, she'd seen the outcome before the battle was at its height, and often before it even started. Now, despite being so late, she saw it, and she felt it. She saw a cliff, and they were headed over it. She didn't know what was on the other side, but it was the end of something. How many times had she seen Ryn charge them into battle? Was this the last time? Would she ever see him again?

A chill went up her spine as she felt it with quick short breaths. She quickly controlled it. It didn't matter. Her goal was the same. Preserve every son and daughter of Crova to the last, cut down the enemy to the last. For the sake of those here, those in the mountains behind them, and the remnant sent away from them. She had to do it. There was no way she could comply with her instinct this time because to comply would mean to run. She did not run! She felt the wind behind her and touched it as far as she could in all directions to make sure she could grab enormous amounts for the moment when the hills were besieged.

As the enemy horde approached, Ryn heard himself roar with mystical authority he barely recognized and pulled back his Yncucyn, now emanating with fire, preparing to swing it upward in a hitch motion. The Crovan line erupted in a roar of defiance, and the two armies came together.

Ryn narrowed his focus and chose to see only his

next target. He burst into the enemy ranks and slashed through bodies as he darted by them. The Crovans again plowed through their opponents. The oncoming horde was without internal energy, like a ball of mud thrown violently at a solid wall. They were duly flung and scattered. Bodies seemed to be flying everywhere as the Crovans trampled their opponents.

It continued like that for an incredible time, more than before. But the Crescendo began breaking down in its weaker parts, and soon it lost its synchronization. As the charge lost momentum, they shot wormlike tunnels through the enemy ranks, around the stronger opponents, who held their ground, stopping the tidal wave of an advance.

Ryn felt the Crescendo break but had chosen his strategy and saw only what was ahead. He plowed straight on through the sea of monsters and mercenaries in an endless flurry of dashes, slices, dodges, and parries. The enemy became more dispersed as he went, and Ryn leapt thoughtlessly into a massive body in front of him. While in the air, he thrust his weapon through a large troll that poorly missed with a mace. The body of the troll scattered around him like a disturbed pile of leaves and Ryn landed on the other side.

He had but only a second to glance up and sense a terrifyingly close intent to devour and quickly noted a Sed Dragon thrusting its jaws at him, swinging from Ryn's right to his left. The Crovan reacted in just enough time to prop his weapon vertically in front of him so as to block. But the weapon could only block the teeth, not the impact. As he was struck by the beast's mammoth snout, he was launched a hundred strides back.

Intuitively aware of the ground, Ryn braced and rolled up into a stand. He then saw quickly that he had successfully plowed his way entirely through the enemy army only to be repelled at the line of trailing dragons and giants. Ryn's army had not made it near as far as him, for as he looked back, he saw a sea of troops still advancing into the hills between him and his men. He also saw the dragons had held back their line from the Olympian regulars, perhaps because the regulars were that much afraid of the dragons. There was a lot of space between the two groups to cover, and it would have been strategically deficient in having cut through them to meet the dragons anyway. His hope of cutting into the dragons to force a withdrawal had indeed been a lofty one that they'd fallen well short of fulfilling.

He was of little use there. Even he would be overcome surrounded by dragons and giants with no vanguard or support. He needed space to draw them out in sparser numbers. Ryn dashed northward towards the flank, trying to stay in between the two masses charging westward. Due to the stall in the battle upon the hills, the gap was shrinking, and he sensed the shrinking space. The dragons chased him across their plane of vision with balls of fire that Ryn could consistently dodge with great effort. Realizing he would be sandwiched between the two lines, he sprinted ever faster, sensing the very breath of the horde barreling down on him.

Suddenly the main army seemed to come to a halt, and the line of towering juggernauts threatened to crush him against the wall of troops to his left. Leaping over a swinging hammer from a giant, Ryn landed atop the head of an ogre and quickly resorted to leaping across opponents to his left to make the flank. The warriors slashed up at him only too long after Ryn had leapt from their bodies, and many of them ended up taking unintentional crossfire from the dragons behind them as they tried to pick Ryn off without regard for the allies ahead.

As Ryn approached the edge, a thick brown dragon on the flank took flight and tried to cut him off. Picking his moment carefully, Ryn leapt high into the air, slightly over the dragon's trajectory. It was far too bulky a flyer to change direction but made a desperate slash with its claw as Ryn flew over. Catching the blow's momentum, he blocked the swing and glanced over it. Spinning over the dragon's head, he came firmly down to the ground outside enemy ranks.

No sooner had he landed than did a giant's sword come down on his head. Quickly Ryn raised his targe and parried it violently. Rising to his feet, he anticipated the next swing and flipped over it, whereupon he slashed his Yncucyn at the giant's abdomen. That landed him directly in the path of another giant's downward swing, which he quickly parried back over his head. Ryn dodged a fast combo from the other giant, barely having the sight to deflect a ball of fire breathed by a dragon from afar by summoning a shield of ice quickly.

Parrying the giant's sword wildly to the ground, he leapt at him with catlike agility and power. Planting his feet into the being's chest, he pushed off, violently swinging the Yncucyn upward with ferocious heat, and his swing carried his body over in a backflip to the ground. Upon landing, he saw that both giants were bleeding but were not subdued while a long green dragon slithered up behind them. Could he take three at once? He nodded. Of course, he could. Today he could.

Ryn blocked and parried strikes as they came. One moment he parried a sword, and the next dodged a ball of green fire. Leaping between the giants, he let loose a sporadic ball of fire that finally blinded one for enough time to work inside the other. Whipping around the giant's weapon, he slung his body across at chest height and decapitated him with a fiery glowing blade. He paid the price for earning that opportunity, and the dragon had slithered to his right unchecked, where it smacked him with a powerful tail. The king rolled into defense only to see more attackers were coming to him. He went into a fighting retreat towards the Crovan line.

The line had been losing ground for some time now as numbers and firepower overwhelmed them. Raiyokyn met a charging Sed Dragon with his comtyr, smashing it into the side of the beast's head. He began to bring the weapon around for another swing when a ball of rich fire caught him full front. Still on fire, Raiyokyn brought the weapon back over his head and, heaving it down, dispersed several limbs in the crowd of enemy warriors next to him. But as he began to pull the thing back into the air, he was pounced upon by another dragon, which promptly began tarring his flesh, satiating its hunger for flesh and carnage.

As Eljaryn flew with too much sluggishness into a troll, he was gripped by the dying beast's arm. He was stuck long enough for an imp to scorch him with a ball of fire. He arose in flames and killed a raging Semaltar and an unidentified furry Nephilim before a

Gullukan ran him through from behind. Even then, he turned and threw several soldiers off of him before being pinned to the ground by the spear of a large elephant creature.

General Calvyn saw Eljaryn fall and, parrying the sword of a Gullukan, rammed him with his shoulder, sending the lizard flying twenty strides back. The general had lost his right arm minutes before but used his left well. He used his girth also and fought until he was alone and surrounded, his men fallen around him.

Rather than pull back to organize a withdrawal that was hopeless, he decided he was best useful in holding his position, striking as many down as he could. He cleverly maneuvered between smaller opponents for some time, keeping the dragons away long enough to rack up a significant number of enemy casualties. By the end of it, he'd lost an eye and a foot. He was stabbed from two directions but found the strength to throw off a pair of hairy Olomers before meeting his end. A preying dragon quickly moved in and impaled him with his talons, pinning him to the earth before intelligently blasting him on the ground from zero distance with a torrent of fire.

Enemy soldiers had overwhelmed Alyra's two fighting companions. She fell back as the blood of another woman sprayed across her face. Out of the crowd, a Semaltar leapt at her coming down on her with a spear. She suddenly filled her right hand with as much White Flame as she had left and flung it at him as he descended. It was the slightest flame, but the being was set ablaze with pale fire. Still, the heavily armored warrior moved frantically in his last moments before melting away and charged her in a blind fury.

Alyra quickly thrust her spear out and impaled him as he leapt at her. His crisping and melting body slid down the pole and almost pinned her to the ground. Throwing the body off, she had no time to react as a troll bore into her with the hard upward swing of a club she partially blocked. The young woman went soaring high into the air and landed several strides limply from Juya on the hill's ridge. The queen did not have time to look but sensed very little spiritual energy coming from the girl.

Ryn had dropped his second giant while also being able to put down a cyclops and a dragon definitively. He had dashed numerous other creatures as well, but they were not worth counting. His progress was slow, and at the rate he was expending energy to overcome the high number of strong foes, it would not be long until he collapsed. He desperately needed his energy to count, and he raced for ideas on how to do just that. Locking himself in an endless chain of difficult melees with multiple enemies was a ceaseless endeavor.

At that moment, he thought to do what was surly suicide, but in a sure death situation, it made hardly a difference. He didn't have time to ponder it too much. He was either doing it or not. It had always been on his mind. Was now the time? He reasoned it was the only time left, so he might as well try. Ryn shuttled back around and began leaping through the attacks of his oncoming pursuers.

Zeus watched intently as Ryn swam through his fierce horde back across the plain. The thunder god was unsure of what he was doing until he immerged from the mass of pursuers still sprinting towards the valley cliffs. Ryn was coming for Zeus.

Zeus' face grew a smirk, and then rose into a full smile at the thought of how desperate his opponent had become. His charge on the cliffs meant delightfully that even Ryn had no stock in winning this battle. He appeared to be making a mad dash at the leader in one last act of vengeance. At least he hoped it was vengeance. A heart of vengeance would sour the nature of Ryn's heart, making him vulnerable.

Accompanying the god on the cliff were his dunataso . There were five of them. Two stood point at the front of the cliff and awaited Ryn. The other three stood next to Zeus. They prepared their steel and armor for the inevitable high profile tussle.

Ryn quickly came upon the rising slopes and began to bound up the rocks towards Zeus's position. He did not know of his army's position, and for the moment, was only concerned with the hope of defeating Zeus. This would certainly be enough to force an enemy retreat as there were no other gods there to help lead the campaign, and it would likely cause a withdrawal regardless, if not a total surrender. A desperate time was the last chance to use a desperate measure.

Juya and the archers had begun carefully firing their arrows as the opponent punched through the scattered and frantic infantry. Most of the women on the hills could not produce deadly force without the carefully constructed arrows and their powerful runes. They were a precious commodity. Those that had learned to do such, however, had resorted to firing scattered weapons from their bows. They fired swords, spears, Yncucyns, even axes, and hammers. Her archers took careful aim and filled their projectiles with ample power to create one-hit kills.

There were only a couple hundred infantrymen and monks remaining, and for now, they created such a flurry of activity between them that the number of troops bleeding through was manageable but soon would not be. Juya had picked up on what Ryn was doing, for she had been watching him the whole time.

As the vision of the battle's inevitable conclusion played out in her mind, she fought the desire to call him back. If that was what he saw as valuable, then so be it. But if they were going to die, she didn't want to die in the hands of some dragon. She wanted to die with him, and she wanted it to be on her terms. As it was, she was devoted to giving him time to see if this could work. His people were devoted to giving him time to see if this worked. But at some point, she would and should call him back.

Ryn bounded up the last crag and vaulted himself over the ledge. Still in mid-air, a gigantic sword was anticipating his arrival with a swing that would bat him right back over the cliff. Lining the Yncucyn up and down, he absorbed the impact of the swing and used it to propel him forward in a front-flip. He landed flatfooted and punched the ground with his fists so as to avoid smashing his head on the rock in front of him due to the immense energy transferred from the dunatas' strike.

There was no time to survey his surroundings. Immediately the same dunatas swung back. Ryn exploded into a backflip, leaping over the swing. His feet went quickly and efficiently into a pivot on the ground. He violently swung his blade left into the dunatas' chest. He blocked with the sword, and Ryn rotated fully and into another more fervent swing; this one blocked as well. Ryn continued his spin into a squat and swung unrelentingly at the dunatas' ankles while avoiding the high swing of his oncoming companion. Crouched and planted in the dirt, he found himself in a free half-second between their attacks, and he made good of it.

He exploded vertically with the Yncucyn and made a thunderous and flashing vertical slice. The unexpected power of the blow off-balanced the first dunatas, and he staggered. Ryn's vertical attack carried him over the dunatas in an arcing front flip, soaring over his head and landing back to back with the enemy. As he landed, he thrust the Yncucyn behind him, underneath his armpit. The blade burrowed deep into the dunatas' unprotected backside, and filling it with energy, Ryn forced an explosion that hollowed out the dunatas' torso.

The monk-king removed the Yncucyn, and his enemy flopped to the ground. The second came down with his sword rapidly. It was instantly deflected to the right with the targe on the Crovan's right arm. Ryn slashed up in a hitch motion, and the dunatas jerked back and came at Ryn twice with horizontal swings. Ryn blocked them and determined to remain offensive. The dunatas snapped the sword down in a quick, half-ax swing.

Ryn skipped into the air and leaned forward to avoid the blow to his lower body. Then in a single motion of midair strength and grace, rolled forward over the downward flat edge of the sword and dragged the Yncucyn around in a violent swing that decapitated the Nephilim. Ryn landed in rotation and brought himself back around to face the god and his three remaining dunataso. He had made short work of the highly trained warriors, and a new aura of respect surrounded the remaining subordinates around the Olympian.

The two black dragons had finally returned and sat behind Zeus. The three dunataso were out in front, and two had already launched themselves airborne into battle. Ryn leapt backward while the behemoths landed in full swing. He landed softly like a cat and darted forward at the one on his right, parrying a quick recovery swing. The two traded positions and took swift swings at Ryn while blocking his fast counters.

The dunataso worked to keep the agile panther from shifting positions, for he was a fiercely agile and yet powerful cat-like fighter. Thinking they had him cornered against the cliff, they came from his right and left, swinging at the same time from the middle, outward.

Ryn flipped over the two strikes and laid into the dunatas on his right forcing him to stagger. Ryn's blade was blocked twice, but he absorbed the energy, bringing it back with more and more speed and power. His last attempt snapped back at the dunatas in a fraction of a second. Completely shocked, the Crovan could muster such power he widened his eyes, expecting to lose his head. But the other came in quickly, and a loud bang sounded as the two blades met and repelled each other.

Ryn flipped over their combined efforts with tireless agility and brushed off his heavy breath. The battle was tedious and tiresome, and the dunataso very strong and skilled. He remained focused on the goal, however.

His two opponents quickly moved in unison,

forcing Ryn to dodge blows in rapid succession while moving back until he was about out of room on the cliff. Upon sensing the edge, he waited until the two swung again to leap over their attacks. The two dunataso had expected him to try something like that and complimented each other with a vertical and a horizontal swing.

Ryn leapt high over the arc of the horizontal swing as it came slightly first and in mid-air changed his body rotation so as to avoid the vertical swing as well. He finished his beautiful mid-air twist on their backsides and quickly spun into a low scathing swing that caught three legs. The two dunataso quickly fell without any feet to support them.

But before they even hit the ground, Ryn felt a sword encroach from behind him. He turned just in time to avoid the lion's share of a stab at his back from the remaining dunatas. Unfortunately, he had not reacted quickly enough, and the sword tore through his robe and caught some of his flesh. Ryn rolled backward into a summersault and got back into his guard fifteen strides away from the Nephilim. He was bleeding, not terribly, but he felt poison had entered the wound from the blade, and it gave him concern.

A shadow began to rise over them, and Ryn saw that one of the black dragons was being sent back across the plains. Zeus had directed his attention away from Ryn and was now staring back at the Crovan line. The other black dragon and the remaining dunatas approached Ryn cautiously.

Juya was now out of projectiles and fighting with daggers and targe against oncoming opponents. She had finally called out and grasped the air to power their defense. Her airscaping abilities could not be compared to anyone but the gods, and she pulled a massive front of cool air that put to their backs a constant heavy wind that swept down the hillside in order to slow the enemy advancement. The faithfulness of the plain's winds amplified her ability to beyond expectation, and there was not a windscaper in the Olympian army that could content with her power. The fierce gale kept flyers from bypassing the infantry and airdropping troops on the hilltops.

Even though it had shocked the enemy to come against such a powerful windscaper, their own efforts challenged her focus and energy. She figured she had a limit; she just hoped it was a limit far enough out to make a difference.

The Crovans had congregated towards the rocky peaks of the hills and fought from the higher ground. One of the monks came to her and helped by refracting light around her to make her image hard to track by those that could hurl elements against her. As the quicker enemy combatants came close, she was able to keep her concentration while slaying several as they approached the rock.

Looking around, she found that little more than forty Crovans remained fighting from high rocks of the hills. A few dozen fought on the slopes; some of the toughest were there. They were Men that caused a serious delay for the Olympians and serious casualty, right up to their last breath. They were the kind dangerous enough to force the Olympians to hold back by the hundreds as they were tepid about approaching.

The queen tried once to concentrate on Ryn long

enough to find out how he was doing. Her attempt was quickly foiled as a Gullukan had leapt off of another enemy's shoulders onto the rock. She jerked back in order to avoid a sword and felt her foot hit something soft as she was backed to the rear of the rock.

She thrust her left arm up and parried the Gullukan's sword to her left, then quickly rammed the blade into his gut with her right. She buried her left shoulder into the lizard and rammed him off of the rock. Turning around, she saw that the soft thing behind her was the body of Alyra, whom she saw now still had a weak flicker of light in her spirit.

From behind Juya, a rapidly pouncing felycar approached. Mounted on top of it was a young Crovan man who held out his arm for her to join him. His eyes were begging for him to be able to save the queen, at least.

Indeed, it was about time for anyone who could make an escape to do so. In seconds, the last of the infantry keeping the army stalled on the slopes would disappear, and then they would be surrounded. But Juya would not leave without her husband. As he went, she went. Shaking her head, she pointed at the girl on the ground and turned back around to throw a troll off of the rock.

The young man did not question the queen's command and at once scooped up Alyra. He then jerked the creature around, and it made a full sprint down the backside of the hills. She saw several other felycars take flight from the hills.

Juya began losing control of her wind, and moments after the young man left, two more Gullukans had managed to climb onto the rock. She finally felt she could not manage both and let go of the air. The power of the front began dying quickly, and she felt the stillness begin to set in. Her very next thought was a scream for help, through her mind, towards her husband. She had given him all the time she could, but they had run out of it.

Atop the cliffs, Ryn received the message instantly. The last dunatas on the ground in submission, he turned and leapt off the cliff without any hesitation. As he left, the black dragon he'd drawn up against made a gaping swing at him with his tail only to miss by a finger. Ryn free fell from the cliff, a good thirty or forty stories above the valley floor. His body struck the ground like a small meteor, and he went straight from his landing into another leap that he eventually rolled out of some sixty strides past and began sprinting furiously towards the hilltops.

On top of the hills, Juya's rock was overcome, and the two or three men that had been supporting her were overcome. Seeking allies, she bolted north, about a hundred strides down, where three men and two women were making their last stand against a climbing horde in the same way she had.

As she ran, the last of the infantry fell around her. One cedentir seemed to race excitedly at her with his blade ahead of the pack. She gracefully parried and shocked him with her fist skills, getting inside his defense and tearing him and his armor several ways before flinging him off and continuing the run. Avoiding a slab of earth and leaping over a ball of fire, she slid to split the legs of an Olomer, gone before he could catch her with his lave.

Within a dozen strides, she saw a mob move between her and the rock. She threw a powerful wind at them and stammered them all but the big one. She had not recovered in time to call on her best athleticism as she passed and, though she should have been intercepted, the weary troll missed her agile frame, and she slid by.

Upon reaching the rock, she was let into a flank, and the six of them formed a hexagon around the rock's ledges. Juya and one of the men, a monk, began creating gusts of wind above them whenever they could focus and manifest them, not many and not strong, but enough so as to keep the dragons and fliers from getting overhead or in the air to rain fire down on them. The others worked the perimeter with them.

Ryn could see where Juya was, and the six on the rock would soon be the only six left on the hills. He sprinted frantically, hoping to get there before the inevitable. As he did, he kept his eye on the enormous black dragon that flew towards the same spot now half an alan in front of him. As he looked ahead, the flying monsters in the army had now begun to hover and encircle above the rock.

On the round peak, Juya and the hexagon were impenetrable. Nothing could get on the rock as the six remaining panthers battled ferociously against insane odds though weakening over time. They were not rigid, for that would be disastrous. Rather, they constantly rotated position on the rock like a tightly interwoven network of traffic. A ball of blue light, not affected by wind, soared in among them, and like water, they let it go by and continued to move around its presence without so much as one of them being burned.

Despite the supernatural efforts of their last stand,

the fight was exhausting. Soon Juya found that they could no longer keep up the wind and fight off the invaders physically. Shadows began to cover them, and Juya knew that the flyers were raising altitude in order to bring down a bombardment that would finish them.

Quickly she tried to create a vortex above them, but she stuttered and found herself unable to as though she was pulling a stone with a rope, only to have the rope break. Pausing for a second in distress, she had not returned to her right to head off an intruder. A Gullukan arose onto the rock and flanked one of the girls on that side. Juya turned to react, but she was too late, and the girl was overpowered by four blades from different directions. A spear from below the rock pierced her side violently.

Juya pounced on the group and sliced through the opponents wildly with her daggers but was sad to see the young girl drop to the ground limply. Rather quickly, a claw came up and pulled the young woman off the rock to finish her.

The Queen thrust herself violently from image to image, blasting them off the rock, and focused all her reserve power into her physical attacks. She was aware in the back of her mind that without the wind above, this battle would be over shortly. Where was Ryn? She had no answer. She could only ask that several times. Live or die; she thought they were together. Where was Ryn?

Ryn was but a couple of hundred strides away when the barrage of fireballs began. The Crovans could do nothing but cover their faces as the hot plasma rained down on them. In those instances, as the fire began coming down, the black dragon swept down on the rock and seemed to pick something up. Ryn did not know what it was and thought it could be a person, but other than that, he his mind only processed the result.

When the bombardment stopped, he skidded to a halt about a hundred strides from the rock, panting and astonished. Nothing was moving on the high outcrop, and the beasts began turning towards the king after he had been noticed.

Ryn stood perfectly still, staring astonishingly at the army that now headed towards him. He thought for that moment that he had lost her, and very quickly, tears formed over his face, even as the enemy approached. A terrible sorrow bled through his iron will. In that one moment, a voice inside him asked him to lie down and die; he had failed. He had failed to protect Juya and had failed to rescue his people.

But it was only for an instant. In the moment following, Ryn conceived that his army was defeated and the war over, but no sooner had he thought it did a voice forcefully urge him that this was not his army. The message was clear; Ryn fought for a greater cause than his people, and the army fighting that cause was strong in existence. He would not believe he was ready to embrace that truth, but something embraced it for him and immediately a lion's spirit within him aroused his passions to fight the ongoing battle.

Out of energy and exhausted, Ryn clenched his fists, and his body began to vibrate. As the enemy was upon him, he exploded northwest along the line of charging enemies, and as he went, he took a hack at anything moving or even unnatural within his field of vision.

As he sprinted, he transcended his exhaustion and

willed his limbs into movement. He entertained no rational thought nor entertained any pressing emotion, but simply dashed bodies as they flung themselves at him. Dozens at a time, he saw them enter his vision, and they would look like a cloud in front of him. But somehow, he weaved his way between them, dashing them as he went with quick and powerful slices delivered at blinding speed.

Zeus looked on at Ryn, and for the first time, he was impressed with the panther Nephilim. The Crovan dashed dozens of creatures in seconds as they flooded around him, all while running into the smooth northern hills. What a powerful warrior he was. It angered Zeus that such a powerful and capable being was not in service to one of the gods. He adhered to an outdated cultic structure. He honored the Primordial. The powerless, the amiss, the deceptive. Something that had reduced itself to irrelevant.

It was ridiculous that such a superior being would adhere to such a foolish outdated belief—to put himself in the hands of a defeated and powerless being—this he did not understand, and Zeus did not like it when he did not understand. The obvious conclusion was that Zeus did understand. Ryn was foolish, despite how noble he appeared. He was still just a Touka.

Zeus leapt off the cliff and onto the plains in order to watch the saga unfold in front of him. He bounded across the fields with a bounce in his steps, majestic and powerful, until mist formed under his feet. Soon a thick cloud formed under him like a rolling fog, and it carried him effortlessly across the field.

He watched the battle come into his view as he got closer. He had to be there for Ryn's fall. Turning to his right, he ordered his black dragon, Ilimat, to finish the king when they got there. Zeus was curious to test the Crovan's strength.

Ryn had stopped on the plains and was taking on warriors as they approached him. The army had encircled him, and had left him a wide space with a radius of about thirty strides all the way around. The troops came at Ryn in a constant supply but were always dispatched in the middle. Even giants and dragons found it dangerous to approach Ryn now. He had downed several of them in the circle already.

Again, a large Sed Dragon approached Ryn in the middle, while at the same time, dozens of others lunged towards him as well. Ryn continued to baffle them as he would seem to dash them a dozen at a time in mid-air and then return to the ground only to do it again in the next instance. The red dragon launched a fireball at Ryn that missed. Ryn countered with a lightning ball that blinded the beast temporarily and stunned it. He leapt out at the dragon in a tornado kick and came down on the beast with his weapon.

The blade sliced through the granite-tough skin from shoulder to groin. The cut glowed with fire, and suddenly, the dragon's innards bubbled out from beneath the hide. In agony, it flopped forward to the ground, and Ryn immediately leapt back into the exact center, awaiting more challengers.

The influx had stopped, and Ryn, in a world that moved much faster than the one everyone else was in, felt like he had to wait an eternity while the circle motionlessly stood around him.

Looking down, he saw that he had taken numerous gashes and hits without knowing it, or at least without feeling it. Ryn stood on a mound of flesh, and could now see Zeus watching from the circle's edge. He was surrounded by his strongest warriors. Next to him, Ryn saw another Nephilim that he had not noticed before. He was another, like Zeus. He was tall and husky and had Zeus' skin color but had golden hair. He wore a lion's mane over his body and had an enormous sword sheathed on his back.

But that was all Ryn got to see because out of the sky fell one of Zeus' black dragons. Illimat promptly swelled a ball of plasma in its mouth, and Ryn instinctively leapt back, arcing behind the pile of bodies. The ball came out and forged an explosion that sent the mound of flesh raining everywhere. It struck with power and extreme heat, but Ryn's sudden shield of air guarded him from it.

He immediately leapt forward, through the flames, and landed flatfooted facing the beast. Bright flashes emanated from Ryn's mouth and hands. Massive energy began to collect in front of him about chest high. The Yncucyn was sheathed on his back and the mass of energy formed with bright light. As it grew, it flamed and spat like a fireball but was expanding to enormous proportions. The dragon reared back again, bringing power up from his belly. He meant to hurl his attack first.

Zeus stood a little shocked. Ryn was going head to head with Ilimat, but he couldn't imagine the touka having the power to harm the dragon. None in over a thousand years had every done anything to penetrate it's hide.

Ryn energized the enormous ball in front of him

as he had never done before. Anger, passion, fear, and confidence all flooded into the ball. The energy was coming out of him at such a rate that Ryn began to levitate slightly off the ground. The ball had now grown to about ten cubits in diameter, and Ryn floated back under the pressure.

The dragon, sensing the power of his attack, wasted no time, and shot a thick flame at Ryn from his mouth like an arrow.

Almost an instant after it did, Ryn burst backward from his ball and sent it hurling at the dragon. The two collided in the middle, and the dragon's fire seemed to disintegrate insignificantly. The huge ball exploded into the belly of the dragon with the sound of thunder.

When Ryn regained his sight seconds later, he saw the dragon's head atop a smoldering mass. A trail of scorched earth and fire lay in the wake of the attack, slashing through the circle of warriors behind it. The beast swayed to the right and then breathlessly fell over onto its side.

The sight sent a wave of fear rumbling through the army around the circle. Even Zeus' demeanor had changed. Ryn continued to astound them. Could he really just be a fifth-generation Nephilim? Where did this energy come from? How long could he keep it up? Zeus had only seen such power in the hands of gods. He was astonished, but again not worried. If Ryn could contend with gods, then the lord of Olympia still had a god for him to fight, and he stood at Zeus' right hand.

Ryn staggered about half-conscious for a good ten seconds until he gained his balance and straightened up into a stand. The blast he had let out had drained him immensely, and it was difficult to believe he had anymore fight in him at all.

Zeus saw this but was not deterred from sending out his champion. All Crovans, most Nephilim, and certainly most gods, had certain elements in which their energy manifested physically. Even knowing Ryn could use all of them, he'd never seen him exert himself like this. This event had finally, at the end, exposed his master element finally. Ryn's soul was one of fire. And if that was the case, then the god next to him was a favorable matchup.

Ryn looked closely and saw the figure that had stood at Zeus' right earlier come walking out to face him. After a few seconds, Ryn recognized him. It was indeed the great hero, the 'People's Hero,' Herakles of Antak. His hair was golden yellow, and his beard was shiny bronze. His skin was covered in smooth golden fur, and his face was a smooth and humanoid lion figure. He was one of Zeus' own children, a second-generation Nephilim, and he was a champion of the Olympian army, even though it had refrained from assigning new champions ages ago.

The army began to cheer, and Ryn knew the fight was over. He had astonished even himself today; he had never fought on this level in his life. And maybe, just maybe, if he were in top health and well-rested, he could contend with an Olympian god by himself, but not in his current state. In the the past, his strategy to counter the gods had been to assign teams and lookouts. He had no such support. He was on his own and no Crovan had ever defeated a god on their own.

Ryn unsheathed his Yncucyn and began to step towards Herakles over lifeless bodies. The fearless champion confidently did the same. The god began circling Ryn, so Ryn did likewise. Looking at the Crovan expressionlessly and still circling, the god reached back and unsheathed his sword, holding it over his shoulder. Ryn continued to walk, waiting for him to make the first move.

Herakles moved comfortably across from Ryn and continued to stare him down. The god outsized Ryn by about two cubits and around four-hundred *mina*. He was a mass of muscle that made Ryn think of an upright walking lion in clothing.

The two finished another circle. Herakles looked poised but made no move to attack. Sensing his wits dull, Ryn finally stopped and began facing the god, who continued to circle as if nothing had changed.

Eventually, the god's footsteps came closer and closer until, without any warning or acceleration, he lunged at Ryn, sword out.

Ryn met the god's sword and parried his first few quick combos. Each one came with about three to four slashes fit into one or one and a half seconds each. Then they came quicker, and Ryn found it difficult to keep up. Unnatural combinations of slashes and thrusts two to five at a time, all within a second. They might be manageable if they were not so powerful. Each one carried enormous weight. The Olympian hero began dropping Ryn's guard enough that he was connecting on occasional slashes. The crowd around them hollered and cheered with amusement and competitiveness.

Herakles continued to be aggressive with the sword until Ryn was unable to block anymore and took several blows. As the champion swung once more at the Crovan, Ryn staggered, and Herakles took advantage of him.

A charged swing of the sword came down on top of Ryn, full of ice. He blocked it with the staff of his Yncucyn but stumbled under its blow. Sparkling ice clouded his vision. In the next quarter second, he brought his sword back across in an upward motion, knocking the Yncucyn free.

He lunged with a kick, but Ryn recovered to block. The Crovan quickly countered with a scathing swing at the god with his left leg. This was dodged, and Herakles came back by disarming Ryn's left arm and punching him in the left rib cage. Shards of ice exploded into Ryn's side, and blood flew out from his body.

Ryn felt numbness and loss of control. He saw what was Herakles was doing, but his body didn't move to respond. The god was inside his defenses now.

Herakles propped himself underneath the caught arm. Forcefully, he used it to pull the Crovan off the ground and sling him over his shoulder.

Ryn felt his arm grabbed and then saw himself go over the god's shoulder. He was in the air and slung to the ground in less than a quarter of a second. He he had one last thought of Juya and asked Teoti why. Then everything went black.

3 A CRY OUT IN ANGUISH

Out of the black surroundings came thoughts, voices, and threats. They came at him aggressively and sounded foreign. But they did not come from the outside; it seemed they were from the inside. Hated, despised, forsaken, hopeless, weak, pitiful, reckless, foolish, lifeless; all these concepts came into his mind. But they were more than concepts. They were entirely self-manifested in that Ryn did not hear them so much as he felt them. They were urges or suggestions that he could not fight off or ignore. They burrowed into his mind and spirit. He desperately fought to be free of them, wading his way through levels of awareness. He fought until finally, as if emerging from a pool of speaking water, he arose from the drifting suggestions and saw light.

Ryn regained consciousness noticing first that he was in pain. Not just physical pain, but spiritually he was hurting. A spiritual presence was polluting and suffocating his energy like debris clogging a flowing river.

As he regained his awareness, he realized that many enchanted bonds had been placed over his arms and legs. These bonds kept him from moving and kept him from amassing charges of energy. He was in a tent and anchored to the ground next to one of four beams that propped the tent up. He sensed it was a large tent that spread eight to ten strides on his right and left and about twelve strides in front of him. There was nothing in the tent except himself and the person across from him who came into focus shortly.

Across from Ryn, Juya lay tied up and bound to the ground with similar bonds. Her face and arms were scarred, and the ends of her hair were singed. She looked very pale and physically bore all signs of death. But Ryn sensed there was life in her, and her soul had not left her body. Still, it was weak, and he actually recognized her familiar body shape and clothing before becoming aware of her faint aura.

As soon as he recognized her, even before her face came into focus, he sprung for her. Immediately the runes lit up, and he was stopped as though he were firmly set in a harness. A red light glowed around him, and he was suddenly thrust onto his back with tremendous force.

He found he could sit up as long as he did not pass out of a small circle drawn around him. Shaking badly, he looked at Juya with desperate eyes. He sensed the spiritual anguish in her, suffocating her spirit, and he desperately longed to release her from it. A part of him was happy she was alive, but for the most part, he was afraid for her. Considering the situation, she might be better off dead. He could only imagine what Zeus was planning to do with her.

Ryn thought back to the battle and conceded that

it was Juya who had been lifted from the rock by the dragon. Tears formed over his shaking cheeks as he realized that Zeus had done this in order to carry out some sort of tormenting revenge upon the two of them for resisting him so long.

Overwhelmed with despair, he found his energy evaporating into the runes that bound him. He immediately stopped the flow of horrid thoughts and grabbed for anything positive and uplifting. Focusing on the simple fact he was still alive; his spirit took an enormous breath as if it just avoided being suffocated.

Juya's bound state brought the flood of thoughts back to him, and he desperately began fighting them. For his own survival, he found himself diving into temporary ignorance. His first and foremost value was staying alive, and the more he thought about the situation, the more he felt the energy flow out of him through the runes. Thrusting his head from side to side, he fought to keep his wind within him. He went from moment to moment, struggling to stay vibrant.

Finally, the still air of the tent was broken. The tent flaps to Ryn's left flung open violently, and Zeus stepped inside, slightly illuminating the room. He said nothing but stood upright in front of the entrance and stared at Ryn, who found himself unable to stare back.

Zeus watched the Crovan struggle against his thoughts and smirked at the powerlessness of his opponent. He shifted his glance over to Juya and gave her a dismissive look as if to question why he was so upset over something as insignificant as Juya.

Bending next to Ryn, Zeus reached down and felt the dirt beneath his fallen foe. It teamed with life, drained from Ryn's spirit. Scooping a handful of dirt up to his face, he breathed in its aroma. It was almost as rich with life as his blood, and to Zeus, it was the tranquil smell of victory.

The god gripped the dirt firmly and, breathing a heavy sigh, closed his eyes, smiling. He soaked in the moment as his enemy thrust his body from side to side. Ryn cringed as he felt valuable attachments tear from his heart; he could not keep them under the circumstances. Tears rolled over his face, and his lip quivered as he desperately tried to hold on to whatever he could.

Zeus opened his eyes and watched the dirt sift through his fingers. Then looking up at Ryn, gave him a pitiful look. His powerful, vivid voice finally broke the monotonous sounds of Ryn struggling through his breath.

"Do you want it to stop?"

Ryn seemed to ignore the god and shook violently as another wave of despair overwhelmed him.

The god leaned his head over and spoke as though genuinely concerned.

"You have never had the pleasure of feeling this concoction, but believe me, thousands of your people have been wasted away by it before you; had their spirits rotted as they still breathed to their last. Trust that it will be the same for you, or did you think I would do any less? But, I can relieve you of it. Even I don't believe in needless suffering."

He paused and pushed his foot forward until it broke the circle. The energy of the ring pulled on his foot, but the presence behind it was far too heavy. It had as much effect on the god's foot as a mule attempting to pull a mountain. It was painful to see that Zeus' aura was that massive. It made him wonder what made him think he could even begin to charge the valley cliff and take him on at all.

The god leaned back and spoke with a calm and level voice as though he were stating common sense. "Bend over and kiss my foot. Pledge yourself to me, and I will make you a powerful prince. You need not endure this anymore."

Ryn shot back a vengeful scowl with a sea of rage bursting behind his eyes. There was no way he would entertain such an insulting and preposterous notion.

Zeus withdrew his foot and shrugged. "You choose to suffer. I care little," the god said with apathy.

Ryn vibrated with anger and, mustering all of his strength, got onto his knees, and stared coldly at Zeus. He shook but maintained an unforeseen measure of strength in suppressing his pain. It was as though he had gotten suddenly stronger. This interested the god, and he stood up slowly, nodding his head.

"My, you're resilient for a Touka," he said softly. Turning around without concern, he stared out the open tent flaps, thinking.

Ryn tried to stand but felt the runes pull on him. He tried to lower himself first, but the runes came down on him with full force.

Zeus heard a thud and turned to see Ryn's face nestled into the dirt. The god laughed and shook his head, shifting his gaze back around. Ryn pushed himself up and got to his knees again. Straightening his back, he caught Juya in the corner of his eye. Quickly he shifted his gaze to Zeus and mustered his defiance.

The Olympian stood with his hands behind his

back and finally spoke. "Why, Ryn? Why fight me?"

He paused and turned his gaze back to his bound prisoner. "You fight for nothing. There is nothing left to protect. No people, no land, not even the worship of your god."

Ryn said nothing but kept his defiant gaze.

"You have been delivered into my hands," Zeus continued, taking a few steps towards him. "Your god has abandoned you; let you fall. So, the question is, did he forget you? Does he hate you? Was he ever there at all?"

Zeus prodded at Ryn, who now looked away, refusing to entertain these thoughts. The two were silent for a minute while Zeus watched the Crovan curiously.

Sensing that the questions would not go away, Ryn realized he would have to answer. Zeus had a way of planting thoughts in one's head. They had to be defied or accepted; they could not be ignored.

"Do you mean to say that the Source is powerless or forgetful?"

Zeus gave Ryn a look of imitated surprise.

"The Source?" he said with slight laughter. "I was referring to Teoti."

Ryn tightened his lips and shook his head. He did not appreciate the god's feigned ignorance; neither was he capable of seeing it as funny as Zeus did.

Looking at the ground with a hopeless expression Zeus spoke apathetically. "Teoti? Source? Such a silly notion, the father of your nation passed down to you. A pathetic crutch, he was the weakest of all hearts."

Ryn's face shook with a horrid offense.

"You disagree? Well, if Teoti is supposed to be the Source, then you have some explaining to do."

Looking up at Ryn from the corner of his eyes, his voice became flat, "If Teoti is the Source, then he birthed these events. Assuming he has power to, and I know you assume he does. Thus, he ordained everything that happened here today."

Zeus stopped and waited for a few seconds before continuing, "You are mine because the Source, Teoti, gave you to me. Your men, your women, every advantage, all of your efforts and… Look." Zeus' head motioned over to Juya, "He gave me your wife."

Lifting his head in a sigh, he suddenly went into thought. "Whatever shall I do with her? Do you have any ideas?" His gaze came back to Ryn with a curious look.

The god tilted his head slightly, "No?"

Pausing for a few seconds, he paced back to the tent entrance. "He gave me your people, your land, your children…" Zeus stopped at the tent entrance, and tilting his head, spoke with frankness. "He even gave me you."

Ryn said nothing though it was obvious that his thoughts were sad.

Zeus continued to stare patiently out of the tent and waited to see if Ryn would respond. After he did not, Zeus laughed and smiled, shaking his head as he watched the exit in front of him. Turning his head and leaning over, he spoke to Ryn with a smile.

"Are we speechless?"

Ryn did not respond.

Zeus walked over to him, calmly. Standing over the Crovan, he watched his eyes shift from place to place on the ground. A fierce and cold stare was on the panther's face. "I suppose the thoughts of a fool never do make sense."

Ryn cringed at the remark and, turning to Zeus, defiantly spit in front of his foot.

The thunder god laughed hard, and, smacking his foot against the ground, he created a loud bang that flung dirt in every direction. It was a contained burst of energy that could have shattered the earth beneath them if he had so chosen to.

Ryn found it amusing the thunder god would use such power to do nothing more than command attention. But Zeus remained ignorant of his thoughts.

With a smile on his face, the god stepped up to the circle. "I see you disagree," he said, still laughing. His face showed how foolish he thought Ryn was, and he expressed it verbally. "Go on. Rebuke me, Arvaita of Teoti."

What was Zeus saying? An Arvaita was a Crovan term used for a monk or monkess who was of the highest holiness and godliness. An Arvaita had an unusually strong flow of the Great Wind, and thus, the presence of the Source's spirit in them. An Arvaita was a symbol of power, and Zeus had Ryn in submission. What Zeus was saying was that the best of Teoti was under his thumb.

He was insulting his god, his people, and within the insult was a questioning of Ryn's character. If Ryn was truly that holy, then how did Zeus submit him? If the Source was the source of all power, energy, and life, then how does Zeus defeat Ryn unless Zeus is holier?

Zeus happily continued this train of thought, "I possess more power, Ryn, more energy, more Source. If the Primordial is indeed closer in character to Teoti than he is to me, then you would have won, for you express Teoti. But I have won; therefore, I have greater power, greater energy, than Teoti and consequently, more Source and more Wind. Thus, I am more like the Primordial. So, you see, might is power, vanity is the spirit of the universe, aggression, and pride its energy. The selfish and proud man, the inward-focused man, will always take from the tender one, the sacrificing one, and he, the loving one, will die. It is this way because the Source made it this way, so you see, he is like me after all."

Ryn shot back with ferocity, a mad laughter in his voice. "You feign ignorance of this thing? He came before all. He IS all. How can something infinite take from that which he took out of himself? He is nothing like you. Why would he give only to take what was his anyway? It's foolish nonsense!"

Ryn arounsed his passion and continued. "He has not taken, he has given! He still gives, we only exist because he constantly gives, constantly animates! He gives! He does not take like you!"

The god did not react in anger, despite the fact that Ryn had shown him a severe lack of respect even beyond spitting at him. Instead, he remained expressionless and kept his voice flat.

Zeus came very close to Ryn and almost in a whisper responded, "And who has the Source given to this day, Ryn? Who?"

The thunder god moved slowly away.

Ryn was now visibly tired and hung his head in exhaustion. Gulping, he cleared his throat and began his rebuttal. "Teoti allows us to choose. We are not like him; we have rebelled against him. But," he said with an attempt to gather courage. "He will bring justice one day." Looking up at the god with mustered aggression, he spoke firmly, "I know that you are not more like him than I. Your time will come. I swear it!"

Zeus smirked at Ryn and moved to leave the tent. Before he came to the exit, he turned around and looked back at Ryn, "If you are correct, and the spirit of the Source is to give life, then why does he take it from you, who protects it, and give it to me, who takes it? Further, why is there death at all? You suggest that death and hate are here because of some rebellion. If this is so, then when the Primordial allowed the rebellion, when he gave birth to the rebellious, he gave birth to that which is contrary to himself. He gave birth to the rebellion. Unless he is a hypocrite and a liar or hiding something, you have nothing to offer but foolishness."

With that, Zeus left the tent and began shouting out orders outside.

Ryn shook his head and, with Zeus now gone, could not help but direct his gaze to Juya. Overwhelmed at the sight, he suddenly wept bitterly. The tears came off his face and struck the ground. Every drop was full of life and love, which bled from his spirit through his tears. Very soon, he began to blame himself. After all, it was because of his inadequacy, his lack of strength, that she was suffering. Heavy drops soon formed on his cheeks, and as each one fell, he sensed his heart shrinking. Frantically he redirected his aggression. His self-blame drained him faster than any other tear he had shed. The self-hatred brewing within silenced his spirit and left his scant energy more exposed to being drained.

Remembering everything Zeus had done, he focused his anger on the god and righteously focused his rebuke toward hate itself. As he gazed at her silent and lifeless face, he thought how terrible a perversion it was to do any harm to such a beautiful being — a jewel of infinite worth. Thoughts of her in Zeus' possession angered him further. Now mad with rage and jealousy, he almost sprung to his feet. Quickly he remembered his bonds and held his ground. He desperately wanted to get up and take her away, but he could not muster the strength to do so. He moaned, and it came out like the wine of a disgruntled cat, ugly and uncharacteristic of his lion-spirit. Unable to react in his desperate circumstance, he finally forced himself to sit down. As he did, the slow resignation of defeat crept into his heart and his feelings changed.

He began to feel cheated and betrayed. He tried hard not to blame Teoti for what was happening, but his heart unstoppably entertained resentment and bitterness. The more he fought, the more uncontrollable it seemed to become. Unsure of what to do as the anger consumed him, he finally let some of it come into his thoughts. In his mind, he tried to manage it, control it. It hurt to do so, and though he knew it would be good for him to allow it full expression, he placed a prudent cap over his emotions with layers of thought. There were many things he did not understand, and now was not the time to take any matter up with Teoti. He was in no mood to pray. But perhaps some form of it was his only outlet.

He chose to direct his upper thoughts toward heaven in a cognitive prayer. "What is happening to me? Do not abandon me! You had better care for Juya!" Cognitively he conceded to the heavens that he trusted Teoti but could not feel it. Every loss for the past thirty-six years begged thousands of unanswered questions, and he could barely contain them.

Ryn was still in this state of meditation when the flaps to the tent flung open, and two dunataso came in. They walked over to him and picked him off the ground. On their arms were silver bracers engraved with glowing runes. These allowed them to pick Ryn up off the enchanted ground that kept him from moving.

As they picked him up, Ryn felt the spiritual suppression subside. They clapped his arms in a brace as they picked him up, moving him out of the tent. Before they exited, Ryn looked back at his wife. Her body was still lying there, lifeless and ragged. She was not far from departing it. Quickly Ryn conceived again that death would probably be a much more humane fate than whatever she faced in the future. Quickly he wished this upon her and stretched for her in love with his eyes as he was led away. The tent flaps suddenly closed behind them and he could see her no more. With a quiver in his lip, he turned around to whatever fate awaited him.

The dunataso carried Ryn outside, and for the first time, he could see that they were in an entirely different location altogether. The country in front of them was very hilly and lightly forested. Behind him was an enormous mountain that was only the forerunner in a field of mountains that lay around it. Endlessly to their left and right were more high mountains, but the one they began to ascend was monstrous in comparison. There were several enormous tents and hundreds of dragons and giants, but the regular army was nowhere in sight. The sky was gray, and after grasping the spiritual feel for the area, Ryn reasoned that they were in a largely human kingdom ruled by the gods, perhaps on the Arvadian Peninsula. After seeing a road marker amidst the trees on a hill below, he saw that indeed they were on the southeast portion of the Arvadian Peninsula. They were on the border between Arovynia and Molnak. It seemed that Ryn had been unconscious for some time considering the great distance they were from the mountains of Aryn in Crova, about 450 alans.

The dunataso drug Ryn up towards the mountain where a path led them high up on the slope. The dragons and giants in company began to follow the dunataso, and a procession winded its way up the path. Ryn felt like he could break the bonds that held him, but without a weapon and in his current physical state, he would stand no chance of escaping. He definitely would not make it back to the tent where Juya was, and although this might be his best chance to get away, the overwhelming odds told him not to try but to wait upon a more favorable situation. Ryn found this difficult because he thought very seriously about fighting just so that his opponents would kill him and spare him the torment Zeus had planned. But the walk up the mountain gave Ryn much time to reason that a suicide was not the best thing for Juya or for his nation, no matter how many were left. There was still a sizable remnant, by all reports he'd received over the years. If there was any hope left, Ryn needed to be alive first. If Juya or anyone else ever needed him again, Ryn would have to be alive somewhere before he could do anything. So, despite the temptation to free himself from the upcoming pain, he remained in his bonds escorted by the entourage.

The dunataso brought Ryn between a number of crags and eventually into an open cavern hidden behind high walls on the mountain slope. Zeus was waiting there with two more dunataso and a black dragon. They all stood around a perfectly symmetrical circular hole in the rock that seemed to stretch into the mountain like a deep cave. On the ground in front of them was a circular pillar about ten to twelve strides long that looked like it had been removed from the side of the mountain, creating the cave. The group in front of the hole watched Ryn as the dunataso brought him into their midst. Beasts filed into the cavern behind them, and Zeus waited until the noise of footsteps stopped, and the place was silent.

With his hands comfortably behind his back, the thunder-sky god moved next to Ryn and began to speak, "I have finally decided what to do with your wife," he said plainly. "I am sending her into the underworld, as a message of victory to my brother Aides. There she will be *gehel*."

In an instant, Ryn's heart sunk. The minions of the underworld tortured with a certain sadism and perversion that was unspeakable. To be in the underworld, as a living being…

Deep within the bowels of the underworld, it was said that the gates of the grave sat like a green-glowing lake at the bottom of a huge abyss in front of Aides' throne. It was in the grave that the souls of the dead came to rest, and there were spiritual entities that brought souls from the earth to the grave as they died. Aides ruled over the pit and often could deny rest to souls he despised or simply chose to torment. Aides could keep Juya alive for centuries of spiritual torment if he chose to.

A chill ran down Ryn's spine, and he was

suddenly weak. Overcome with anguish and disgust, he violently croaked, and leaning over, physically vomited. Unable to stand, the dunataso held him up.

Zeus watched amusingly as the Crovan regained his breath and panted heavily. His face, for an instant, grew compassionate, and Zeus spoke tenderly to him, "It might be wise to petition your god for her death."

Looking at his enemy, he saw liquid vomit still running over his short beard. How pitiful he was, terribly pale, deathly sick, with vomit on his chin. Zeus looked at the ground for a few moments and soon chuckled. Looking up at the panther pitifully, he reached up and stroked his long mane-like hair. Nodding his head, he spoke as though Ryn were a naïve child. "But then again, if the prayers of the past have brought you to your current destination, it would be fearful to think what lay ahead should you ask for anything more."

Ryn was unable to respond. He actually cared little for what Zeus was saying. Deep within him collided waves of anger, self-hatred, despair, and confusion. Zeus backed away from him and took a deep breath. Then he motioned for the dunataso to throw Ryn into the cave. The dunataso complied and quickly shoved Ryn into the hole. Ryn was completely befuddled. He could not move and lay in the cave as activity went on behind him.

The black dragon lifted the pillar and moved toward the cave with it. "Goodbye, Ryn, king of Crova," Zeus said. "May your days still be many and your prayers many more," he said with a humorous air. With that, the dragon thrust the pillar into the cave. Sensing the pillar come towards him, Ryn quickly awoke and crawled down the tunnel. After about ten strides, he felt nothing and fell into black open space and onto a wet rock. The pillar came behind him, and with the sound of crashing granite, he was sealed in.

Zeus motioned to a hooded figure to seal the prison. Almost reluctant at first, it came over, and a slender apricot arm covered in smooth stubble fur reached out. Zeus took a deep breath and held up his hand. Opening his palm, he revealed a glowing cartouche, the likes of which seemed brimming with power like that of a thousand peals of thunder. The feminine figure carefully took the ovular item and held it flat against the pillar's outward seal where a hole lay for it to be inserted. She began mumbling slowly, and her voice showed the ancientness of her being.

Zeus seemed uncomfortable for a mere moment before covering his discomfort quickly.

As she sighed, she took the cartouche and turned slowly to hand it back to Zeus. "No living being will ever enter this place," she said softly.

He nodded, "At least I still have use for you," he said with a certain bite. The hand retracted, and for a moment, her blond hair and silver eyes were noticeable before retreating back into her cloak.

Before he turned to leave, she bowed shortly, "Do you have anything else I can be of use for?"

Zeus sniffed. "No. Go back. But if there is any indication this has failed, you will be coming back here to see. And if it is found your seal failed, I will put on you the punishment of Ryn." He turned away, and the slender feminine hand remained motionless in submission until he was no longer there.

*　　　*　　　*

A set of soft humanoid-canine eyes followed their movement from hidden trees. If there was one thing she did well, it was staying unseen. They had the young ones with them. It was not apparent what they would do, but she didn't need to know for sure. A set of Centaurs traversing as a party in the deepest parts of any Novan territory were up to no good. It mattered not that this land had passed from her king's control to Zeus' plenty of years ago.

The children struggled as the armored horse-men drug them along, bragging about their escapade. She knew, in close proximity now, that they were human children, likely from the nearby village. There was a group of settlers that had not lived here before the war, but innocents in comparison. She reached back and clutched a long thin wooden shaft and swung it to her front with smoothness and ease, all the time making not a slight disturbance in the mist, lest she be given away.

The husked voices of the captors were bellows of terror in their ears. The mist was cold that day, and it spoke an omen of death. The child wanted it to end, wanted the horror to go away. He wondered why it didn't just go away. Why wasn't it turning out to be fine? In his bleeding thoughts, he didn't notice anything had changed until he heard the thud of a body against the ground. Thinking it was the body of his sister, he shook his eyes open only to see the confounded horse-men looking down at the ground. One of their own was on it, covered in ice.

A scream of air like a whisking insect came out of nowhere, and the second, who held his sister by the hair, lurched back with a thunk and gawked through his horse-jawed mouth as an arrow now lay in his neck. Falling back, the boy saw the man's neck freeze like a block of ice before falling to the ground.

He didn't think to do anything but lunge forward and cover his sister. If they were going to die, he would die covering her. Gripping her with his face planted against a mossy tree root, he didn't hear what happened. It was a minute before anything caught his attention. But when it did, it was unexpected.

"Child, get up."

He shot his face over and saw a cloaked figure. Under the cloak, though well covered, was a fair-skinned being that, spirit-wise, felt like a wolf that lived in the mist. Was it perhaps a Novan, one of the original inhabitants of this land? He got to his knees and did the only thing he knew to do. He bowed down.

"P-please spare my sister and me. We mean you no harm, and we do not mean to intrude upon your territory."

A soft hand touched his shoulder, and it was accompanied by a gentle young, almost innocent voice. "You are fine. I will show you back to your village if you go."

The boy wanted to cry, and he almost did. Jumping to his feet, he led his sister up, and they followed the mysterious stranger southwest to where they had begun.

When they reached their destination after the long silent journey of half a day, he ran into the village with his sister in tow. Their father came out from the meeting hut, a husky man with a black beard. Shouting loudly, he went to embrace them.

The wolf-eyed wanderer of the mist made her way toward the forest from the edges of the village, but was soon found. A young man of the village had eyed her and wanted to get her attention, then the boy's father, still holding his war-ax, came bounding toward her; his fur-padded shoulders bouncing off his frame.

"Wait! You must!"

Sighing, she paused and looked at him.

Stopping short, he felt at a loss but got his words. "You are Novan, are you not?"

She gave him the slightest of nods.

"Then please, let me thank you for my son's life."

She answered back, "You are not afraid of drawing Zeus' ire for entertaining an enemy?"

He was obviously shocked by her youthful and feminine voice but did not seem to mind after a brief pause. "No. I had lost my whole life, and now I have it back. I ask you to come." She could not complain about that. She was quite hungry and in need of a good sleep anyway. She relented and came back with the two.

In the main hut, the people noticed her, though many tried not to pry. She was obviously happy to have a good meal and very friendly to the chief and his family. She was very fair, and she seemed so innocent and non-aggressive at times that one young man out of a group of four found it in his nerves to approach her.

"My lady, might I ask you if you are betrothed to anyone?"

Seeing his friends shocked at his forwardness, she responded with tact, "Cool your heart, son of man. Such a thing is not available to any here. Though take heart, you have a fair continence. I'm sure you will please someone's eye."

A little stunned yet not harmed in any way, he walked back to his chiding friends. In the midst of them, he defended himself, "I have a fair continence."

That made her laugh. They were a pleasant people. This experience was a very good change.

Going to bed that night, she kept her bow at her side. She was used to the suddenness of the night by now. A lot had happened that had changed her, and it had everything to do with where the dreams took her. She kept seeing it. A light. The dragon-lion. She kept seeing it. She was waiting for it. The light was so bright over it that she knew that wherever it was, she had to be there, and she wanted to be there for who it was. She didn't know where the light was now, but she knew, in each dream, it was getting clearer.

She fell asleep soundly, with faith that tonight she might get her answer, and sure enough, she did. Awaking before it became day, she packed quickly. She now knew where she needed to go, and she needed to hurry. She could not miss his arrival. If he left before she got there, she could not think of it. She had to be there. Both of them. The dragon-lion and the panther. She had her next target, and before anyone knew, she slipped into the mist to continue to quest for the familiar place, the person around whom she knew she needed to be.

*   *   *

Now awaken from a cognitive slumber, he quickly tugged at the brace shackling his arms and shattered it. There was silence. There in the dark, he was awake and began to make observations. At first, he could see nothing, but shortly he saw that the walls were illuminated with a glowing purple light. It was not bright enough to illuminate the area he was in, but it did reveal to him the contour of his location.

He seemed to be in a square room carved out of the rock. The ceiling was high above him, around forty cubits, and the walls were about fifteen strides apart. The floor glowed as well but was not smooth like the walls around him. It seemed to be jagged rock in no particular pattern or contour, and it was also wet. That was odd. Over time the water would surely wash out these runes. But then again, he realized that if they had left the floor unshaved, then they had embedded the affective runes deeper in the rock below. The top layer was the padding of the armor, while the iron lay far below. After a few seconds of listening, Ryn realized that running water entered the room on his right and exited on his left.

His first reaction was to try and find the entry and exit points. Ryn could not believe that Zeus would be so careless as to leave him a way out through a spring inside the rock, but it was worth looking. Ryn felt his way across the jaded rocks and found the entry point, which was a small hole in the wall that was no more than the size of a finger. He followed the trickling water slightly downhill across the room until he found the exit point, which was slit in the rock floor too narrow to fit a finger into.

Earlier, he had thought to blast his way through the rock but now dismissed the idea as he realized what the glowing lights were. They were shield-casting runes, enchantments that were meant to make the rock indestructible. These runes were not unbreakable. The fastest way would be to use the water in the room. But he had very little water, and the walls were littered with them. They varied in size and covered every small part of the room. When a weapon-smith wished to remove a rune from a blade, he bathed it in the river for 20-40 days. There was no telling how long it would take with what he had. It could likely take him years of spiritual battle to break enough runes so as to blast enough rock away, and that was assuming there wasn't a layer behind the first layer. And even then, that calculation was given that he could stay spiritually and physically healthy, which was impossible in such a place. There was no access to the Wind. Everything was blocked out — this was a tomb.

Ryn was not surprised. Indeed, Zeus had thought of everything. But why would he leave Ryn in a place with running water? He listened further and also noticed that air was creeping in by way of the tunnel. He felt his way over to the pillar and felt air coming in and going out through notches in the sides of the cylindrical rock. Not only this, but after listening further, he observed that small creatures existed in the room as well. They were insects of some type, and soon, Ryn felt a fly land on his arm before he brushed it off.

In all reality, the room was a viable cage, allowing interaction with the outside environment while keeping Ryn sealed in. At first, Ryn did not know what to think, but he soon realized how this was intentional. Ryn had been left with breathable air, running water, and insects with which to live on. It was Zeus' every intention that Ryn be alive for years to come in which he would agonizingly contemplate his defeat and Juya's torture.

Indeed, this was a devious plot by Zeus. Ryn may have fared decently against methods of torture and humiliation leading up to an inevitable death, but here Ryn was left alive with only his failures and his thoughts. His only escape from the prison was to die by volitional starvation or some other means of suicide.

"This is what he wants," he said to himself. It was not enough to kill Ryn. He wanted Ryn to give up and bring death upon himself. It was the spiritual victory Zeus sought. Such an assassination was not how one ended a soldier's life. But it was how one ended a god's. A god could reanimate another flesh. The only way to ensure a god could not do that was to destroy their very wind with entropy. This...was a god's execution.

Ryn leaned back against the upper wall in a trance. His body dropped lifelessly as his mind began to wander. Was this really it? Had he been resigned to this tormenting fate? Ryn felt he was strong and resilient. He had been a powerful monk for many years before he was made king, and his spiritual and mental durability were like no other. Deservedly Ryn had been called an Arvaita. But in this dark place, in this dungeon, Ryn did not think that even he could survive the long and agonizing days ahead of him. He felt tired. He felt drained. Even before he had been put behind these walls, he had been stripped of his strength.

Ryn slowed his thinking. Thousands of ideas and arguments flowed into his head every second, and he had to stop, simply to observe. Too much rational thought was a quick road to a deteriorated spirit, and because of the troubling thoughts he faced, it was likely he would be driven mad. Trying to reach a state of meditation, he found himself moment by moment, attempting to divert his attention from the abstract.

The room smelled like rust and mold. Most likely, due to the interaction the water had with its environment. Vividly he heard the clicking and chirping of insects as they scampered across the rocks and in and out of tiny crevasses in the walls. He heard the patter of their little legs all around him. He also heard the air wisping in and out of the room through the notches in the pillar. Other than that, there was the faintest of trickling of the water. He heard the noises blend together and found the rhythm and melody in them. He appreciated it. Then he disliked it. What was it compared to the melody of the Wind?

After what seemed hours, Ryn attained cohesion between his mind and his heart and resumed thought. He was surprised it had taken so long, but there was a lot of shock to work through. He began to contemplate the fate of his wife and the words Zeus had said to him. Indeed, Teoti was watching, and this event had been allowed. All manner of sins had been allowed. Did this mean Teoti was unconcerned? No, Ryn knew Teoti was an interactive god. In fact, he felt compelled to expect him to act. How could the Source, the author of life, not act against death? Why was he not acting now? He'd asked that a lot over the years, and every time he did, he'd received no better answer. The only difference was that now there was time to think, and it was irritating him to have to turn the same unanswered question over and over again as though it would suddenly change colors.

He tried to listen to the Wind, but the energy of the universe was indeed hindered by the runes of the chamber. What came through was like sawdust while he likened his task to building a temple. It was hopeless.

Ryn was confounded. It didn't make sense. None of it did. Why? What was the reason for this? He found no reason. He didn't know it. When he didn't know, there was only one recourse. But did he even bother? If he could not hear, then why bother? But Teoti—if he was truly as they knew him—couldn't he have the power to hear Ryn anywhere? He paused and meditated on that thought.

After turning his thoughts and emotions over several times, he began to pray. Did he make a plea, or did he need to understand? Both, he conceded. But practically, he began to wonder if it really mattered. After all of his prayers over the last 30 years, he watched Crova evaporate in front of him; he found himself tempted to be numb. If Teoti wanted Ryn to live, he would live, and if Teoti was going to let Ryn die in this dungeon, then it would be so. But he could not help but speak. There were things he wanted his god to hear him say. He found it trivial to close his eyes or change his position but rather sat and spoke aloud.

"Are you here? I am afraid," he began. "You have brought me to a place of uncertainty. I… I am…"

Slumping over, he grabbed his chest. His heart was aching. From the pit of his body, he felt nausea, and a very real physical illness came over him. It resonated from his pain and anxiety. It seemed to swell within him, pressing against his soul. It was as though his inner organs were bloated and expanding, ever aching as they stretched beyond what they were meant to; only it was his spirit that was in pain. The pressure was great, and his lip quivered with anger. Soon he found reverent restraint to be useless in comparison to real expression.

Ryn rose to his knees and, holding his head up towards the heavens, roared from the top of his lungs. The roar of despair was soon followed by speech.

"WHAT ARE YOU DOING? WHY HAVE YOU DONE THIS TO ME?"

The anger moved fiercely in him, and it shook him as it came out. Somewhere he felt ashamed of his lack of restraint but reasoned that Teoti was big enough to handle him. If he wasn't going to say it now, he never would. He deserved to hear it.

"TELL ME, HOW HAVE I BROUGHT THIS DOWN UPON MYSELF!"

He shook at the ceiling and groaned.

"WHAT HAVE I DONE TO DESERVE THIS TORMENT! WHAT DID I DO TO YOU?"

He threw out in condemnation. A single thought hit him right away, and his pride instantly evaporated, leaving his anger with an empty center and nothing to stand on. The panther let out a loud wine and slumped into a sob as reality suddenly struck him. He felt it. He felt the truth of his condition and situation. Ryn did not deserve Teoti's favor. No creature did.

What had he done to the Source? Against that pure and original origin, the Source, he could not hold a light. His own darkness, his own evil, had brought about more death and darkness by happenstance alone. He was angry but relented to the obvious. Deserve; that was a dangerous word. It meant 'balance.' If everything was balanced right now, evil against good, what would befall him? The truth was; more disaster and more death.

He wiped his face while shaking. It was odd that both humans and gods were capable of ignoring reality. Both could act like infants, ever wanting and expecting, never realizing the full extent of their contribution. No creature had healed more than they'd harmed, not one. That was unavoidable. How did they get past that? How could he not deserve death? He didn't have an answer for that.

Hunched over on his knees, he continued to sob.

"I am sorry. I am not worthy of your response."

He paused as fluid fell from his eyes and nose. "Do whatever you want."

He could not even wipe his face but soon tightened his fist, mustering all his hope. "But in doing what you want, know that I am in pain," he said sternly. "And I don't want Juya to suffer…"

Remembering his wife, Ryn brought his face to the rock and wept. There was no way to express his sorrow with words, nor was there a need. The horrors Juya faced came flooding into his mind, and he no longer restrained them. He contemplated it fully, and soon, an ocean of emotions found their way to his lips. He could no longer hold them back. It would be like trying to stop water with a fishing net; it could not be done.

He groaned with sorrow and rage together as he felt her fate. He shook and pounded his fists. In between each blast of sorrow and belt of anger, there was a gasp for air. Every blast of anger simultaneously relieved him of something and heaped something upon him. He shouted at the situation, at anything that would listen in defiance and terror all at once.

His spirit roared like a lion, desperately proclaiming protection over her. But he could not. He was bound, enslaved, and his body and spirit found its only outlet in roars and screams that truly only the Great Wind could hear and were truly meant for only the Wind to hear.

Every living thing had fled the room in fear of Ryn's vicious spiritual presence. His body knelt hunched over his knees, trembling, but his spirit lashed out at the walls and the ceiling, unable to be released, like a tethered lion. His spirit was violent and without restraint. It wouldn't stop either. He knew that with every shout, he was sending away his vitality, but the rage forced it out of him as though he were having to vomit.

After hours of shaking the walls with his roars, he was exhausted. Still trembling, he resigned himself to a fetal position and lay helplessly on the jagged floor. Worn out from his shouting, Ryn slowly became still, and the lion lumbered down to the ground in weariness. As he lay there, his spirit howled every so often like a wounded cat lying helplessly on its own. Ryn's body came to a stop, and finally, his eyelids dropped over his teary pupils, and his body slept.

4 THE ARVAITA EMERGES

Ryn found himself floating through a thick white cloud with a warm light on his back and a breeze blowing in his face. The cloud was thick in front of him and blew past his face as a matterless vapor. Though the air behind him was brightly lit and warm, as he flew farther through the clouds, the wind in front of him became colder. He could not turn to look behind him but felt as though he were falling from the sun to the earth.

Suddenly, he had begun to accelerate, and the air in front of him became uncomfortably cool. The cloud became thinner until he finally burst through its bottomless white blanket and into a clear expanse. Below him, a dark storm cloud covered his entire range of vision. As he lifted his head to look to the side, he saw that two blankets of clouds continued endlessly in every direction, clearly separated by the expanse. The light penetrated the white billows above and fell onto the black storm clouds, raging chaotically against the light with spits of lightning.

As Ryn fell frightfully fast towards the dark clouds, he felt distinctively that the light was not impressed upon by the coldness, but it simply faded and penetrated the air below less and less. Now rushing by, the cold air approaching him began to blast against his body. The solid dark clouds beneath him raged at him from below with a certain maliciousness. As he approached it, he realized suddenly that he might be splattered against it as if he had fallen from the sky onto a hard rock. But as he accelerated into the dark mass, he instantly fell through it into dark smoke.

The earth below him pulled him down faster and faster through the swirling dark clouds raging with violent flashes of lightning as he went. Their chaotic and violent dance followed him down, swirling all around him until he exploded from it with great force. He was suddenly falling through a vacuum onto a desolate and dark plain where nothing grew or lived.

The dark and lifeless desert charged fast upon Ryn, and he accelerated to such speed that he became sure of his own demise. He could see his body instantly being shattered upon the dry, cracked earth beneath him. But just as he approached, in less than an instant, the ground rushed past him, and he saw himself falling into a black pit. The pit grew icier and icier as he fell through it. The light and warmth from above seemed to fade like a distant memory and vanish deep in the pit. Ryn fearfully rushed straight into its cold darkness.

Suddenly he flew into a wave of foul odor permeating from the spiritual presence below. The repulsive aura of decay permeated everything, and he gagged under it. As he descended further, he found it impossible to breathe; the foul air and icy atmosphere shut his lungs. Unable to close his eyes, he saw everything but perceived nothing. Everything was black.

Falling at immeasurable and indiscernible speeds, Ryn gazed at the vacuum beneath him until he found himself floating downwards from the top of a monstrous cavern. Soon the cavern became clearer as green light illuminated things from below. Out of the rock wall jettisoned a cliff upon which was a fearful black silhouette seated on a rocky throne. In the figure's right hand was a staff and over the being's body was a triangular robe. It sat perfectly still upon the rock like an unmovable shadow. The cliff towered over a black lake that filled the bottom of the cavern. From the black depths emanated green aura. Its waves cast a green shadow and rolled up against the walls of the cavern as the waves hit it. Ryn fell unnoticed past the cliff and down towards the dark waters until he plunged headfirst into the murky liquid.

He did not stop or even slow down but continued to pass quickly through the lake towards the bottom. The souls of the dead swirled around him in the thick and dark waters, and their deadness filled Ryn with terror. Even though Ryn plunged through them at an alarming speed, he felt deeply fearful that if they so much as touched him, their lifelessness would defile him and that he would quickly decay. He was relieved that they did not seem to notice him as he plunged ever deeper towards the bottom.

As Ryn fell farther and farther, the lake seemed to disappear, and the souls became less and less frequent until he saw only void beneath him. Quickly, the significance of the blackness below came to him as he sensed nothing underneath it as though the universe were coming to an end. Ryn was filled with helpless terror. He was falling into nothingness, void, a place of non-existence, without movement and without mass. It struck him that upon collision with the blackness below, he would instantly disintegrate.

Ryn looked down and suddenly saw two enormous eyes of putrid fire open beneath him. They locked onto him slyly as he fell. Screaming with horror, he grabbed for anything to stop his descent. The unspeakable power seemed to arise out of the void as though the monster's very skin was somehow coated with nothingness. It opened its mouth, and a vacuum caught him, pulling him down.

Then he saw nothing. His vision remained black, and he began lashing out at everything around him. Finally, seeing the familiar runes under his hands and feet, he saw that his body was bouncing off the walls frantically. Quickly Ryn became aware of his body again and, forcing himself to a stop, planted into the dark, jagged floor.

His heart breathed a gasp of spiritual air. It had been a dream. Ryn's heart immediately rejoiced in the fact that he had not experienced the terrors he saw. Thankful, he kissed the stone beneath him and clenched his fists.

Quickly he remembered all that had taken place: the battle, Zeus, his wife, and his confinement. The sound of trickling water and whistling wind brought his memory into reality, and Ryn's heart sunk back down into despair as he lay on the cold rock.

The sounds of the elements filled his head as he analyzed his dream. Had he lost favor with Teoti? Ever since Nova had been invaded, Ryn had wrestled with this. Such a dream of the Source casting Ryn from the heavens to the abyss was terrifying. He feared judgment, the inescapable judgment of his kind, for everything his ancestors had done. Their sins were in his blood. That was the problem, a problem he could not figure out. Teoti called them to reconcile, but the sin was in their blood.

He pondered that. Laying back, he had plenty of time to reflect, and he recounted the history of his people.

Many hundreds of years ago, a prophet and holy man named Ano had told that the Primordial would bring judgment upon the world because of its wickedness. The entire earth would be wiped out, and all things made new because of the existence of the Nephilim. Their existence was the result of Stars, who had come to earth to conquer it and bare their own kin through humans.

He called the Nephilim a curse upon mankind, leading them astray. Ryn was the king of such a race. The father of the Crovan nation was a son of Yhadyal, one of the fallen heavenly beings. Yhadyal had many sons, but his favorite was Onal, an enormous giant. In his carnal form, he was gray-skinned and thick of body and limb. He had a trunk for a nose and mouth with tusks. Onal had a very cruel heart and a sadistic taste for human suffering. He became just like his father. Because of this, Onal was looked upon with favor. The lanky and very humanoid dragon-like son, Traijyn, was despised.

Traijyn tolerated humans and kept many as servants. Early in his life, he had a love of violence, but it was kept in check by his intellect. He was said to always be calculating. He soon realized that a god who is loved by his worshippers has something more valuable than one who has fear. Thus, he treated humans well.

Traijyn's docile and favorable actions towards humans earned him the distaste of his father. Eventually, the distance between them became intolerable for Yhadyal. Traijyn refused to do his bidding, and Yhadyal disowned and banished his son from their home in Canaan. He moved east, into Emade, and it was here that Ano came to Traijyn and befriended him. Ano had profound wisdom and understanding that Traijyn was enamored by. Never had a son of man shown him such understanding and clarity. Traijyn was soon won over and recognized the Primordial as in control and the rightful king of the universe.

Traijyn's proclamation of this was inconceivable. No one had ever heard of a god worshipping another god. It was seen as a betrayal of all gods. The offense spawned a war between Onal and Traijyn. Traijyn was fortunate that by that time the Titans had been bound and imprisoned in the abyss by the Stars. Had Yhadyal been there, he—and likely all the Titans—would have descended upon his house to destroy it.

Traijyn's armies fought better, but Onal received mercenaries from Egypt and Sumer. By the end of the war, all Canaan, the Elo Ijuma peninsula south of it, and the plains east of it, the land of Tobol, were all under Onal's rule. Traijyn, rather than continue to fight with his brother, took his clan away from the eastern plains and moved north to the Ystrafe Mountains. This location far north of Sumer and between the Dark Sea and Crystal Sea provided excellent space to start over and spawn a new nation.

It was here that Traijyn settled the tribes of his two wives, the panther-like Crova, and the wolf-like Nova. These were the two women that rebelled against the way of the gods with him. The two tribes would become two powerful empires, one in the north and one in the south. Both followed in Traijyn's tradition and believed all the prophecies of Ano. Despite their uniqueness as a Nephilian race that worshipped Teoti, they had not been spared. All this time, how had he explained that? Why was this happening? But that was just it. This judgment must have meant that the sins of the blood were too important to forgive.

Regardless of anyone's actions, the blood spoke to everything. Traijyn, Onal, Zeus, and others like Poseidon, Osiris, Enki, Ziva, and Labak, were all sons of Titans. They were all commonly descended from the black holes of Heaven. Ryn had the same darkness in his blood as Zeus, and his ancestors were guilty of the same crimes. They involved the destruction of mankind, and for these crimes, Ano had prophesied judgment upon them. That blood and its legacy stood and condemned him, no matter what truth they adhered to. He could not escape the sin of his blood.

That was what burdened Ryn's heart the most. The earth was meant for mankind, not for Nephilim, and though they revere and worship the Source, the Source had in mind that there was no place for them in this world. Yhadyal bore Traijyn, who bore Alyn, who bore Jyrai, who bore Amyn, who bore Ryn. Ryn was born because mankind fell into slavery. The fact that all of his fathers since Traijyn had been holy men and monks did not matter. The blood was the blood.

He could try and argue against it. But he was too wise to be in denial. The fallen stars and their ancestors had brought to mankind knowledge of divination, astrology, windscaping, and metallurgy for weapon making. Darkened and malleable in their innocence, their faith quickly went from his own abilities to their tools, and then to their gods. Weakness, ugliness, and death came on swifter wings because of this. Knowing Crovans and Novans used this knowledge extensively further condemned him in front of the Primordial.

Ryn quickly began to drown in sorrow. He was a curse upon the earth, not by his choosing, but simply by his being birthed.

"Our annihilation is righteous and just," he thought aloud. "You have it in mind for all of us to perish to make it right. I am a curse!"

Every failure that Ryn had suffered over his lifetime came back to him in his misery and told him of his accursedness. As a monk, he'd learned his value was not his to determine. But what he saw…he saw. Perhaps, in this space, he had to come to the reasonable conclusion that he was being informed of his value.

Ryn wanted desperately to believe he was worth something to the Source, not just a mistake, but he could not hurdle the truths that tore at him. In sudden betrayal, a faith that had taught him how to connect with purity and goodness now turned on him and condemned him.

In a mess of self-anger and defensiveness, Ryn began tarring his spirit apart from the inside. With every insult and accusation, he broke down further. This whole time, what had he been fighting for?

He longed to be of value, to be accepted by the Source. There was no other reason to exist, yet he couldn't have that reason. What good was it to be when you were not meant to and then not wanted? He simultaneously hated it and was angry, yet found it easy to accept and strangely appropriate. The burden of value could go away, and he could leave this world without remorse, for it would lose nothing.

He countered with the thought of what he could do if he made it out. But he asked, what could he do? Was he not just another mistake making more mistakes? He had no reason to save himself. Why continue to fight for an accursed mistake? But if he died, didn't Zeus win? But why did he care if Zeus won if he was a mistake? If his kind was filthy and corrupt, it didn't. But Zeus was real, so it did matter. It mattered because Zeus was evil. He knew it.

Ryn cried out in desperation, pleading with the Great Wind. "Don't let me destroy myself! Help me! Don't let him defeat me!"

Ryn's body trembled and convulsed in agony as he battled his self-destructive torment. A powerful and subliminal spirit began to grow and manifest itself around him. It hovered over him and condemned him for all his sins. Was that his heart manifesting an eon? It was ugly. There had to be another option. He dug deep and heard it. There was another voice that was very faint that tried to comfort him, telling him of his righteous heart and acts of love—rebutting, briefly, the idea of his people's filth and corruption. But it was vague and difficult to grasp. It fell in and out of sensibility. Was that one fake, a made-up counter to the other like an imaginary rope a man sees as he's falling to his death? He couldn't grasp after a fake. He could not commit to either, and his desire to have the answer given to him was unsatisfied.

Finally, weary of the inner conflict, Ryn screamed at the walls one last time, feeling his frustration with his situation. It was an angry scream of defiance, imbued with temporary hatred. No sooner had he released the air from his lungs did he suddenly feel he was in great error. A correction came, suddenly, as though he'd been in a box the whole time, and the lid had finally been shut.

Immediately he shut his mouth. His scream died as soon as it took off. No monk would ever do what he just did. He had acted in folly. The condemning voice, the dark spirit, ridiculed him for it and tried to arouse his anger, accusing the Source of not having compassion, but Ryn quickly realized its game. Sitting up, he chanted a holy prayer, and soon, a dark aura dissipated and vanished. The Wind had spoken, even in this suffocating spiritual coffin, and Ryn became silent and listened.

After a while of meditating, he bowed his face to the floor and prayed. As he did, he became aware that his acts of sin and acts of love had nothing to do with whether or not Teoti cared for him. He could not be righteous enough to deserve his respect; neither could he sin enough to diminish his value. Likewise, neither blessings nor curses were reflective of what he deserved, so how could they indicate favor if they did not indicate justice? It was like starting with no fish, being given two, and then feeling angry he didn't receive four. The point was that he received fish when he had none, and that was that.

His anger was misdirected. He made a silly association. The Source would do what he would do.

He knew Teoti. He saw Ryn and watched him as he battled for him in this wicked world. That should be enough. It was enough to be known. That was all there really was, wasn't there? When a being died a thousand deaths and entered the depths of the underworld, was there anything left than to be known by the Source? The Source was the Source, who could tell him what to do or enlighten him to justice or reason? "Ymaiyel abanad, Saiyan ala ja," he said genuinely.

At this, Ryn felt satisfied. He had been very prideful. Despite the pain, he was feeling, and despite whatever grief he was enduring, he would not bring accusations against the Source, nor did one blame the Source for pain and suffering. A monk knew from his first initiation that it was not the Source who brought pain and suffering. It was not the Source who instituted it as Zeus had alluded to. Rather, the Source molded pain and suffering into character and acts of surrender and love.

Ryn knew that the Primordial was there first. Death came with the actions of creation, not the creator. Perhaps, the Primordial felt every bit as much of the pain as he did, perhaps even more so, for he was not limited in his experiences and could perceive all anguish where Ryn's suffering was isolated. If he thought of it, what man does not suffer when his own son does? What man does not suffer when his creations are damaged? If the Primordial did not at least feel sorrow for creation, he was less than creation, and that was not possible.

Ryn lay back against the rock and accepted his condition. The truth was that as far as he could perceive, he was not going to escape. The enchanted walls kept any manner of positive spirit from flowing into the room, and without divine intervention, Ryn would eventually lose his hope and die. There was no use in being angry, and Ryn saw that now. He was still furious. There was much to be angry about, but powerless to change anything and to having to place all his hope in Teoti; he found his spirit relieved of any responsibility at the moment.

It wasn't a place of no hope. Quite the contrary, it was the opposite. He had outrageously high hope. There was simply nothing he could do but wait on his god. All of his hope was in Teoti, and for the moment, that felt perfectly fine. Once again, he was exhausted and had little energy. He laid down on the rugged rock and became comfortable.

It was in those moments that he began to realize something. He felt sustained. That was odd. He looked around and was certain no Wind was entering the area, yet, he felt it. How had the Great Wind entered there? No. It hadn't entered there. It had entered through him. Sensing within himself, it was almost as though he felt something touching his heart, a source of Wind. How was this possible? He felt it, sensed it. Before long, he got an image, perhaps of a finger.

As he was contemplating it, his senses suddenly pulled him out of his inner self. Still spread out face up on the rock, Ryn took note of the wall to his right, which had slowly begun to collect a red tint. The runes on the walls seemed to diminish in brightness until Ryn found that the runes did not seem to glow at all. In fact, the walls all began to collect the red tint. Furthermore, a circle of about seven cubits in diameter at the bottom of the right wall was now brightening in a red glow. Eventually, the room was illuminated by the glow, and Ryn sat up, seeing the room lit for the first time by this strange red light.

He stood up and watched the glow intensify. He felt the heat begin to permeate from the circle. An unfathomable amount of energy was bleeding through the other side of the wall, and, for a moment, Ryn thought that either the mountain was a volcano now erupting, or someone of great power, the power of several gods, had come for him.

The wall now glowed brightly as if it were on fire, and from the dead center of the circle, a ray of white light blasted through a small hole. Ryn backed away, and the hole increased in size as the rock melted away from the center.

He was astonished by the energy coming through the rock and was even more astonished that the runes on that wall had been rendered impotent by the spiritual force behind it. The sheer power of whatever melted the wall struck Ryn with fear, and regardless of who it was, he had psychologically begun to expect death.

The walls melted back in a circle, and as the rock on top of the circle melted, it broke off in chunks and fell to the ground. The white light had filled the entire room, and it became so intense, Ryn had to shield his eyes. Even after turning away, it was too intense for him to keep his eyes open. He also soon realized that with his eyes closed and his hands covering them, the light was penetrating his flesh enough so as to cause him pain. Quickly he fell to the ground and shielded his eyes against the rock floor.

The light began to diminish, and Ryn felt a fresh cool breeze enter the room and halt the sound of bubbling lava. Everything became silent, and he feared looking up at the circle but knew it was pointless to cower like this, for whoever had come for him was not oblivious as to his presence. Ryn slowly began to lift his eyes and saw the room was illuminated by a soft white light coming from the entrance of the circular cave now carved out of the rock.

Looking closer, Ryn saw that a humanoid figure stood at the entrance. Its skin was solid and intense like the purest bronze, and its hair was long and a shiny black that reflected light like a pool of water. Its eyes were a sky blue, and it wore a snow-white tunic that stretched down to its knees and was tied around the waist with a golden sash.

Ryn had never seen so white a garment, and its sleeves were folded inside so as to stretch over the shoulders but leave the arms bare. It wore golden sandals that basket weaved up its shins. Tucked into the left hip of the sash was a long double-edged sword. Its blade was as clear as water, and it was sheathed in gold. The sheath was smooth and unornamented, just as the tunic was plain and undecorated. The being had a shine to him that illuminated the room, and his spirit was strong, authoritative, and masculine but pure of any evil or darkness.

The purity of the being struck him with fear. He backed away from him and dropped to his knees out of natural submission and respect. As he did, the being took a step towards Ryn and spoke softly and casually.

"Stand on your feet. I am not so far above you as to deserve such homage; rather, it is he from whom I have been sent that deserves your admiration."

Ryn slowly arose and made eye contact with the being. As soon as he saw the being he had known he was a Star. "Who is this that Teoti has graciously sent to me? I fear I am not worthy of such an audience?" Ryn spoke softly and carefully with respect.

"I have been in audience with your people a long time, Ryn. I am Amaras, and you are not so far kin from me."

Ryn bowed his head, "I am honored by your visit, Amaras. I am humbled by your presence."

Amaras, Teoti's messenger to the Crovans. Throughout the nation's history, Amaras had been a guide to Traijyn, and subsequently afterward, to Crova and Nova. Every proceeding king of Crova had been honored by a visit from him. It was now Ryn's turn, and the fact he was here was incredibly important because why else send him to Ryn if Ryn was not meant for something noble?

Amaras stepped comfortably close to Ryn and spoke with frankness, "Ryn, the truths you hold are not in error. Teoti has indeed decreed the destruction of this world as you heard from the prophet Ano, but that will not happen during your time. Teoti has set you apart to bring judgment upon Zeus for his terrible deeds, for they have reached a full measure. You are being sent to do this so that the righteous may not be wiped off the face of the earth. Teoti has in mind to save a righteous remnant of mankind, and you, Ryn, are Teoti's tool for ensuring this."

The news struck Ryn with a shock of varying emotions. Here he was, hearing it. He was not Teoti's enemy but his servant, and he was joyous almost to tears because he would be the tool for such a righteous and important mission. But soon, Ryn realized all that lay ahead of him, and he became concerned; how would he defeat Zeus and his army?

He began to speak when Amaras headed him off, "Do whatever you feel is necessary to defeat your adversary. Build an army to attack Olympus, increase your abilities, and gather allies so as to defeat Zeus, and wherever you fall short of victory, Teoti will do that which is necessary to lift you up, for Teoti has decided to make foolish the wisdom of the self-appointed gods through you in a way all the world will recognize."

The Star reached behind his back and unsheathed a long lance that Ryn had not noticed until Amaras had reached for it. It wasn't that it hadn't been there. It was simply that Amaras' presence was so large it hid it. He pulled it out over his back and held it out for Ryn to take.

The shaft was about eight cubits long and appeared solid silver but with an organic quality to it. Upon the end of the shaft was a blade, well over a cubit in length and half cubit wide. The blade was flat and thick, with edges cut at perfect forty-five-degree angles. It was in the shape of a hexagon and was transparent like water.

Amaras extended the weapon to Ryn and urged him to take it, "Here is your new weapon Ryn. It is pure and untainted and will make your energy flow stronger than if it came straight from your hand."

Ryn reached out and took the blade, and as soon as he did, he felt his energy permeate the entire thing and radiate with some unseen powerful presence as if the weapon were a spiritual conductor. In the proceeding moments, he felt a heap of warm energy enter him from Amaras.

With suddenness, it came, and in no time at all, he felt restored. His wounds were gone, his fatigue was lifted, and his boundless energy had been restored. He was instantly rejuvenated as though he'd just awaken from a long, comfortable rest. In that one moment, he caught a glimpse of a realm that was untainted by darkness, and suddenly his concept of purity was enhanced like never before. Did Amaras and the Stars really come from a realm like that? It was like the sky, but above the sky, neither here nor there. It was, all at once, reality, and yet removed from it like a dream. Where was this place?

"Its name is Arvaita, for like you, it is able to manifest many forms of energy. You will have no need for a wet stone or any other enhancing device, for you will not encounter any force or material in this world capable of damaging or dulling its edge. When you have no use for it, keep it sheathed and do not lend it to anyone else to use. Remember, the blade will destroy the tainted things of this world, so be very careful with it. And remember that although the blade may take life, the hilt may channel it from you, should you ever need to give it away."

Ryn broke from his trance to twirl the weapon from hand to hand and enjoyed the glide that it seemed to have to it. It seemed to be burdenless, almost weightless and did not meet the normal wind resistance that he felt it should have. As the wind carries a leaf over a field, so the weapon was carried through the air, effortlessly and relaxed. It puzzled him, for the weapon seemed to have incredible mass—more than he could see yet seemed to support its own massive weight. Ryn looked once more at the weapon in awe and then sheathed it on his back.

Amaras spoke again, "When you leave, go through the tunnel that I have left for you. That tunnel will lead to the underworld of these mountains. Go up until you come to a tunnel above you and a narrow path beneath you. Follow the narrow path until you drop into a large passageway. Continue upwards until you get to a large open cavern at the top of which will be a staircase that will lead you into the tombs of Molnak. Use the Arvaita to light your way in the darkness and to defeat any foes you may encounter, but use it reservedly. Upon reaching the tombs, proceed up the stairs through the winding caves until you come to the hall. The entrance to the hall exits into the hill country of Molnak."

Amaras smiled at Ryn, who stared graciously at him in anticipation. The Star almost looked as if Ryn had begun to ask a question and had not finished. Ryn looked back at Amaras and realized that he was waiting for Ryn to ask the obvious question he had on his mind.

Ryn awoke from his listening mindset and blurted out quickly, "What will happen to my wife?"

Amaras smiled at him with compassion and responded almost reluctantly, "I do not know what your Juya's fate will be, whether life or death. However, I am to tell you that Teoti will intervene for you so that she will not suffer more than she can bear. Neither will she submit her spirit to anyone other than Teoti."

Ryn dropped his head and sighed heavily as he closed his eyes. Was it enough to know that? It would have to be. She would not taste spiritual death. Though he would have liked to know her physical fate, he found her spiritual health beyond the grave to be much more important to him and to her, and he had to be satisfied.

Amaras spoke again, "When you exit in the hills of Molnak, do no go to the south back across the mountain or southwest into Akola to summon allies. Zeus' army will be on patrol in all of those surrounding regions, rather, go west, north and then east, into your home country until you get to the high mountains of Ystrafe."

Ryn was still in contemplation when Amaras stopped speaking. As Ryn looked up, he heard Amaras bid him blessings, and when his eyes met the space where Amaras was supposed to be, he had vanished.

5 THE GOD'S TEMPLE

Ryn lit the Arvaita with his fire, and it made a bright yellow light. The tunnel that Amaras had created was as smooth as skin and extended about 120 strides before opening up into a natural cave burrowed out of the earth. This cave was no more than five cubits high and four cubits in width. It was fairly smooth and was probably created by some sort of burrowing creature. Ryn followed it upwards for about two alans until it emptied into a wider room. The tunnel Ryn had been traversing came out the side of a high wall. He looked down and found a pool of water below him, clear and untouched. The rock in the room was splashed with various colors of red, yellow, and brown.

To his left, the room emptied into a narrow corridor about twenty strides downhill. It came together into a small tunnel to his right about twenty-five strides uphill. The ceiling, a good twenty cubits in the air, was hung with long and sharp cylinders of rock that dripped water onto the floor. The pool did not cover the entire floor but only space around six strides in diameter below the tunnel. The opposite wall was littered with holes and small tunnels and stood about twelve strides away.

As he had pointed the weapon into the room, he saw dark figures begin to move into the shadows. He moved the light around to see what was present in the room. As the light passed over the holes on the opposite walls, he saw a few tails scurry back into the darkness. It was true that the creatures residing under the earth were fearsome, but they appeared to be terrified of the Arvaita's intense and pure light. This behavior explained to him why he had not encountered any creatures thus far. The light was probably visible for some distance through the tunnels. Perhaps he would encounter few problems as long as he had the weapon glowing brightly.

Ryn jumped over the pool to the rock floor, and his Arvaita lit the entire room. He turned to his right and began to walk uphill towards the tunnel carved out of the rock. This tunnel was very jagged and narrow and likely formed by water erosion. It continued upwards for about two hundred strides. Eventually, it took a sharp turn upwards, and Ryn climbed up a jagged ascent. As sure as Amaras had told him, there soon came a split in the paths. A wide fisher in the rock opened above him, and a small water trail weaved around sharp ledges beneath him.

Climbing out of the tunnel, he began the crooked descent through the maze of turns ahead of him. There were times that he had little more than a couple of cubits of space to move through, and he found himself having to navigate the superbly tight spaces in the darkness. The thought of being between such mountainous masses of rock like that was crushing. Willpower was needed to continue.

As Ryn squeezed through small, jagged openings, he thought the trail would never end. Eventually, it did, though. As he finally made his way over the last jagged rocks, he found the water path dropping into a smooth and narrow tunnel. This went on for a few alans in steep ascent until it opened into the floor of a wide arching cave. The ceiling was some thirty cubits high where the arch reached its zenith. Ryn climbed out of the tunnel and found that the cave stretched far behind and in front of him. The cave seemed to open up ahead of him, but behind him, it seemed to disperse into several passages. Ryn pointed the Arvaita towards the back and was suddenly surprised.

At the cave's edge, in the darkness where he had not seen it previously, was a golem, enormous and hunched over on the ground. Just as the light passed over the beast, it rose up and turned its head to look upon him.

Golems were not uncommon and could vary greatly in strength and ability. They were created when a spirit manifested itself within a rock or a mix of metals. The rock and metal formed a humanoid body driven by the spirit within. This one stood up and reached fifteen cubits. Its body was a mix of granite and iron ore. Without eyes to perceive the light, the golem functioned entirely by senses of sound and awareness of spiritual presences of life and death. The lively essence of Ryn's spirit and his weapon had immediately grabbed the thing's attention. It was not happy that Ryn had invaded its territory and did not seem aware of the Arvaita's pure light. It lunged at him, striking the ground with its right fist.

Ryn reacted quickly and hopped away from the attack. Golems were extremely difficult to kill, having no life source that could be drained like blood. Rather, one had to sever the head from the body. But the head could be anywhere; it was not necessarily the physical head. One could also incapacitate a golem by severing all its limbs. A powerful spiritual tool could also cast the spirit from the body, but most of the time, it was grunt work.

The creature swung its fists in a fast combination, Ryn flipped back to evade. This thing carried itself as though it were very efficient at crushing multiple enemies in a short time. Fortunately, it wasn't nearly as fast as him.

The thing charged again, and this time the Nephilim turned and ran up the left wall. Ascending the arching wall, he rose above the beast, then fell into a spin and opened up, swinging the Arvaita. He had had little time to endow it with much energy, but he endowed it with water, which was his best tool against a rock monster. As the Arvaita fell into its shoulder, it glided through the rock, and when Ryn landed, he saw that he had detached the right arm of the thing entirely.

Astonished at how such damage could have been done, Ryn paused in silence while the golem also gazed at his disconnected arm in bewilderment. He had not swung very hard, but the blade had gone through the stone like a knife through papyrus.

Ryn remained still in wonderment, shifting his glance from the golem to the Arvaita. The golem was frozen in its tracks, with its back turned to Ryn. It too shifted its glance from Ryn to its arm and back to

Ryn. Eventually, Ryn stared at its head as though he were making eye contact with it. The golem stared back motionless, and he could tell it had decided it could not win. Ryn decided he could slowly walk away without continuing the fight. He felt compelled not to destroy it, as though this golem served some noble purpose. Never turning his back to it, he kept walking until the golem too, picking up its arm, began to back away into the darkness.

The Arvaita had proven itself more than adequate. To defeat such a thing with one blow was indeed impressive. If he could slice through a golem if that strength, there was simply nothing that his blade could not cut, and no manner of material could deflect it without some sort of enchantment or windscaping. Ryn wondered if the weapon had favorable performances spiritually as well and thought it probably did. Perhaps it could break runes if endowed well or even scatter spiritual essence. Its potential was endless now, and Ryn found himself dreaming so much about its possibilities that he had to hush himself, lest he begin to put faith and hope into the weapon.

The cave emptied into a massive cavern. To the left, a water-formed tunnel emptied onto the smooth floor. Ahead of him, the far wall showed a staircase that ascended high up into the rock, disappearing into a passageway. Pools of water filled the smooth, shallow depressions in the floor, which covered some thirty strides separating the staircase from the cave entrance.

As he shined the light over the floor, he saw small, scurrying silhouettes running across the floor away from the light. Some of these were amphibious and plunked into the pools of water. As the sound of the golem rustling around in the background finally disappeared, Ryn could make out the splashing of these little creatures.

The water-formed tunnel on Ryn's left was faintly lit, and it was obvious that it opened up somewhere. There were mosses and insect nests nestled into the tunnel. It was a wonder to Ryn how a culture of insects could live so freely down here. He figured that predators from the surface or from the deep would be feeding off the nests in this room. The area was possibly inhabited by much larger predators that did not feed upon the critters, like the golem, keeping visitors at a minimum.

Now aware that there could be other predators, he looked around the cavern with the light of the Arvaita. It was here that he noticed the ceiling disappearing into a massive overhead cave. It tunneled forward over the staircase ahead of him. The large cave above was most certainly inhabited. It was the perfect place to launch an attack.

He continued his cautious walk towards the staircase and began the ascent up the crudely cut rock. He reached the point where the stairs ended in a platform. At the end of the platform was a passage that led deep into the wall. Upon the platform, he could now see a carved granite pillar with artistic features of a bear upon it. Engraved into its side was a spiritual ward to repel the weaker visitors.

A few broken pots that were filled with dust and dark organic substances surrounded the pillar. This indication of intelligent existence meant that Ryn was likely approaching the entrance to the tombs. This looked to be where the tombs connected to the underworld, often called the Path of Souls. Before he could enter, he had to break through the ward.

Reaching up with his hand to the doorway, he pressed on it. Like a soft tent sheet, yielding before his spiritual weight, it seemed to break it. Rather unexpectedly, it popped. The odd spiritual essence filled the area like a plume of dust and covered him.

Looking down, he remarked how it seemed to coat his essence from bleeding out. Perhaps this was a blessing in disguise, for it actually concealed his identity and nature. At least until he was outside the tombs and the fresh wind drove it off him like an old scent.

He looked back over the room one last time from the high platform and saw the insect life carrying on without concern. As he turned around, he dimmed the light of the Arvaita, for there seemed to be a faint presence of lumination coming from higher up in the tombs.

The stairs ascended through winding passages that eventually turned into a maze of catacombs. He was surprised at the freshness of the air that came down the passage and knew that an opening lay somewhere ahead. Ryn followed the stairs all the way up and did not take time to search through the various caverns of tombs that branched off in many directions. The people of Molnak were mostly human in bloodline and therefore did not have large or oddly shaped nooks in the rocks in which to place bodies. But a splash of Nephilian blood added power and beauty to some family lines. But to the same degree, they had the opposite effect on others.

There was almost no human settlement not subject to some sort of ruling Nephilim, whether it be a national or patron god. Usually, in exchange for food and other sacrifices, a god would offer protection in a territorial sense. The people in the region of Molnak were no exception. Molnak's territory was north of Arovynia on the southeastern quarter of the Arvadian Peninsula. There were thousands of patron guardians and gods in any given region, but the patron god of the powerful central city of Molnak was said to be an enormous bear. Ryn had never met him.

It was fabled that this flesh-devouring beast was fiercely territorial and protected the people in exchange for human sacrifices. The sheer power and savagery of the fabled beast were truly disconcerting.

Traijyn had passed down only one teaching concerning this god, and that was not to bother him or his land. If that didn't say enough, he didn't know what did. Given the ferocity of the beast, it may even seek him out, being an intruder upon sacred sites. Somewhere inside, Ryn got the distinct impression he would be confronted by this very god. Somewhere in his mind, he felt it was destiny.

He would slay it, of course. But as soon as he tried to muster spirit against the unknown beast, he found himself checked as though doing such would constitute an unrighteous act. Confusing to him, he wondered how slaying a territorial flesh-eater was unrighteous. But he was one who knew that sometimes an evil authority existed to protect against an even greater evil.

All this ran through Ryn's mind until he had passed half-noticing into a very well cut and ornamented hallway that was well lit. To his surprise, this opened up into a huge hall. The stairway rose out of the floor in the back center of the room. Across from him, two enormous double doors stood about fifty strides away.

The walls to his right and left were about fifteen strides away from the tomb entrance and were ornamented with carvings of the bear in strong and majestic positions and poses. Rings of gold and jewels were often inset as the beast's eyes. Stone and wood pillars surrounded the room. The stone ones actually served a structural function. There were four thinner ones on each side, and towards the back of the hall, there were four thicker ones that were richly carved and lined the back wall. The wooden pillars were ornamental, and eight of them surrounded the edges of the room in a semi-circle from the double doors. Six large rectangular windows were cut high into the rock wall above the massive doorway. The daylight from outside lit the room well as it bounced off the hall's white granite.

The edge of the hall was lined with hundreds of pots. The center was kept perfectly clear with a large circular symbol on the floor. The symbol was not magical or endowed with any enchantment but was probably a character representing the patron god. Indeed, Ryn did not see any indication of spilt blood or torn flesh anywhere. For the most part, the hall was very clean, and not a lot of stagnant dust was around either, for the hall was well ventilated. The air from outside poured in through the windows, and a breeze went past him into the tombs.

Ryn looked up and noticed that the ceiling did not seem to stop but kept going on, high up into a cave. The cave above disappeared back into the mountain and was extremely spacious. Ryn theorized that this cavity was connected to the one he saw above the cavern in Molnak's underworld at the catacomb's entrance. It was very dark, and Ryn could not see where its ceiling was, but the point at which the light stopped illuminating was nearly two-hundred cubits up.

Ryn thought to light the Arvaita in order to see into it but soon noticed movement from above. An enormous silhouette that seemed barely to fit into the massive cavern began to emerge from the darkness and descend from the high ceiling. At first, the form looked ape-like, but as it descended, its head came into the light and was distinctively bear-like. At this point, Ryn was certain that the beast was indeed the notorious patron god of Molnak himself.

He was not disappointed by the creature's physical prowess. It hung limberly from the ceiling like a chimpanzee, with long and massive arms, but its legs were thick and powerful like a bear's. Its upper body was massive, and it carried very broad shoulders and spacious pectoral muscles. Its body was covered in long black hair, and its eyes glowed with yellow brightness. These eyes came out of the darkness like two stars in the night, and the beast stared at Ryn without moving.

Ryn sensed anger emanating from the beast, probably for impeding upon his temple. However, Ryn did not sense a spirit of extreme selfishness or vanity coming from it, which shocked him cognitively, yet spiritually he had somehow expected this. Ryn gazed back at the being and did not show fear or a sense of respect, which the beast was looking for. Ryn would not betray his confidence and hide his strength from the beast, so he stared back as if to say that by divine right, he had every reason to be there. The being did not appreciate this lack of respect, and his agitated spirit was obvious.

The black beast suddenly jumped from the cave, the height of a small peak, down to the floor. But as he landed, he fell gracefully and gently into the stone below. He did not displace or shake one thing, not even the ceramic pots around him. Hunched over on the ground, he made eye contact with Ryn and did not release his gaze from him while he rose from the floor into a four-point stance on his knuckles and ape-like hands. Standing upright, the beast would be around forty-five cubits tall. It was no wonder the hall was so spacious. The god itself emitted an overwhelming presence that rivaled the black dragons of Zeus.

Ryn took a few cautious steps forward but pulled the Arvaita close to his chest so as to show that he would rather not fight if it could be avoided. The bear leaned forward a bit and spoke to Ryn in a low but surprisingly gentle voice.

"Who are you, and how have you come out of the underworld and into my house?"

Ryn was, at first, unprepared for the creature's gentle tone but adjusted quickly, "I am an Arvaita of the Crovan Empire, and my intentions are righteous. I have escaped the underworld, into which I was imprisoned by an enemy."

Ryn was hoping to keep his identity a secret; it would not be good for anyone to know that Ryn, the king of Crova, was walking around. In this regard, the broken ward had, indeed, become a blessing. But he thought then that the essence would soon be gone, and this being of great power could surely sense his unique essence through his own ward.

As the god looked at him, it came to him that holding the Arvaita alit in front of him obscured his genuine identity, for it gave off such a vibrant and fresh presence. At this point, it may have been the extra help he needed to remain obscure. If Ryn had considered it, he could have prepared an enchantment to cover himself.

"Your spirit is proud, and indeed it appears purer than most," spoke the creature; "But the underworld is a place of darkness and deception. I control the only passages in and out of this mountain's underworld. I do not see how anyone could have put you down there. Therefore, I have only to consider that you are a powerful windscaper and filled with the glory of the Stars, but your intentions are questionable. You have invaded my home, and I am unwilling to let a being of your power walk freely upon my territory and down the mountain into my city of Molnak."

Ryn sensed a fight was coming; the beast was simply unwilling to trust Ryn despite the spiritual presence he carried. Ryn looked to create a new line of reasoning with the beast since it seemed to reason out its course of action well. "Are you not the patron god of Molnak, a son of Romael the Titan, one of great power and authority?"

The beast leaned back in a more relaxed physical position but was still staring intently at Ryn and still aggressive in spirit, "Yes, I am En Ju Mogon, a son of Romael the Titan, the guardian and patron god of Molnak, capital and cultural center of the people of this region. And yes, I have much authority and power, though I see that you do not fear me, son of Yhadyal."

Ryn took a soft step forward and spoke intelligently, "Surely you can see that I too have been in authority and that my spirit commands it. Having been a governor myself, do you see in me a respect for the authority of another governor? How can I respect my own authority unless I respect the authority of others? I have no intention of diminishing your rule or desecrating whatever rules you may hold in the land. I realize that I have intruded upon you in a disrespectful manner, but I have no choice. I have been placed here by my enemy, who hollowed out a new passage in the mountain, and my mission is, indeed, of the utmost righteousness. Thus, I am confident of my safe passage, whether that be through conflict or not. However, I apologize for the intrusion, and give you my word that I will cause no upheaval in your lands."

The beast did not change its facial expression. Ryn wanted to say more, but he had relayed all the concepts that needed to be relayed. If the beast still fought him, then it was destined to be. The god looked intently at him and, in particular, the Arvaita. It was obvious that he was put off by Ryn hiding behind it.

En Ju Mogon brought his head and its gaze down and narrowed his focus, which told Ryn that indeed a fight was coming.

"The presence of one such as yourself in the underworld is indeed questionable, and it is known that Crova has just fallen to Zeus. And I do know of one being, in all Olympia, who is capable of hollowing out my mountain. You very well could be a friend and an ally. But these are presumptions. All I know for sure is you are a being of great power that has ascended from the underworld, and part of my agreement with my people is that I keep the underworld in the underworld no matter who it is. So I conclude this, I fulfill my promise and confront you in hopes that you will not even be in my country to threaten it. If you win, then it is because the Great Wind has allotted it, and you will go on regardless of how I feel about it. If I win, then it is also because the Great Wind has allotted it, and I will have done what I believe is wise, fulfilling my oath to my people."

Ryn bowed his head in respect. It was not out of the creature's wisdom or his insight, but because he conceded to the power of the Great Wind. This showed that En Ju Mogon had great wisdom and humility and, quite frankly, was somewhere close in understanding to Traijyn. But alas, Ryn did not know what relation this god had to Zeus. To this point, Molnak had been an ally of Olympia. There was certainly a chance their relationship had changed in the past years, but he knew nothing of it, and neither would there be a chance to find out. It was apparent that En Ju Mogon had to fight to fulfill his oath, and an oath was so important, it could not be disregarded for anything. The only thing that could change the path of an oath like his was the outcome.

Ryn readied the Arvaita and moved slowly forward away from the wall. En Ju Mogon slowly strafed to his right in readiness. For a single moment, Ryn entertained an escape down the catacombs and out the wet tunnel he had seen. But in his spirit, he had expected this fight and considered it part of destiny. Besides, En Ju Mogon's cave above offered quicker movement than the catacombs. He could never get there before the god. Amaras had indicated that this was the path Ryn was to take so he would not stray from it.

Ryn continued strafing diagonally to the god's left. In an instant and without warning or windup, the beast lunged out with his right fist and drilled it into the earth where Ryn stood. Ryn had reacted just in time to hop above the attack as the stone beneath him shattered under the powerful fist, now ablaze with yellow energy.

Another swift fist came, and Ryn backflipped hard away from the attack and into the empty space to his right. The bear kicked and followed with a tight combination of punches that Ryn dodged acrobatically. Shifting to his right, En Ju Mogon came in again. His right fist came low to sweep Ryn, but he jumped over it. The left fist came while he was in the air, and Ryn met the fist with a powerful swing of the Arvaita. The two collided in a flash of bright light that resulted in a deflection.

Ryn spun off and raced to the nearest pillar to launch from it. En Ju Mogon moved to attack with his left fist but found it was out of power. Launching off the pillar, Ryn flew into the beast's chest feet first, and upon planting his feet, swung his blade dancing with fire.

With exceptional speed for his size, the bear blocked this attack by striking the shaft with his right arm. The deflection sent the Crovan back. He landed and immediately avoided another low-high combination by hopping over a low right arm sweep and diving to the floor to avoid the left fist, which was still not yet ablaze. As En Ju Mogon took more swings at Ryn, he missed once and shattering a wooden pillar. Ryn countered quickly and dashed towards the bear. But as he moved to swing, he was cut off by the right hand, which grabbed at the weapon.

Ryn spun counter-clockwise, away from the arm, and into a mid-roundhouse kick that jolted the beast. The bear instantly countered with a left paw that flung Ryn across the room into the right-hand, double door side pillar. The Crovan fell off the pillar and watched En Ju Mogon regain his balanced and move to rush him.

Ryn lashed out with his left leg and blasted the cracked pillar, kicking the shattered stone. The spray of shattered rock flew at the beast, who halted his progress to block and protect his eyes but only for a second.

Ryn rushed him and stopped to block an instantaneous left swing followed by a right hammer fist that missed Ryn and broke the stone floor. Ryn planted off the right arm as it was in the ground, and leaping, meant to plunge the Arvaita into his right shoulder. En Ju Mogon ducked, and the shoulder fell out of range. As he arched over the bear's backside, he stretched his weapon out and caught him softly on the backside right rib cage. The cut was hardly deep, but it drew blood.

Before Ryn touched the ground, En Ju Mogon was swinging both fists vertically down at him in a single hammer. Sensing the blow, Ryn thrust the Arvaita down and vaulted his body back into the air, gliding into a backflip over the attack. Turning around in mid-air, he brought the Arvaita over his head in a large downward arch towards the beast's left shoulder. It was an instant counter that turned the tables of the attack, putting En Ju Mogon into a helpless position to block.

Yet instantly and with panic, En Ju Mogon lunged backward and brought his hands together in a clap in front of the approaching blade. There was a thunderclap that thrust Ryn back, and he sailed to the floor now across the room from the beast with the tomb entrance at his back.

At one point, En Ju Mogon's fisted energy attacks had been nullified by the Arvaita, but they were now restored to their blazing glory. Ryn saw now that concentrated spiritual energy could block the blade. He would simply have to endow it with more than his opponent could meet it with or get around En Ju Mogon's fists.

The bear moved at Ryn, and Ryn ran at him. He juked to his left and drew out his right fist, then leapt from the attack and apparently right into the bear's left fist. But Ryn focused his energy into a small wind vortex that caught the fist swinging and spun him like a swirling coin towards the beast's chest. Ryn was going to come out of the spin with the Arvaita and slice the beast straight through the chest!

Yet, as he spun, he felt a powerful urge not to strike with the blade. So, when Ryn came out of his spin, he came out with all that terrible energy and momentum in his left leg, which blasted into the beast's torso with incredible force. En Ju Mogon flew back across the temple and ricocheted off one of the front pillars before crashing into the front wall, bringing rubble down around him.

Ryn still stood at the ready but waited to see how the god had made out. Dust from the broken stone around him began to settle, and En Ju Mogon sat blinking his eyes in the position he had hit the wall in.

His gaze was not on Ryn but on the floor in front of him, and he was not in a spirit to fight anymore; rather, he was entirely confused. Ryn stood calmly as he allowed the bear thought. He reasoned that the god was probably wondering why Ryn had not run him through with his blade.

En Ju Mogon lifted his eyes up from the rubble and looked at Ryn, this time in a measure of wonderment and some admiration. This being had not killed him when given a chance, and he surely had the chance. He had out skilled En Ju Mogon, plain and simple. Never had the god encountered such skill in combat and that weapon…

En Ju Mogon winced and began to notice his pain. There was a slash on his back, and the bruise in his chest that could have shattered his heart had it been two or three feet to the right and higher.

He coughed and saw blood coming from his mouth; he was bleeding inside. Ryn saw this and became concerned. He approached a few steps and asked, "Are you going to live?"

The beast looked up at him in amazement. "What kind of foe cares for his enemy's health? I will heal from this," the beast spoke and returned his gaze downward toward his chest.

Ryn looked at the bear and had compassion on him. Indeed, this was not the creature of the fables, and Ryn matched up with a lot of foes and never ceased to learn a great deal of them during the fight. Unique to En Ju Mogon was a measure of trustworthiness and ungodly humility. Much like that of Traijyn.

Ryn looked at his blade for blood but saw that there was none. The intense energy had slowly burned it all off. He sheathed it and returned his gaze to the bewildered bear sitting on the floor and the destruction that lay around him. The double doors had been flung open by the force of the beast's collision with the wall. Ryn now saw a canopy outside supported by pillars that were erected from a stone deck. Stone steps led down to a dirt road that smoothly trailed down the mountain through grassy slopes. It was sunny outside and a very beautiful day.

The bear began slowly to climb to his feet and stopped at various moments to regain his focus. When he finally stood up, he gazed away from Ryn and opened and closed his eyes as he battled against unconsciousness.

He kept his back turned and spoke, "You have taken power from me to stop you, so go and do as you wish. But if you respect my people and me at all, despite the fact that you have bested me, I ask you to be generous and responsible with it."

With that, the bear sluggishly and painfully climbed up the pillars and then up jagged rocks into the cave above until he was gone.

Ryn stood unsettled. He felt somewhat disappointed at the damage he had done to the beast, for he felt that he was honorable and undeserving of defeat. Ryn decided that the least he could do was be a kind traveler in his land and perhaps earn an ally. Of course, Ryn still had no idea where En Ju Mogon stood in relation to Zeus. He had to have some kind of treaty in order to remain, for Molnak was well inside the areas of Olympia's influence, but perhaps his heart could be won over.

In any regard, the king of Molnak would be someone else to speak with. Often politics were not handled by gods; they simply had a symbiotic relationship to the kingdom. From the way En Ju Mogon interacted with him, he felt that this was a case of a more symbiotic relationship, rather than one of ruler and subject. The king would still make the political decisions, and Ryn would have to see how Molnak's king felt about being an ally.

6 THE PEOPLE OF MOLNAK

A stone stairway wound its way down the side of the mountain. Surrounding him was green grass and patches of brown dirt, and he had never been happier to see the outside world. He began to walk down the path.

Every two or three hundred strides, there were stone pillars about five cubits high on either side. They were simple pillars with rough surfaces and writing carved into them in rings. They formed basic wards against those detached from the mountain. Ryn found it interesting these wards didn't affect him at all. He paused only a moment to view the landscape. The sun was bright and penetrated the thin blue sea that extended over the face of the sky.

The mountain descended into grassy fields where he could see a large settlement with roads winding in and out of it. It was a city and doubtless the city of Molnak. The buildings were constructed of cut wood and mud bricks. The city was surrounded by a wall about fifteen cubits high, out of which stood a bronze gate to the east and the west. It was a medium-sized city, but the scattered farming villages and livestock settlements around it made it much larger. It was very odd to see a wall with no runes on it. It served no purpose. It kept out nothing.

His attentive eyes scanned the area until he found out why he'd not seen any. Upon the ground was a colorful banner some fifteen cubits from the wall on the near side. He was certain the banner had held a sutra. The sutra came from the wall, and its being on the ground there meant only one thing, that someone had wished it removed. He went closer.

The town was still. The fields were not being tended to, and there were no animals about. Was this city abandoned? It couldn't. He could smell the presence of the people of the land. An image of a discarded tool alerted him that something might be wrong.

He looked up the mount to En Ju Mogon. The idea of informing him passed quickly. Ryn had injured him badly. If there was an issue, Ryn would fulfill his agreement and be a responsible guest of the land.

He raced down the path and came close to the gate. At the edge of the path was a young man that had been cut down on his way up to the mount. He hadn't made it far. As he looked through the gate into the town, he saw several humans in retreat who were being followed by the familiar lizard figures of the Gullukans. The Crovans had seen many of those since they had hired themselves out to Zeus in a one-way alliance.

He eyed the city wall. He traced the scent of them. They looked to have entered the city from within. That could only be done in one of two ways. Either they came up from the underworld, which was unlikely, or they had their scent covered by locals working in league with them or under threat. Either way, they had come under attack suddenly, and somehow, the bear-god had not been alerted.

He stood and smelt the air for any other presences. There were none. This was good. If their enemies were Gullukans, their relation to Olympia was tepid at best and in full-breakdown at worst. Molnak would be an ironic ally should fate fall that way.

Ryn sheathed the Arvaita and gently ascended the fifteen cubit wall, perching on its ledge. Inside one of the houses, Ryn witnessed the lizards break down a door and slash a defenseless woman. They grabbed articles of value, and one of them grabbed a small girl. It appeared that they were pillaging the city, but not looking for anything in particular, nor leveling the place.

Ryn looked down to his right and saw another house, empty and ransacked. Gracefully he fell to the ground and crept through the near doorway. He would need a disguise that was just good enough to cover his distinguishing features like his ears and the colored hair over his forehead. He didn't have much to work with physically. He supposed he wasn't concerned about his small fangs, or feline nose; only that he remained obscure to any survivor that might pass a word that could travel back to Zeus.

Finding a large black blanket, he draped it over his head and his body, tying the waist down with a piece of rope. Ryn took the Arvaita and hid it under a bed. His weapon style would be identified as Crovan, so he would have to battle without it. Finally, now that he was outside the underworld where the lively wind blew, he was able to perform a technique called mymtai. It concealed his spirit so he might not reveal any of his wind.

Such tricks did not work well on beings of great spiritual power, but on the general human and Nephilim population, it was absolutely reliable. He hadn't performed the technique since he'd taught at Alvyn his final year as a monk. He recalled the last young man he gave an exam to. Ryn smelt right through his mymtai. He told him where he'd been, where his family was from, the character of his mother and father. The man was despondent. Ryn assured him he'd seen little. Should he encounter a god, he'd reveal so much more.

The memory was in his mind a moment until he saw the inhabitant of the house, an older man now crumpled in the corner with a slit throat. Ryn snarled. The very youth he'd given that exam to had fallen in the battlefield in a similar fashion some years ago; such an unfortunate death. He had work to do.

He stepped out of the house, now facing the city wall. Just as he did, two of the lizards came running by. They did not notice him as he came out of the darkness, or at least the one on the right didn't. The one on the left did when an arm came out and whipped him from the head to the ground. The second heard a loud thud and turned around to see the cloaked man standing over his comrade's body. He screeched to a halt and let out a call for help. Ryn dashed at him, and the Gullukan moved to swing his sword, but Ryn got quickly inside him and grabbed the hilt with his right hand. He then proceeded to thrust that same shoulder into the lizard's chest, sending him promptly soaring backward, smashed internally before even hitting the ground.

He heard three more racing around the sides of the building, two from the north and one from the south. He hid against the wall. As they came, he could sense their presence step by step. A weakness of the Gullukans was their soft belly and light frame. Fighting their kind had been perfected after so many years.

As the first came around the corner, Ryn lashed out and slung his body into the air with a thunderous fist. The blow sent the pulverized lizard out of sight. The other quickly lunged at Ryn to stab.

The Crovan pivoted to his right, avoiding the blade. He grabbed the stabbing right arm and pulled the lizard around his shoulder, slinging its body off of and into the adjacent wall. The body smacked and bounced off the crumbling structure, falling limply to the ground. Ryn had now caught the attention of others in the middle of the street. There were about six of them, and they left a cornered group of spearmen to confront the new opponent.

Ryn turned around and darted back around the corner of the building, meeting the third Gullukan. He dashed by the blade of his outstretched sword and shoulder blocked the lizard into the adjacent wooden wall, again pulverizing his insides with the fearsome technique. Ryn kept running and turned between the next two houses on his left and came out in the middle of town. Seeing the other's coming, he darted to his right. In front of him stood an utterly surprised Gullukan pulling a sack of plunder from a house.

The lizard backed up in astonishment as Ryn approached and, not knowing what to do, and obviously being under experienced, raised his sword to block. Ryn swiftly grabbed his sword arm and pulled the lizard over his back, hurling him to the ground. He then moved two houses down and interrupted a plundering in progress.

Coming in the door, a lizard had his back turned to him, shouting at the people inside. Ryn reached around his chest and swung him over his hip, hurling the lizard out the door. There was a second one that had no time to react. Ryn reached around him and grabbed both his arms, then flung him over his shoulder to the floor. He ensured each strike channeled enough energy in the right spot to be lethal. Immediately he was out the door and moving to another building.

Ryn played shadow games like this for some time, moving from building to building and alley to alley. This group was obviously amateur. He'd encountered only one that reminded him of the formidable strength Gullukans could possess. As he took on three by the wall, he slung one into another and left a third to try his luck on Ryn. He mounted a rather forceful kick that actually backed Ryn off his footing. Being much quicker, Ryn still was able to finish him shortly. But he needed to remember that Crova's great experience with them did nothing to detract from them being a formidable and accomplished warrior people.

As he dispatched more and more, the city's soldiers made gains on their invaders. Ryn found them coming from the corners of the city, making a push to the center. They were spearmen and axemen, mainly; many civilian conscripts as well, barely able to contribute. Many were frightfully engaging and looked fortunate to be alive.

Eventually, they grouped the remaining lizards into the center while some had fled the city. The rest found themselves dispatched by Ryn on his way there as well. The men of the town grouped and fenced the enemy in, while their mystery ally dispatched the remainder. When it was all over, Ryn stood over bodies of lizards in the town square with fearful soldiers and citizens of Molnak watching from the street and surrounding houses.

He remained there, unapproached for some time. The town's people came out of hiding, and Ryn saw very soon that there were far more than he anticipated. Thousands began appearing from inside hundreds of houses. They did not confront him, only looked at him bewildered and afraid. The soldiers kept their distance as well. Standing in the street, they felt a duty to engage him but did not. Few beings could route a battalion of Gullukans like this.

Finally, an older man with a now broken bronze sword with furs indicating he was an elder, came forward and shakily began to speak. "May we thank you, traveler?"

"You may," Ryn said, "By giving me an audience with your king if he is still here."

The man looked somewhat afraid.

He looked at another with concern, and they hinted at one another. But after a minute of silence, the obvious became clear. Whether or not his intentions were good, the old man felt like this mysterious warrior was able to take whatever he wanted anyway. Turning around, he gave instructions to two soldiers, who promptly ran westward down the street. Ryn waited for them to come back with word.

The city soldiers retook their defenses at the gates and walls while a group of maybe a dozen saw fit to escort the unknown hero warily. There was a lot of happiness and tears as the Molnakians found loved ones both alive and dead. The attack had come very suddenly, it appeared. There was a general spirit of admiration and thanks focused on Ryn, but the overwhelming fear of his power masked it. The mystery of Ryn's identity scared them the most. A being that obscured his spirit before others was deceitful and most likely of ill intent.

Ryn detoured momentarily from the street. Walking into a house calmly, he took the Arvaita out from under the bed and wrapped it in a large skin. After he had carefully done this, he emerged from the house again and resumed his position in the street looking down at the palace, all the time the dozen or so men stood around him.

The two men came back to the old man and whispered something to him. Then the old man turned around to face Ryn again. "The king says, come! But he wishes to hear the reason for your visit?"

Ryn looked back at the man making sure to keep his face and skin under the hood obscure, "You don't need to worry. I am not here to begin conflict. It was in my heart to rescue your city, for I am from a nation of allies."

The old man immediately responded with gratefulness, though, in his heart, he was not entirely persuaded by his words. Once again, the obscure identity was a stumbling block, a universal sign of ill-intent.

The people of Molnak were a plain people,

dressed in simple skins and wool tunics. They lived communally, raising crops and tending livestock. They knew mining and stone cutting and could even dye their textiles, but these were skills they called *daicome* and was thus too good to be used on their own accommodations. The Molnakians found themselves content to live by simpler means while using their skill to adorn the halls of their patron god and the graves of their ancestors.

Their warriors were equipped with bronze headed spears and did not have any armor. Armor was either endowed by the artistic expressions of windscaping, such as runes or sutras, or a hindrance and restrictor of movement. The material itself was of little protection. The weakest of men could put iron through iron. He learned that as a child. Still, the material was becoming more important to the sons of man. With each generation, they liked the stronger materials just that much more. But perhaps that was expected, for it seemed, in general, that people were getting weaker.

He'd learned, from those who'd lived long enough, that the tales of things done a thousand years ago far outweighed those done now. So it was said that Ano's ancestor Syet pushed a mountain aside to reveal the hiding place of a menace. Syet was human! It appeared that mankind, like the Nephilim, lost his divine wind with each passing generation. But if these men had not accepted armor without runes yet, it meant they had more faith in their skill than those he thought of. Their hearts were healthier.

More than a hundred men came to them from the direction of the palace, and it appeared that the battle had moved to the palace in defense before Ryn arrived. When they had all gathered, there were about two hundred warriors of Molnak escorting Ryn. They left the main road and ascended a hill with a palace atop it. This palace was built against the city's western wall. The two-story house of logs and mud was not particularly impressive, but it did tower over the other buildings in the city.

A platform of stone was laid in front, and stone steps descended from it in the middle. This architecture contrasted sharply with the temple of En Ju Mogon in the mountain but made sense. This was a nation of men; they still had the "Chieftain mentality" of leaders. They carried an idea of chief more in their minds than in their architecture. The latter was a practice brought by the gods. In its simplistic ways, Ryn loved the purity of human thought and loathed the corruption of their minds. How did fancy architecture make a better king anyway? Besides, there was no point in bringing stone down the mountain if structurally it did little better than what they had. However, Ryn did notice that most floors and foundations were of cut stone.

The men opened two large and intricately detailed carved wooden doors and showed him the way in. This display of daicome on the doors showed their patron god in his strength.

He ascended the stairs and walked into a chamber where across from him sat a throne of stone, upon which sat a tense and concerned man. The king was bearded and very large for a human, perhaps six cubits tall, and he was broadly built. He was obviously strong and probably made king by warrior code. His right arm was extended over the hilt of a long sword. Around his throne, wooden pillars cut from thick trees lined the center of the room, keeping the log floor above from bowing. He wore a black tunic over his body with edges of white fur, and his dark hair was long and tied back in a ponytail.

The men circled the room as their guest stood before the king. To all of their surprise, Ryn bowed in reverence. The king was wide-eyed but remained calm, "Thank you for your respect and for assisting my warriors. Please do me the honor of speaking your mind," said the king.

"King of Molnak," the Crovan began. "I must say, for as large a nation as Molnak is, it has a small army to defend its cities."

The king did not take offense; the powerful stranger's perception was accurate. The king could tell he was wise and that there was no hiding anything from him.

"My forces are detained elsewhere, and a mere two days ago, 500 of this city's choice men were dispatched to the southern mountains. These mercenaries surprised us by coming through our back door, over the southeastern mountains, and came upon the city while there was a failure in the watch."

Ryn questioned for a moment how the aura of such majestic mountains had failed to keep back lower Nephilim, such as the Gullukans. However, the range housed an ever-encroaching underworld that weakened the resolve of the land and their bond to it. Still, there was more as he listened for it.

His eyes diverted for a moment. "This army was in the barracks behind the palace when they attacked suddenly. Believe it or not, the front line of this battle was the front door of my palace." He smirked, now a little more comfortable with giving his guest details.

"Thanks to your efforts behind their main offensive, we cleared the city of them rather quickly."

The man's first two sentences were the most telling. His ability to hide thoughts was not above Ryn's ability to read them. Within his words, he heard far more than what was spoken. The men at his outpost, he assumed, had sold out their people for a price and allowed the Gullukans through the border, neglecting to report it, of course, and ensuring they made it to the capital without being spotted. The benefactor was obvious.

Ryn made his voice very calm and inquisitive. "I see that you struggle under the hand of Olympus. Tell me, for the sake of my people, do you consider Zeus an ally?"

The king began to laugh but caught himself, feeling that this might offend his mighty guest. He bent over his throne in a strained voice, "We are certainly not friends of Olympus. They have pillaged our towns for months. Our patron god, who lives in the mountains, has been overwhelmed by the flood of beasts and spirits coming over the southern highlands. When we go to him, he is not there, and when he is, he is exhausted and unwilling to give us audience. So, you see, strange traveler; we are not allies of Olympus, we are under its thumb. But, we do not make war against Zeus despite the size and population of our nation because Zeus is powerful, and we must respect his power."

Ryn smiled slightly with delight. The man's spirit and words made their relationship to Olympia obvious. They were oppressed and taken advantage of. Zeus did not ask for their allegiance because he did not need it. Molnak was a nation of men, relatively weak and of little value as soldiers, and the king's openness about it told, even more, their desperate situation.

"Is this what you wanted to hear?" Asked the king.

Ryn looked up for the first time and made eye contact with the king, and his gaze shocked the man. Behind Ryn's eyes, the king sensed a fearsome being with the power to tear them all to pieces if it suited him. The king was petrified and became locked into the stranger's gaze, unable to look away though wanting to.

Ryn spoke calmly and gently, attempting to alleviate this fear, "I too come from a nation that has been pillaged by Zeus."

Calmly he spoke the word "*Yshalyr.*" He did not, however, remove the blanket from his head.

The soldiers in the room gasped and took steps back. The sudden unveiling of Ryn's aura filled them with immense fear of his strength. They all stood perfectly still in awe of Ryn while the king was made awestruck. Yet, he felt no need to flee from Ryn, for he did not feel that his life was in danger. Perhaps this was the stranger's good intention showing through as well.

Ryn spoke to the king with urgency, "I am a Crovan, a son in the house of Jyrai, the great chieftain. Surely you know that Crova's land has been taken, but Crova has not fallen. We fight now and always to end Zeus' tyranny abroad in every nation. That is why I delivered your city from him; he is my enemy."

The king grew a look of concern. His fear was that Ryn was going to make him swear some allegiance to him or make him confront Zeus hopelessly.

Ryn saw this. "I am not asking you to declare war right now, but I am asking you to make me a promise." He let the room stay silent and waited on the king to respond.

The soldiers to his right and left fidgeted but remained frozen in a gaze upon the drama unfolding before them. The king took a deep breath, and it came to him that Ryn was not going to force him to do anything. This realization changed how he perceived Ryn entirely, and his face relaxed, and he lost his fearful tension. Ryn liked this and smiled at the king, which brought the tension down in the entire room.

The king leaned forward slightly and asked Ryn, "What do you want of Molnak, son of Jyrai."

Ryn continued, "I am traveling from kingdom to kingdom. I am giving trusted information to trusted nations and asking them for their help. If I fail in my quest, then you will never hear from me again, but if I am successful, and I amass an army of nations to march against Zeus, I will call for you, and I want you to come."

Ryn stopped momentarily to straighten his stance, then continued, "I would not ask this of you unless I felt that it was for the greatest good and the desire of Molnak's people. I see that you are tired of this oppression, and I see that you are willing to do this. I also see that I can trust you because you are a man of integrity, a man I see light in. And also understand that I would not ask you if I had any doubt within me that you would not say yes."

The king was impressed. The Crovan knew what

he was saying and thought he had a voice somewhere in him that told him not to trust this Nephilim; his heart told him that he could. He leaned back in his throne and nodded his head in thought all the time, looking into Ryn's explosive eyes.

"All right," he said. "Send word to us as to who is fighting, and I give you my word we will be wherever you ask."

Ryn bowed to the king in humility and thanks.

The soldiers in the room became excited. Things had been set in motion to destroy their enemies. Finally, something was being done, and by a powerful ally.

"What is your name, gracious king?" Ryn asked this, knowing that a formal introduction had not been conducted.

"I am called Riglan, Compassionate, and Wild, and you son of Jyrai, what is your name?"

Ryn hesitated slightly, "I do not mind telling you who I am, Riglan, but I can entrust this information only to you and not your servants."

Riglan looked around at his soldiers and, without hesitation, asked them to leave. He did not have to question Ryn's motive. He saw in his spirit that he could trust him and that he was a being of integrity. Perhaps a decision his mind would question later, but his heart led him to make. Ryn loved utilizing those decisions.

Once the hall was empty, Ryn pulled back his hood and shocked the king once more, for he had a look of majesty, and his aura came through vividly clear. Riglan almost shook his head as he waited for the stranger's most fantastical answer.

"I am Ryn, son of Amyn, son of Jyrai, son of

Alyn, son of Traijyn, son of Yhadyal. King of Crova, commander of her armies, and spiritual guide of her people."

Riglan rose from his throne, shaking. There was no doubt in his mind that Ryn was who he said he was. The Molnakian king had heard tales of Ryn and his power. He never envisioned that he would get to meet him. Crova had never had relations with Molnak.

Naturally, the king leaned forward as if to bow to the Crovan, for his aura nearly demanded subjugation from him.

But Ryn approached and put his arm on Riglan's left shoulder. "You and I, two kings united in our struggled against Olympia, have made a pact here today that will not be forgotten."

Riglan, his eyes still wide, swallowed the saliva in his throat and nodded his head. "Tell me, Ryn," said Riglan, "How did you come to be by yourself and not with an escort befitting a king?"

Ryn smiled, "Some things don't make sense but suffice to say, I am a king disconnected from his people by this war. Fear not, I am coming to them. Let us talk of pleasant matters, and if you wish to hear the pleasant parts of my story."

So Ryn told him of his marvelous rescue but little more of his recent events. Riglan would ask him many questions, all the while careful not to give away his identity. Ryn appreciated it all that evening.

For the first time in a long time, Ryn relaxed and enjoyed a good meal. King Riglan was a course man for a king; sophisticated in his own right but certainly from hardy stock, not educated stock. He was a joy to be around and loved to laugh.

His men were the same sort and seemed to compete with each other over who could tell the funniest story or tell the funniest joke. Looking at their hard and worn faces over a low table he reclined at with them in a wood hall by firelight, Ryn felt purity.

It was amazing how Egyptian, Sumerian, and even some Crovan scholars and monks could dismiss humans as lacking in intellect, knowledge, and power. Yet when he was among them, they seemed to have an ability so gloriously pure and different, it made him envy them. Nephilim were so good at raising power and knowledge, but it was humans who knew how to raise joy, faith, and hope. He looked at every one of them and could not remember one Crovan who could laugh so freely and joyously as he saw them do despite the indisputable fact Nephilim felt sentiment deeper and more complex than their human cousins. It was a mystery. Almost as though that depth was drowned out by the myriad of other things that drowned out their conscious mind. In simplicity, they were able to grasp the full vision of life's experiences. He would never feel the same way about the sons and daughters of man again.

Before leaving in the morning, Ryn went up to the mountain to see the god. As he walked in the double doors, he called several times for the beast, without an answer. He stayed some time and then finally conceded to leave his gift and go. Ryn peeled the wrapping skin from his object and left it on the floor in the center of the room.

It was a peace pillar that Ryn had carved from wood himself. It depicted En Ju Mogon and Ryn going into battle together with their people behind them. It was a common gift between nations of great trust. The pillar showed a bond of absolute faithfulness in one another, a mutual relationship of unconditional protection, and an indication that the two nations lived with the same spirit. Crova had a pillar with only one other nation; it's sister Nova.

"It has finally become time," he thought to himself, "To stop doing this alone." The silliness of saying that now saddened him. He stopped short in his thoughts, however, and let it be.

Ryn left the item and began to walk out when he heard a faint rustling in the cave above. He looked up to see the same two glowing eyes peering out of the darkness that he had seen before. The beast stared at Ryn from the darkness and, without words, accepted his gift. His body language said he had one of his own, though. His arm gently tossed something in his direction.

As Ryn caught it, he saw that it was a Fire Stone. Fire Stones were incredibly rare and had to be made by someone of great skill and power. When given the proper command, they exploded with the sound of thunder and with tremendous brightness and force. Glad it was a gift and not an attack, Ryn was very grateful for the weapon, and it showed En Ju Mogon had offered Ryn his trust. He looked up and saw the god turn and disappear into the darkness. He stayed and gazed upwards for a minute, then tucked the chicken egg-sized stone in his pouch and left.

Ryn walked away from Molnak, very peaceful. His first ally on his quest had almost come directly to him. Was this a gesture of affirmation from Teoti? Most certainly. Perhaps a small voice inside him that wondered if this incredible feat was even possible was silenced that day. Whatever it was, Ryn did not feel above enjoying the memories of men, women, and children shout blessing at him as he left the friendly human city.

7 IKOWO IUBAITA

It was as if acid had come down on them from the sky. She tucked her body under her wide circular shield, hoping the runes were strong enough to save her the fate of a young soldier in front of her who screamed with agony as his body began to fall apart in ways it ought not to. The acid produced an aroma that stung the nostrils, and behind it came a stale air that washed back the fresh arid mountain air produced by months of attacks of nature sent at them by powerful windscaping.

"We are dead on this hill!" Shouted a fur-covered Crovanar behind her. "We should go!" He should have known by the colors and ornaments of her vest and skirt that she would never do that. She was a monkess, not a conscript. But then again, he was still a foreigner, ally or not. He probably didn't know that.

"We are not ordered to! We must hold!"

A terrible screech was heard as an incoming force clawed at them through the air like some ghost or screaming banshee. She held fast behind her shield and prayed. Blue fumes of putrid plasma poured around them and saturated their group of a hundred or so on the slope of that yellow short grass hill. Some caught fire as the stuff ate them away. One soldier went rolling down the hill toward the line of rocks below. The enemy was behind that line of jagged rock fighting the last remnants of an ill-fated counter-attack. They would break through and make the ascent in minutes; time they may not have.

Suddenly an old Crovan with wild hair and a bushy beard came thundering in with heavy footsteps. Taking a deep breath, he filled his lungs and prepared to bellow. "WITHDRAW! RETREAT TO THE MOUNTAINS!"

As soon as he said it, nearly everyone remaining was gone, sprinting up the slope to the goat path under a rise that led into the highlands between the mountain peaks.

She also stood and caught his eye. "Is it over?"

The rough-looking man with a lost eye bellowed for lack of tact. "Vundar's battalion has already fled! It's over monkess! Save yourself!" With that, he ran only glancing back for a moment.

She sheathed her sword and climbed the slope watching dozens of others running uphill ahead of her toward the high ground painted pale hues by a dark gray morning sky.

She reached the goat path but was slowed by a line of soldiers running up its trail. The officer with the bushy beard was just ahead of her when the path ahead shook with force. Several men were thrust off the path as a thick-bodied, red Sed Dragon dropped down ahead of them where the path was widest. It breathed fire from its mouth, and though several men were consumed, they attacked with their remaining strength, wildly flinging themselves at the beast. Another winged beast came down behind that one, and yet another was on its way. She knew it was hopeless.

Suddenly the bushy-bearded officer turned and, with a gleam in his eye that was nothing short of prophetic, shouted, "RUN, NOW!"

She was shocked. She couldn't run. No, she may have been a lady but save herself despite another?

"GOOO!" The man wasn't having it and shoving a shoulder into her chest, thrust forward and threw her a dozen strides or so back in the opposite direction, down the goat path's descent. Then with a wild glaze over his eyes, he turned and launched himself at the dragon.

Skidding off her bottom, she found her footing, and rather than question, she chose to do as she was told. She felt guilty; she felt wrong; it was not her place to sacrifice another, not like this. But in the midst of running, it was not time to disagree; the choice was made. Running down the goat path, knowing she was surely pursued, she swore...she swore she had to be alive to tell what had happened.

*   *   *

Ryn hung his head in frustration as he began scaling the Arvadian Peninsula's eastern mountains. The more he thought about it, the worse it got. He was conflicted, though. He was certain he was back on the right track. The question was whether or not he had always been on the right track, or if he should have changed his course sooner.

What he'd learned from his seven-day detour into Arvadia was that Zeus had reconciled a lot of power in the shadows. Ryn had witnessed no troop build-up in Arvadia, and all along, he and his generals had assumed that Arvadia was blissfully ignored by Zeus. He had learned the real reason for the lack of armies.

Inner Arvadia consisted of rich farmlands with numerous ranches and mines. They were protected by numerous patron gods, minor gods, and isolated communities of Nephilim. Many kings and gods ruled over its plains, and no one person would decide their fate like in Molnak. In the past, they had used a large war council to make cohesive decisions. Ryn had hoped the council had started meeting more frequently. But despite the encroachment of Olympus, it had met less and less. Perhaps it had even been four or five years.

It took Ryn a full day to see two governors and one king in the southeast region. Neither of the two governors gave him an audience out of fear of Zeus. The king of Ugolomon, the principal tribe of the northern hills, saw Ryn but made it very clear that his people acknowledged the authority of Olympus. When Ryn had suggested to him that he was not under Zeus' authority, the king was anxious and asked him to leave for the sake of his people.

Two more failures followed Ugolomon in Arvadia. In Kumatun, Ryn felt immediately that the spirit of the people was under Olympus and did not even try to negotiate a treaty. Rather, he went through the town, only gathering food, and marching on to Adaijan, a fortified city in the heart of Arvadia.

If Arvadia had a cultural center, it was Adaijan. It was one last effort to make sense of the trip. If

Adaijan could be convinced, even to subvert Olympian cooperation, he could use it. But upon arriving, he learned that they had since his last word of knowledge concerning them, replaced El Muget Omo, their previous patron deity, with Apollo. The prior relegated to a minor position of honor in the city.

Ryn went out of town and sat on the high hills overlooking the city. It was evident that after fifty years, Arvadia was little more than a vassal state of Olympus, such a far cry from their former glory. Perhaps a token trade nation they had marched over apathetically. He recalled that Amaras had said nothing specific about Arvadia, but had only mentioned going west and not south nor into Akola.

He sat and listened to the wind. Peering ahead first, he saw two paths up ahead. The road to the left took Ryn to Aupur, a once-proud commercial city that had a long, but in the past tenuous, relationship with Olympia. It had avoided punishment due to its geographic isolation. The people lived in the mountains.

To the right, a road took one into a forest some ways off, beyond which were many logging towns in Northwest Arvadia that had historically been neutral. He whispered to the Wind, so Teoti might hear, that he knew a fork presented three choices, not just two.

The Wind spoke in whispers, but it was heard. It seemed, whether left or right, his quest was doomed. The Wind over the land was dark and stale. Their hearts were hardened by fear, and their minds closed by resignation. To move a king, it was possible; to move these people, impossible.

He sat in the tall grass and meditated. He found it

wasteful to proceed. There were important things to do. Ryn was the type who hated missing an opportunity, but at that point, the opportunity could be elsewhere.

It then came to him that Zeus' control was often not material, but rather, spiritual. Sumer had conquered first and done it by the sword and only the sword. When they lost the greater power of the sword, they lost near everything to Egypt. Osiris understood the need to demand worship, so Egypt demanded reverence. But when things fell for Egypt, they found reverence had saved them a harsher fall, but what was missing was devotion. Zeus understood devotion. He used his patron gods and cultural power to acquire it. His hand was steel against strong hearts that opposed him and gentle to those he might win over. Zeus had, indeed, conquered Arvadia, and no surplus of steel or vast army was needed to do it.

As he prayed, he performed a monk's ritual. He filled his hands with water and lightning, at the exact same time, with the exact same effort. Then he prayed and brought them together. What was left was a small spark of lightning in his right hand.

That was it then. The wind was fresh going East. It was time to turn around. He sighed and reconciled with it. It may not have made sense, but it was his path. He could not change it now, only trust I had lead to the best outcome.

Now three days after the prayer, Ryn was moving quickly and cautiously through the unclaimed and unsettled territory east of Molnak, the mountainous country simply known as "The rugged place." It was a rough terrain filled with crags, cliffs, caverns, desolate rocks, and oddly grown forests of dark and hard-barked trees. Cutting down a tree in these woods was a tedious task. There were also the left-over enchantments from too many battles waged with careless cursing of the earth. Such warfare made whole corners of landscape impassable, and those enchantments would remain for centuries. Only a great downpour of waters could remove them. But more fearsome than this was the vast array of rogue Nephilim and offspring of evil that inhabited the place. Everything that the patron gods worked to keep out was homed here, and it was a savage place of constant death and devouring. No man dared enter its borders.

But as he entered, he felt no fear. He held onto the ever-present sense that he was being watched by Teoti, empowered by the Great Wind. "Aren't you forgetting your failures?" Something spoke to him, trying to erode his confidence in his safety. He fought it with his triumphs, triumphs that made him one to be feared as well. He was aware that the legend of him had spread abroad, and it all began during the Major Sumer War. A mere youth, he was only thirty-five years in existence. Ryn had been brought to the front lines with his order of monks. It had happened that Juya was part of a regiment of warriors at the same front at that time.

Ryn's order was assigned to bombard the enemy lines, and Juya's battalion was given orders to charge the battlefield when Sumer began to advance on their ranks again. In the fighting, Juya held fast as the line fell, as she so often did. Her intuition often inspired others back to the line when she sensed they would win, a trait she would become praised for. But in this instant, she became isolated by the advance and was set upon by the god Istaran.

Ryn, filled with passion for his lifelong friend, rushed to her aid. He defeated the god. Beheading him and undoing his flesh, the god descended to a lesser form, in the likeness of an animal. Ryn was immediately promoted, and whereas a great victory would be an opportunity to be known for one's power, Ryn made it an opportunity to do even more. But from that very day, Ryn's victory over Istaran spread throughout the kingdom, and word grew of his power.

When he made general, he had a moment where he doubted if he should have the title since he was commanding men hundreds of years his senior. His father explained it best for him. There was a spirit about him that commanded the respect of others, and his spirit was that of a king's as well as that of the noble lion's. Every new campaign was not a reward for his efforts but a chance to do more for his people. Each battle earned him another great achievement, and his name grew and grew among the people. It was his heart to refuse to focus on his own satisfaction that freed him to do more with the opportunities fate put in front of him. All of that led to him lining up victory after victory until he had impressed every naysayer of his that could possibly arise. Born in another nation, he would have likely been deified.

Ryn's name had been exalted to such proportions that there was likely no being in all the centralized world that had not heard of him. A poem made it back to him during their 50-year war, one that came all the way from Udete, far west of Egypt. In it, he was painted as a fierce dragon-lion, strong and proud upon a hill which Olympus itself could not seem to overcome despite throwing wave after wave of monsters at it. He had often chuckled at that image. Looking down, he contrasted that with the frailty of his very mortal hands that were, by no means, that of a legend. Yet, he'd often remembered that image to put his own self-criticism into perspective. He did that even now. He'd truly done great things, had he not?

But against reality, the image broke apart. That hill had been overcome, and his pride of lions had been scattered. Ryn had watched as the world's power had passed from empire to empire, and somewhere it just made sense that his time had come. Empires didn't last forever. None of them had.

From the beginning, the Sumerians were the center of civilization, not even known as Sumerians at the time. Very soon, however, Egypt and Akunan grew powerful. Within a millennium, they had slowly overpowered Sumer in culture and each traded rule over the lands in between them. After centuries of war, the three reached a stalemate, all the time ignoring the growing Olympians.

When Crova defeated Sumer, Crova and Nova were acclaimed as being the most powerful nations on earth. So powerful they were that the world's nations controlled their pride and refrained from warring with their neighbors out of fear the Crovans or Novans would make a move on them in their weakness. Without reluctance, it could be added, for the nations were still recovering from the long ages of war.

They were all fearful, except for one, Olympia, which seemed to expand on its neighbors not by open war but by pushing its language, ideology, and gods on the soft-hearted, weak-willed, and weak-minded nations around them. It was during the time of peace that Olympus grew to the strength it now had. It was a sly nation that had not fought a major war since its successful campaign against Egypt over a hundred years earlier. Terror and manipulation were its favored tools of conquest, picking out one territory and using it to leverage the next. That was until the invasion, the invasion that dispersed the Crovan and Novan people.

Ryn finally felt it prudent to sit a moment. His heart seemed to need a chance to sort itself out and perform some reconciliation. His mind wandered, and almost like a waking dream, he had deep troubles turn to images in his mind.

He looked around. He was alone. Where were they all? His heart asked. He had to be honest with the response. His heart heard that and was saddened again. The loss of the war had also meant the loss of allies, companions, the loyal, all of them.

He looked off into the charred hills. The evidence of ancient war was all around that place; jetting rocks, caverns, places where all that had lived had been turned to ash or mineral by an incredible power. It was barren, despite the colorful broadleaf and sturdy trees there.

Then his mind began to show him things. He saw a group of Crovans. Men, women, children, all coming up the path, suddenly ecstatic to see him. He embraced them all and kissed the little ones, assuring them it would be okay. Teoti had defeated their adversary and given them peace, and forever on, they would not have to worry if they would be alive the next day.

It was a sweet dream. Then it faded. It saddened him. He asked for them to come back, but what came back wasn't them. It was Juya. His heart leapt because the image in his mind was so powerful. He could smell her and nearly feel her body heat. In the moment, he actually reached up a hand for her, only to see that she was not there. He put it down in a bit of embarrassment.

He took a deep breath and felt the wind. He listened. Yes, she was gone. But she was not gone forever. That didn't satisfy, but he was trying. He went deeper. But it was no good. Something dark was there; a wound. Where she was, he couldn't consider it. It was still difficult. He couldn't go any deeper, and he felt the wind blocked him. He sighed with disappointment.

He tried focusing again, this time on the task at hand. He regathered his wind. He had to. There were only two ways a being's wind could move. Hot and fierce, ever-expanding, and going forward despite any obstacle, or it could move cold and passive, ever begging to die and sink into nothingness.

He clenched his hands. They felt weaker than when he was young. This was it, the experience of death, decay, dying. It was the passage of age, the bleeding out of his wind, the settling of his blood. He could feel it. Sensing the inevitable, what point was there when all things died in the end?

He broke his thoughts. That wasn't who he was. He did not lay down and die. He did not accept his fate like an ascetic. He was a mover. He was vibrant like the Wind. Zeus' prison had tried to kill his wind. He could not let it. He'd learned just how vital the aim of every monk really was. It was everything. It was life itself in his fingertips.

He prayed for Juya. She needed to know that, to

feel that. If he could send a message through the stars to her, he asked it to be done. Could Teoti preserve her? Could he save her? Could he save any of them? He didn't know. But the more he pondered it, the more Teoti had to save them. Why else do it? Why else trust. Trust...

He wasn't upset by this anymore. He entertained his questions while his heart maintained his devotion. Thousands of men and women since the dawn of creation had invested their lives in figuring out Teoti. He was no exception. Teoti loved creation. He awaited their devotion. Yet how did one love another and allow him such misfortune and devastation?

He tried to understand that, but no one really could. He was about to give up and move on, leaving it to be reconciled another time, when another image came to him. He saw his oldest son. There he was, when he was a youth, reaching out to the fire outside their home. Ryn didn't stop him. He let him touch it. Why? Why let his son get burned? Because he learned something. He let him get burned there, so he might not be consumed by it later on. There was an answer there.

What a simple explanation. How had he not known that? Perhaps he had. The monks hadn't been satisfied with that. Why? Because they still died, that was why. The fire consumed anyway. So how did the dream make sense? Unless the plan was the son's preservation...

He suddenly began turning his wheels. How was it possible for a father to want to save but not to? He wrestled but soon came by the only logical answer. Because the son turns away from his father, that was the only way a son did not have his father's protection. Otherwise, the father was always over him, never abandoning him. Suddenly, his heart was filled with hope. Was that it?

He saw his own children, and he was living this out in his mind. Another image came. They were all on a journey, and along the way, he asked them to stay away from the plants that were sullied so they would be clean. If they touched the sullied plants, they could spread it to them all by touching one another. It was dyer that they be pure. But one by one, they kept getting sullied, and he realized he would have to leave some behind to save the pure ones. His heart suddenly had more than it could entertain at the moment. He sighed and left the deep thought.

He set his mind on his children and had fond thoughts. He had not thought of them in days. He meditated on them little these days, not because he failed to love them, but because he knew they were safe and he could afford not to during such times.

There were seven of them, and they were all in eastern Omoka, a secluded land far north, all protected and away from the wars. Seven was an unusually low amount, especially for Ryn's age, and considering he had been married to Juya 76 years. They were different than other kings and queens, though. At war their entire reign, the fact was that Ryn had a wife who was constantly in the field. With both of their lives lived in constant command and service, they were together rarely, right up until the last year. Even then, they put off any more children until the battle could be decided.

He wondered if they should have just made everyone understand; done what they wanted. But she was needed as a commander. She was priceless to the nation as a general. Besides, Ryn knew that she would go insane kept in a house somewhere while there was fighting going on.

Juya loved to be in combat, and he was always anxious over it. She had offered her husband only a brief window into her psyche when she told him once that she only felt alive in the thrill of battle when her life was on the line. It seemed that the mere realization that her demise was imminent seemed to be an incentive for something, a hope that she longed for. Yet, after every battle, she felt let down, yet she never once backed away from battle. It was as if she was designed for it.

He'd contemplated discharging her if need be or forcing her into a stately role. But he couldn't do that. Neither would he want to. Juya was not the bureaucratic type and would hate being resigned to the city. If he had ever done that to her, the Juya he loved would slowly disappear. Thankfully, she loved life, and she loved her station. She did not succumb.

Being in Hades, she would be in the shackles of death constantly. Over and over, they would bring her to the point of giving up and then pull back. Physical death would come when she finally conceded her spirit. If she did this, she would be lost, and her spirit tossed into the lake of the dead.

Ryn suddenly felt the ache again. He was pushing himself with this reconciliation. This was supposed to be done in rest. He supposed the humans did something a lot better than him. He smiled at that. His mind saw the beaming faces of the Molnakians. That was encouraging. He took hold of that and restarted his trek.

In the high hills, the trees around were of a

vibrant wood that spoke of aggression and vengeance. There were rocks strewn about of great size, as though a battle had taken place there at one point. Ryn made his way around a bend quickly and came into a small clearing between two heavy rocks about forty cubits high in a space ten strides wide. Then he saw the figure in the path.

"It is you. Why am I not surprised?"

The smooth yet mellow voice spoke from the middle of the road. Ryn stopped, and his first reaction was to wonder how he had not sensed him before. He sniffed the air and sensed a powerful water-based incantation that blocked out every spiritual sense. He had camouflaged himself. When he realized who it was, his heart almost skipped a beat, but he held it down. He was fine. He had Teoti watching over this; he could trust it was enough.

"It's been a very long time, Enki."

The figure was about eight cubits tall and had a turquoise tint skin with black hair. His butted gold tunic was held down by a belt of dragonhide. A particular dragon he'd slain early in his life that he now wore to signify his power. His gray-blue eyes looked inquisitively and showed a massive presence. Were it not for the water incantation, the trees and rocks might be leaning away from his body from the sheer weight of it.

"Yes. It has, Ryn. You masked your presence extremely well. You simply failed to realize that Boktom owes me a debt. So I have made myself the exclusive inheritor of your trek out of the underworld."

Ryn had feared he'd be identifiable in the depths. He'd done nothing to mask his presence until he'd approached En Ju Mogon's temple.

"I'm sure you are wondering why I am here."

Ryn took a breath and maintained his demeanor. "It is on my mind."

Enki took a slight step, "Zeus doesn't even know you broke out of his prison. And it will stay that way."

Ryn smirked. "So, you were predictable, after all."

Enki murmured, "Call it what you will. But yes, I am happy you are still a thorn in his side. But let's not waste our time. I came for another reason."

Ryn nodded and relaxed slightly, "Of course." He breathed, recalling that his former rival to the south had always been a bit wordy in conversation compared to others.

He looked out over the area and took a deep breath. "I enjoy a good frivolous gallivant from time to time. It will be interesting to see what happens when everything is destroyed, the sweetness of life gone. It makes you wonder why he'd want to do that." His sly look told Ryn he was not referring to Zeus and knew right away who he meant.

"So you take for granted the warnings of Ano. You always seemed to hold a certain fear of Teoti."

Enki had a look that was offended, nearly vomitus, but he refrained. "Your interpretation is...sordid. I have no words of favor for Apsu I care to express,"

Ryn sneered, "That is your derogatory word for him. That's not his name."

"It will be," said Enki. "You haven't bothered to ask yourself, what is this battle really over? Hm?"

Ryn waited patiently.

"This is not a war of flesh. I actually agree with you, Ryn. All flesh dies. It can't be sustained. So what is there left? What does it mean to be a god? It simply means to be remembered, venerated, even after death."

Ryn started feeling where he was going.

"Osiris, Akunan, all the others, even Zeus; fight with all their might to deny that. Perhaps a hallmark of their youth compared to me, but I am different."

Ryn found that amusing. "Is that your way to lay a claim over them? Being the eldest? Despite the fact Zeus is the leader's son, Osiris was the priest, and Akunan was given the keys to the mysterious?"

Enki laughed, feeling the whip the Touka had put upon him. "That's funny, Ryn. But let's not get distracted. What makes someone a god?"

Ryn was quiet.

"It's worship. Even you're father, the ol' renegade himself, saw that."

Ryn almost smirked as he saw Enki's aura do a slight fidget in remembrance of Traijyn. Perhaps he was remembering that great battle of old.

"But what keeps Apsu from being worshipped?" Enki went on. "It's called knowledge."

Ryn humored him a bit more and listened.

"Knowledge is the only true way to win and gain immortality. Zeus, Osiris, and Akunan can fight over a bit of political power for centuries, but it will all mean nothing when they die. Knowledge, that is what keeps us going on. Knowledge will mean worship for generations. That worship will mean life given to us after this…destruction."

He turned to the side and seemed to bemoan his thoughts. "I am here to make you an offer. Since we squared off against one another so equally all those years, slayer of Ishtaran."

Ryn shook his head, "That is so kind of you," he said sarcastically.

Enki found that amusing. "Every god makes his own history. You can walk into the temples of Osiris and be told a different story than the temples of Zeus. They're all competing for the same thing. They all want their worship. The problem is, who is going to understand it after such an event as this destruction? So between you and me, I am building a library, one that can survive this destruction. In it, my priests will tell my story, for all the nations to remember. Even the story of mankind himself."

Ryn shook his head, "It won't be nearly as good as the one Teoti will tell with real people. Not mere stone and papyrus."

Enki smiled. He looked up at the sky. "You miss something, Ryn. Did you know the stars up there are already telling the world how this whole story will go? How it all comes to an end. Did you know that?" He looked at him provokingly. "You say Osiris was the priest to our fathers, but I taught reading the stars to this world. There is nothing that cannot be divined from the stars. All of the events from the past and future can be read like a cosmic book. Talk about predictable," he laughed.

Ryn heaved a breath. Enki came back to a more somber state, allowing his bemusement to exude a bit much. "But seriously, don't you want to know something? Isn't something...on your mind? Go on, ask me."

Ryn sensed the temptation, the temptation to know. But he knew it was a trap. Enki could predict whatever he wanted to, but even Ryn knew the stars were vague. They didn't tell you specifics. He knew that. Traijyn knew that. On top of that, there was no way to trust his words, and that meant there was no use for anything Enki could say. "No." Ryn said.

Enki was surprised. "Interesting. Well…you may well decline my real offer."

He started to walk a bit to the north. "I suppose I was going to offer you a place in my story. A minor one, but I would have written you in as a hero." He somberly turned to Ryn, "Are you sure you are fine being forgotten? That seems like an awfully harsh punishment coming from your god."

Ryn thought it over. Enki was very real, far more real than Zeus. He had, surprisingly, come to terms with his condition. That was interesting. But centuries of having Ano and Gilga in his own land preaching might have finally persuaded him to take it seriously. Still, what he offered was not life. It was a substitute. Where Ryn agreed with Zeus was that life was one's prime value. Next to life, no other value mattered. There was no way to actually be comfortable with death. He had proposed an interesting thought, but in the end, it was nothing better than the path of the ascetics, a way to feel better about dying.

"I must decline. I reserve that honor to Teoti; for him to decide."

Enki chuckled bemusedly. "I really expected you to see it differently. I'll admit."

Ryn didn't know what to say to that.

"After all these years, after you had so thoroughly frustrated Zeus, I suppose I expected a higher level of reasoning of you, oh mighty Crovan King. But I suppose once a zealot, always a zealot. So be it." He started to turn.

Ryn watched him go but then plant his feet and

look back in preparation to leave.

"You had your time on top, Ryn. I suppose your Touka nation's fall was expected. But please do harass Zeus for me. As for myself, I have made it clear; I have no interest in it."

Ryn nodded, "I remember."

Enki smiled crookedly. Then he spread his arms out and began to fade from view. "I don't know what you will do after you fight Zeus, Ryn. But if you happen to have an evolution of thought, come and see me."

In a moment, he was gone. Ryn had to wonder why he had been allowed that visit. Was it a test? He had to admit, for a brief moment, he wondered if Sumer might help him. He wondered if they might fight Zeus. But he had already known, long ago, that none of the southern powers were going to do that. They were content to watch and wait for the right moment. He supposed it felt like a shame he had ever thought to go back and try to rely on those rivals.

*   *   *

The Sumerian god soared through the air, seated on his sails of water. A stream came from the back of each shoulder, and he glided serenely through the sky. He surveyed the Crovan land beneath him and eyed its possession. His thoughts were many. He had expected a rather boring flight when some excitement showed unexpectedly.

Ahead, in his path, was an old acquaintance from the East, from the hermit kingdoms. "Well, well," he said to himself. "What have we here?"

He slowed, and his water began to settle,

falling softly from him. In his path was a man stading on air. He was dressed in a long and shiny robe of intricate design, blue and red in color. He had a long black beard that thinned to a point, and under his robe were ruddy trousers and a vest that gave away his combat prowess.

"Enki, old friend," said the hovering god with a wide smile.

"I don't recall us ever being friends." Came the sordid reply.

"These are words. Let's be amicable to one another. Perhaps we have the same aim."

Enki seemed doubtful. "What do you want? Fan Gi."

The golden olive-skinned god looked at him slyly and pointed non-threateningly. "You found Ryn, didn't you?"

Enki rose an eyebrow. "And how did you surmise that?"

"Because I set out to do exactly what you did."

Enki laughed. "I love these games we play. Why don't you come out and say what you mean."

Fan Gi took note of his directness and simply smiled. "It's all a game, Enki. If the games end, we get too serious. Like ol' Zeus. So upstading, reasonable gods such as ourselves, have to poke back a bit. Right?"

Enki had a flat and fake smile. "I am done in this tale. I am not poking anything."

Fan Gi chuckled. "We are always poking, aren't we?"

Enki didn't respond, and Fan Gi shrugged. "I say, we see what happens. And maybe I'll go in to watch at the end of it all."

Enki found that amusing. "If you can resist."

Fan Gi's face suddenly showed a seriousness slightly behind his smile. "I've resisted quite a bit. It is no trouble. Life is about games. Let's play them."

Enki nodded. "Then, we shall see. I am satisfied to watch."

$$*\qquad*\qquad*$$

He had passed through a thick forest and had ascended into the mountains where he now walked passively around scattered rocks. The splash of rocks on the jagged hills leading up the slope would indicate that they had fallen from the cliffs that peaked the mountains and towered high in front of him. Lacerations upon the cliffs showed where forces of impact had rattled rock loose from the tall face. Ryn sensed a violent spiritual atmosphere and woke up from his thoughts.

The air was supercharged, and one could tell that blood had been shed there. It was possible that something was still there. Many Nephilim were fiercely territorial and attacked intruders. For the most part, rogue Nephilim had a disdain for community and sought solitude. Vanity was only threatened by others, so many fed their vanity until it drove them to wander. This was what the Crovans and Novans called "going rogue." A rogue being could be in any stage of severity of this spiritual disease, but seclusion and self-reliance accelerated it. The symptoms were always the same; aggression, autonomy, and self-absorbed survivalism in all functions. Where he was traveling, anything he encountered would invariably be rogue.

Ryn treaded more rock until he was forced into a narrow passage between two high cliffs. The passage was a three to four-foot-wide slot in the side of the mountain, cutting through the rock separating two high and thick pillars of the mountain. If anyone was expecting to attack him, they would find it easiest while Ryn was inside this passage. Reaching back, he kept his left hand on the Arvaita, ready to swing it out at an attacker. The passage was a little over a hundred strides long, and with every step, he felt an impending ambush.

He sensed nothing near him in the spirit. The cavern was so charged with rushing wind of the spiritual kind that it would be unlikely for him to sense anyone until they were right upon him. Just as heavy physical winds make it difficult to locate a thing by its scent, so Ryn was impaired from pinpointing any opponents. It befuddled him to think about that strange place. It was a place where the aura of the entire land to the east rushed into this chasm and into the void behind the ridge. It was like water pouring from one bowl to an empty one. It made him aware of the goodness of the land ahead, the Crovan land that lay just over the areas held by Omaika.

He intensely traversed the trail for about a minute, not running through but shuffling through at a pace where he was a faster-moving target and had time to catch a booby trap or an ambush. As Ryn approached the other side, he was slightly surprised to be unchallenged but not off his guard. He still expected something to jump out at him.

It was as he came near the end that his deep memory caught up with him. He had heard of this place. He began thinking of everything he knew of it.

Coming out the other side of the gash in the rock, he stood on top of a high cliff. Ahead of him, the mountain chain grew intense and below Ryn was a deep depression in between the surrounding peaks. At the bottom of it sat a crystal lake surrounded by evergreen trees. It was very beautiful, and Ryn admired how the green mountains rolled into the water smoothly. It was astonishing to him that such beautiful land laid hidden to mankind deep within these violent mountains. It was almost sad that they were unable to see the most beautiful parts of their own world. And it was land mere alans from Crova's western border, at least in their days of glory.

Ryn moved to his left along the cliff's flat edge. There was space of about a stride between the rock face behind him and the drop in front of him. The flat walkway disappeared into the rock to the right, climbing up until it was no longer a path but a fold in the side of the cliff. After following it a bit, it seemed the cliff to his back ran about a hundred cubits up and flattened into a jagged mesa at the top. Ryn watched the top suspiciously and winded his way around this cliffhanging path.

The path turned the corner that had concealed the rest of the mountain from Ryn. To his surprise, the flat path opened up as the rock face receded back into the mountain, leaving a flat area overlooking the cliff to his right about thirty strides by fifteen. What Ryn saw next immediately put him on his toes, and in reality, he only had tenths of a second to react after he had processed what was happening.

In front of Ryn was a large cave, obviously hollowed out by a creature, in the rock face thirty strides in front of him. As Ryn had turned the corner, he saw two red eyes, dragon-like in shape, peering out of the cave's darkness. From them immediately came a bright light that turned out to be a streaking stream of molten plasma. There were only tenths of a second for Ryn to bolt into the open space and out of the way of the plasma before his face would have become a dripping and melting mess.

The dragon emerged and immediately pounced. The beast was around fifteen cubits tall and thirty long, bearing narrow jaws with sharp blades running down its back in thick clusters. The blades glowed like embers where it drew in spirit and turned it into fire. This creature had a godlike ability that made it capable of creating incredible heat.

It snapped and charged for a burst at the same time. He was quick and fluid. Flowing to the right, Ryn slashed out with the blade and severed the left foot to drop it.

Un-thwarted, the dragon swung its bulk counter-clockwise from the ground and delivered a massive blow with its tail in an instant. Ryn only had time to block the blow from making direct contact. Unfathomable to Ryn, the blow came with megaton force and flung him high into the air off the side of the mountain. Twisting around in the air, he saw that the blow had propelled him far past the cliff's edge and about a half alan from impact with the forest lake below. Falling towards the depression, Ryn quickly sheathed the Arvaita and flattened out his body. He then massed explosive energy into his loins and flung himself, sprawling back at the cliff, where a slide of volcanic powder with rocks and trees jettisoning out its side awaited. The cliff sloped a fierce seventy degrees, so Ryn dug in and anchored his weight to the side of the mountains solid underbelly.

Ryn finally came to rest against a jettisoning tree and regrouped. Swinging himself around, he flung his body another twenty cubits back up the mountainside and landed on a protruding rock. The beast was at the top about three hundred cubits up, unhappy about the resilience of his opponent.

Ryn now recalled who this was and why he'd remembered it. A villain, his people, often called The Gatekeeper. Its purpose was amicable to Olympia's, and it had a bond with these mountains. In fact, this was his mountain. It had menaced his people in the past. It was a hard task to challenge something like that on its own mountain, but knowing who it was, he could not leave it there. It began charging plasma, and Ryn did not hesitate to start hopping his way to the top.

The beast fired shots of plasma down on Ryn as he leapt from tree to tree and rock to rock, advancing towards it. The beast made efforts to catch him by spraying combinations of shot at him and sped up its frequency, but it could not connect with the Crovan as it pounced up the slope with catlike precision.

When he was about the height of three men from impact, Ryn hit the last rock and exploded upward. The beast unloaded its last glob above Ryn so as to catch him in his jump; it didn't. Ryn accelerated in the air and, at the peak of his jump, advanced above the beast so quick that he spontaneously appeared over the thick chunk of fire. Absolutely astonished, the beast had no time to react, and it only took Ryn a blink of the eye to unsheathed the Arvaita and plunge it to the earth, slicing the head into two halves.

Most all of the force of Ryn's advance went into

the swing, and he nearly floated above the falling body before finally descending softly to the earth.

The dragon backed up, sprawling on the ground and flailing its limbs, the spirit struggling to regenerate cognition and regain its strength.

Ryn poured his spirit into the Arvaita, and it began to glow brightly. He charged it more and more until it outshone the sun and then spun into a horizontal slice that went out in a flash. The fierce energy burned through the body and turned about half of it to ash before slowing to a ring of embers around the husk. He looked at the corps for a second and then decided against doing anything with it. He supposed it was enough to leave it there, burning. Something about how the fire burned told him this corpse would not return to any form of life.

The victor left the cave area and followed the path downhill along the mountainside into another high chain of peaks. Gone was the fierce dragon that owned the gateway from The Rugged Place to Omaika. The beast was widely known and sparked fear into the hearts of would-be travelers. It was a less noble offspring of Romael and was even considered an uncle to the Algeh Dragon race. Perhaps, had it remained in its original station and not made a deal with Zeus, they could have discussed things. Allegiances meant more than what man or god took for granted. They determined who one became. And where they had come to was unfortunately unreconcilable. Too often, the games of the gods and the way they conduct their affairs made violence inevitable.

He stopped. Why had he questioned that?

Ryn wondered, there, what the difference was

between this being and En Ju Mogon. Both came against him due to allegiance, both were gods, sons of Romael, yet he reconciled without death with the latter. Was it the humans? Had their humility and curiosity allowed for that, or was it the aligning with one another? Perhaps, and yet his fight with En Ju Mogon, before anything else was known, ended in peace. He honestly didn't know. There was something within En Ju Mogon and himself that made that possible. Here, it was not. What did he call that?

Now headed into higher mountains, the air grew colder, and the hues of green, brown, and gray were now covered in thick white blankets. This was the territory known as Omaika, home to a secluded and fierce tribe of Nephilim known as the En Ar Mujan. A faint hope was present in approaching them. Perhaps it would be thought well of that he had just slain Ikowo Iubaita, the Fire Mountain God.

8 THE EN AR MUJAN

White powder began to collect on Ryn's feet as he walked steadily through the high mountain country of Omaika. He ascended the ridge of Mount Ju Ogo, which climbed through the atmosphere about seven thousand cubits above the lush green and blue lake valleys below. Ryn could look to his left and see the places where he had come from, and when he looked to his right, he saw the Yzke Mountain chain.

Smoother and higher mountains, the Yzke was separated from Omaika by a series of deep gorges and valleys of crystal blue lakes and evergreen forests that ran into the Euphrates and Tigris rivers. Ryn stopped and watched, briefly held in awe.

This was the first time Ryn had laid eyes on Crovan soil since his capture at Raijyn. He recalled the spirit of the land, a spirit of love, justice, and peace. Now overrun by the hordes of Zeus, it felt sullied. He sat and beheld it. He shed tears over it.

He would spend the night on the ridge overlooking the Yzke. It was the best place to be for the night since his path took him around. He lay down and listened to the land. It was in confusion. It didn't know who it was anymore.

He sat up just before dawn and made a lament for the land. It was in honor of Crova, and the hundreds of thousands that had perished in the houses of Crova because of Zeus. The growing temptation among the sons of man was to write down such laments. He did not. Songs and stories should be carried orally with mathematical precision. Not subject to change, destruction, or errors, such as in the case of written tablets.

While the wind blew over Ryn, he poured his heart out to his god and stared at Crova under the waning moonlight.

O precious soil, pure and sweet to my senses;
Guardian of Crova's mighty wind, you were like a father to me,
Teaching me to survive and challenging me;
Begging me to press on despite any cost or pain.
Irreplaceable Aichokyn (personable living ecosystem),
Gift of life, inspiring beauty;
You nurtured me with sweet nectar and
Earth's most powerful beings nursed on your lavish milk and honey.
Glorious, a jewel of the Source, a trophy of inspiration and joy,
What tragedy has befallen you?
That such pain could be bore upon a diamond such as this
Testifies to the darkness, arrogance, and wickedness

Of your enemies who now plunder you.

For we who are dark and lost, you have sacrificed

And such sacrifices do not go unnoticed in the heavens.

When all is forgiven, and all debts are settled, your price will be glorified for eternity.

The next morning Ryn stood and bade the land a blessing. It responded with recognition. Part of it cried out. He remembered his lament and then continued.

The path took him up the mountain ridge and towards the frozen plains on the plateaus of Omaika. The inhabitants of this land were the En Ar Mujan. Their appearance was like that of a Chimpanzee with long white fur and a dog-like face. They typically fought with long arched blades in a crescent shape that they handled like a handheld elbow blade.

Their relationship with Crovan had been tepid. A coup, inspired by Zeus, had detained the Crovans, and they had left the Yzke defenseless. King Raiyn was assassinated, but Zeus's candidate did not ascend to the throne. Alvyn assumed leadership over much of the west and secured the mountains to keep insurgents from coming into the nation from the Arvadian Peninsula. Many of these insurgents were En Ar Mujan.

In time, Alvyn closed the western border through a show of force. Unable to profit off Crova's civil war anymore, a band of unified raiders, numbering around two thousand, came into the Northern Yzke in mass. Without hesitating, Crova's mountain rangers mobilized along with a battalion of the Northern Army.

When the En Ar Mujan lined up across four thousand plus Crovans, they did not bother to call for reinforcements and conceded the Northern Yzke. Ever since then, they had resided in Omaika, high in the mountains and apathetic toward most political activity. But if the En Ar Mujan had made themselves a stink in the nostrils of anyone, it would be Crova.

They'd been a constant supply of mercenaries for Zeus. A worrier culture high in the mountains with few direct foes, they found successful mercenary work admirable and found Crovans to be difficult foes. Killing a Crovan warrior in battle bore one merit in Omaika.

So indeed, there was bad blood there despite hardly any formal campaigns against one another. But in Ryn's mind, reaching out to them was worth the risk. Omaika was on the way to Alvyn, a Crovan city on the coast of the Dark Sea as well as his next destination, and it was quicker than going around. The En Ar Mujan had never bothered to make an alliance with anyone, and despite their warriors having a long contract history with Olympus, Ryn felt they were one of the least likely nations to submit to Zeus' power and hated authority. He also knew that Zeus treated his mercenaries like chafe, often sending them to their demise. Surely there was a desire to throw off Zeus' yoke there. So Ryn's goal was to make contact and seek an audience with the current chief.

Now leaving footprints in the snow, Ryn looked around and saw the disappearing tree line replaced by crags and collections of rocks. It would reappear in the middle of the plateau, but for now, it disappeared. Beginning to cross back into inhabited territory, Ryn pulled the cloak over himself as he had done in

Molnak. The air was thin, and the wind was fiercer. It made visibility minimal. Currents picked up snow and blanketed the sky with it. Snow was created through windscaping or it's after-effects. In the same way, deserts without vegetation did not exist naturally but were created as a bi-product to the scorching of the earth.

In Omaika, the windscapers of the En Ar Mujan created snow in order to blind their enemies if they ever invaded. It also deterred strong travelers from braving their mountains. Ryn found it difficult to navigate in the snow. It's sheer cunning as a weapon was unmatched. To make something that pulled the heat right out of one's body...it was insufferable, to say the least. The rising cold moisture in the air also made it difficult to perceive other spirits around him. He walked on quickly, hoping to find a dry place to warm his feet.

After some alans of walking, Ryn noticed an evergreen forest around him, and he also felt as though he had passed a high barrier, perhaps a high wall. He looked around but saw nothing, though he could faintly make out the silhouettes of trees. The wind had turned the area into a blizzard, and Ryn found it hard to see four strides in front of him. This was unusually fierce weather and fairly deep into Omaika's proper territory. It likely meant that Omaika's windscapers were targeting his region.

They were likely aware of him. He traveled on. They were likely trying to get him lost. The spiritual trail of travelers diminished in the snow. But Ryn was adept enough to see it.

Several alans later, Ryn's feet began to grow sore and irritated. He found himself concentrating energy on keeping them warm. While looking at the ground, preoccupied with his feet, Ryn suddenly became aware of a weapon, some four or five strides to his left.

It was motionless, and above him, possibly in a tree. He did not see it, but he sensed the spilt blood that had not been fully washed from the blade. Blood was very noisy in the spiritual sense, and blood on a blade gave a worrier away all the time.

It was clear that the En Ar Mujan were watching him. How many were watching him was unknown. As Ryn trudged the snow, he locked in on the presence surrounding the blade and began to track it uniquely in other places around him. After another alan of walking, Ryn had become aware of twenty or thirty independent signatures surrounding him as he went.

Needing a moment, he stopped at a fork in the road where a wooden sign stuck out, indicating the destination of each path. The sign pointing right had "Eo Ujan" written on it, which stood for some type of towering fortress. It probably faced the plains of the plateau to the east towards Crova. The other sign indicated a city, "Juku Okaimo" which was probably on the way to the capital. He took a moment to remark on how odd it was for anyone to actually make written signs for directions. Did they have a lot of outside travelers…of the kind that couldn't sense the most basic spiritual aura?

Ryn burned a dry area to sit down on and reached into his flat-sack, pulling out a woolskin given to him by the citizens of Molnak. Tarring it down the middle, he wrapped one side on his left foot and the other on his right. He had to have a plan to get through the aggressive and blade-happy warriors so he could talk to an authority. This way of making his feet warm provided a deception for the En Ar Mujan spying on him. Clothing his feet meant that he could not use his fire in his kicks, which they had just seen when he cleared a spot for himself. It was to make them think he was not aware of their threat. For good measure, Ryn also pulled out a wool fleece to cover his hands. He then got up and began moving left towards the capital.

The air was getting clearer, and the wind less violent. Simultaneously the entourage following him began to fall back behind him and out of sight. The forest around him was growing scarce, and occasionally Ryn saw their white fur shuffle from behind trees. He wondered how long they would do this and gauged whether or not he should let them know he was aware of them.

While in thought, he became suddenly aware of a signature right behind him. It had appeared there without giving itself away to his physical senses. Making a quick turn would be taken aggressively for sure, so Ryn slowed and came to a stop in the path. The sky was still gray and cloud-covered, but the wind was light, and Ryn had full visibility through transparent gusts of snow and wind. The being seemed to stop as well, and Ryn waited until things were very still to speak to him.

Still turned away from it, Ryn spoke, "I am not here to fight, plunder, or take anything. I am an ambassador, seeking a political audience." The words hung in the air for a few seconds as the figure behind him remained motionless. It spiritually began communicating with the surrounding forest, and soon rows of warriors emerged from behind the trees.

There were more than Ryn had anticipated, about forty, and he was impressed with their obvious stealth.

After some time, the being moved around to face Ryn. The intention was to peer into Ryn's spirit to see what his motives and thoughts were. Ryn didn't make eye contact, not allowing the aggressor to see his inner spirit.

He approached Ryn, aggressive, and bold. To the ape-like warrior, a deliberate attempt to conceal identity and intention was a clue as to malicious intent. "What are you trying to hide, ambassador?" He spoke in the common language of the Sumerians. The others started to come closer.

Ryn had to be careful. The En Ar Mujan thought communally. If he aggressed one, he aggressed them all. There would be no reasoning and no discussion. His window to their leader would be lost.

He brought his hands up, relaxed, and moved his eyes down towards them as though he were concerned about their coldness. Then dropping his shoulders and his arms, he gave the warrior an aura of diverted attention. He had a matter of great concern, something a leader might find valuable to know, and something the warrior may be punished for by not collecting.

The warrior stood soaking in the presence that Ryn was giving off, as little as it was, and began to cling to it. Revealing so little else, the Nephilim had nothing else to decipher from him. Ryn left the warrior with no other conclusion. He would have to deliver him to the leader.

The Nephilim looked Ryn over for a second and then turned to face the rest. Without speaking a word, he directed Ryn to follow him, and he began down the left path. The group closed in and followed, tensely. En Ar Mujan weapons could not be sheathed, so all of their weapons were brandished.

The warriors had studied him closely in the last half-day of tense travel, but Ryn had also been studying them. He sensed tenseness and agitation, excitement over an oncoming fight, and malicious intentions for him. These reactions, he expected from their aggressive people. But what frustrated him was the inability to decipher their relation to Olympia.

The group walked another full day and into the night. Early in the morning, before the sunrise, the group stopped and slept in the open plains. They had been moving frustratingly slow for Ryn, and he figured that it was meant to test him, to bring out his fight, or to stall long enough to gather reinforcements to Ryn's location for a fight. In either case, Ryn chose not to sleep but meditated through the night under watch. At daybreak, it was clearer and warmer, and the group began moving again.

Around noon they began traveling along the western edge of the high plains where the grass became yellow and then green. Over the side, Ryn saw the land slope down at a sharp angle. It was full of outcrops and other small hills and mountains that merged into the side of the plateau. Ryn saw many cities lining the tributaries that poured down the sides of the mountains.

They traveled along the ridges overlooking the horizon until they came to a large city with shrines, temples, and centers of activity. The shrines and temples were sacred places and not necessarily grand buildings. In that regard, he wondered what was better. To leave the space open, perhaps designated by a ring of rocks, or to build a grand structure laid over with runes. Was one given more to the madness of *Aryfaran* ?

Ryn had once met a man who was mad like that. In his insanity, he used coverings such as leather, rocks, and steel, for armor. His mind somehow associated the privacy of a wall or a tent with protection. Ryn had tried to break his insanity by asking his commander's human companion to crush the wall and expose him. It didn't work, and the man cowered under a piece of wood.

This madness had somehow grown. Some of the sons of man began to live with an illusory sense of security when they were in structures without runes. Ryn knew it was part of the disease, a spiritual disease of putting faith in materials rather than themselves. Buildings only made sense to those who used them as a medium for runes or other techniques that provided actual protection and true privacy. For others, structures paid homage. Yet, for the rest of the world, like the En Ar Mujan, building large structures was pointless. For a people like the En Ar Mujan, structures seemed less useful. They used tents of leather and foliage for their privacy. Perhaps there was hope there. Perhaps the madness was not as prevelant there.

There was, however, one noticeable structure. A square edifice made of large cut rock stood in the middle of the town. It could only be a political office or sanctum. The stones were coated in vines and green plant life. The presence of living things concealed the spiritual nature of what took place inside. Somewhat. It was better than nothing. Such a design's function was exclusively secrecy. This confirmed with him that not even the most skilled of them knew how to use runes. Without them, this was the only way to conceal an aura without advanced levels of windscaping. The stones absorbed it, over time bleeding the aura of what was within. The vines were an attempt to overpower it like a stronger fragrance.

Ryn was led through an archway and into the main hall. A wall of vines hung over the entrance. Ryn pushed through them and stood in the middle of the room to face the platform ahead of him. There were no columns, for the roof was constructed entirely of wild vines over wooden sticks. Spots and speckles of sunlight shone through the green ceiling. The En Ar Mujan made a circle around the outside and gave Ryn about five or six strides of radius between them all. One went back to another room and was gone for some time. Then a vine-covered doorway split open, and the chief walked out.

Only a red bandana around his head set him apart from the rest in appearance. On the bandana was written a word of power in gold. It wasn't just a symbol, such a piece was helpful in blocking out manipulative suggestions and efforts to sway his mind. Perhaps the En Ar Mujan's chief was weak-minded. He might be arrogantly stubborn if this was how he'd prepared for this meeting. It did not bode well.

He walked out to the platform accompanied by two very large warriors and stood looking at Ryn with intent. Ryn did not look up at the king but bowed his head in reverence and kept his gaze low.

It seemed as though the chief had an agenda for

Ryn already. Judging by his demeanor, it wasn't a good one. This was a disaster. In the few moments that he had been exposed to the chief and their place of negotiation, he had become aware that this was ill-fated.

The chief spoke, "You let me know you are Crovan, but you let me know nothing else. I am told that you are an ambassador; I was unaware that Crova had any nation left for which to negotiate."

Ryn diverted to a backup plan he had ready for such an occasion. "I represent a small band of survivors. Your people are good warriors that have been hired hands of Zeus for a long time. Now that the war is over and Zeus has moved on, we seek to know whether you intend to continue hostilities with us. We prefer to trade and benefit one another."

The Nephilim responded immediately, "My dear ambassador, my peoples are servants to Zeus in exchange for wealth and glory, as long as Zeus continues to pay us, we will continue to make war on your peoples. Whether or not you still have a national territory is irrelevant."

And just like that, days of effort had received a conclusion. Very tense, Ryn folded his hands and gripped them so that he could pull off his gloves in a moment.

"Are you still receiving payment from Zeus?"

The chief looked brazenly at Ryn and spoke confidently, "Yes." At that moment, if the En Ar Mujan had weapons that could be sheathed, Ryn would have heard the entire hall unsheathe them. Their spirits moved out in front of them, and they waited to attack him.

The chief spoke once more, "So ends our

negotiation, ambassador."

As soon as his lips ceased pushing out air, Ryn was sprung at by three warriors, one from each surrounding wall, while the others shrunk the circle. Because of their weapon style, the En Ar Mujan did not charge opponents in mass and the others seemed to rank up to decide who was next for a shot at him.

As they came, Ryn performed a move where he thrust air into the ground, and it produced a gale of wind that stuttered the attackers. Then he spun counterclockwise and came around, unloading a spinning back heel at the chief. The move had been seen by his two largest warriors, who stepped up and promptly took the blow for him, flying back into the wall. As Ryn connected, he unloaded fire on them that burned through the shoe on that foot.

This unexpected show of power shocked them for a second. Recovering quickly, the unarmed chief bolted to the back room, and the other warriors covered his escape.

Ryn unsheathed the Arvaita.

They came at him in threes, and they were very skilled. They would challenge him in fast combinations of attacks. Ryn found himself performing some split-second aerial stunts to avoid blows. He also blocked and parried rapidly. The attacks came at him so fast that he had no time to counter. Each warrior had two weapons slicing at him, and Ryn realized that he would not last in the confined structure. Somersaulting underneath a mid-range swing of one's left arm, he burst from the ground to avoid the right, trailing his rolling body. Now moving towards the bare wall behind the platform, Ryn bolted for it, running up its side until he was at the top. Leaping at it, he burst through the roof of vines.

After landing outside, Ryn saw that a few hundred warriors were camped at the entrance. He was obviously the local attraction at the moment.

He bounded over a line of them before they were ready and began north.

The small army gave chase, now joined by their comrades in the palace.

Ryn sprinted at full speed and began covering ground quickly. His first thought was to escape Omaika northward and continue his original route. But Ryn was now pretty sure that this army would follow him for hundreds and hundreds of alans. He would have to lose them at some point.

Ryn continued sprinting down the cliff-side road for alans, hoping that he could thin them out, when he was surprised again to see another army headed down the road towards him. Had they known how strong he was, or was this just the local excitement?

Ryn ran straight at the horde, and he moved quickly, near a felycar's pace. Just as one warrior leapt out in front of the others to strike, Ryn exploded left over the rolling edges of the plateau and soared into the valley. He skidded down the slope until he gained his footing and began the sprint again.

The warriors changed direction and followed suit, flooding down the valley slopes towards the river at the bottom. Ryn came to the river and sprinted through the forests surrounding it. Dashing through trees, he heard the agile and ape-like Nephilim right behind him. There was suddenly a lot of them. Ryn thought perhaps that a good five hundred were pursuing him now.

As they came pouring in from around him, he saw that they were very adept at propelling from tree to tree. From the side, one jettisoned into his path, and he dodged. Soon another, and then another, as they sprung from twenty or thirty strides away at the speed of an arrow, hoping to catch him and tumble him so they could circle him up. His agility, balance, and skill in midair helped him avoid their assaults, but they were increasing in number as more and more permeated the forest around him.

After many more alans of pursuit, Ryn decided that the plains above would serve as a better place to make a stand against this enemy. Executing a series of airscaping maneuvers that stifled the attackers to his right and glided through precise paths between the trees, he moved out of the forest and began leaping up the slope of the valley's eastern wall back up to the plateau.

The alan long ascent put some distance between Ryn and his pursuers, who did not bound from the dirt nearly as well as him. After rising over the top, he saw another group who appeared to be waiting for him. They now closed in around him. Ryn parried off the first attackers and sliced one down the middle. The other continued to unload two-hit combos in rapid succession, and he was joined by two more who came from the circle developing around them against the cliff.

Ryn spun in between two of them, swinging the Arvaita left to right. His blade severed the limb of the far-right warrior. Another quickly replaced him, and Ryn again found himself barely fighting off their combinations. One warrior lunged forward while Ryn parried the four blades of the others in one swing. His right blade lashed out as Ryn turned to smack him with his hilt. The metal cut through his arm, but while the third one was on the ground, having been flung there by the hilt of the Arvaita, Ryn worked the other two back and decapitated one.

Someone from the crowd bolted for Ryn, and it happened that the other two recovered and ran at the Crovan at the same time in the same distance. Ryn quickly ducked their charges and swung the Arvaita about knee level in a circular sweep of the battlefield. With the help of a stretching aura from the blade, it caught six legs, and all three warriors collapsed at once with their feet severed.

This clearing of his opponents gave Ryn the time he needed to get out of there. He bolted at the left side of the circle and planted the Arvaita into a warrior's chest. Then he vaulted from it, flinging his body over the group and northward back on the road again.

In the moments that followed, warriors began pouring over the side of the cliff from below, and the army of around six hundred and fifty continued its pursuit of Ryn northward.

The air started growing colder, and the snow began to pick up again.

Ryn raced alongside the cliff until he saw yet another group of warriors coming at him from the north. This time the cliff had actually become a cliff. Ryn spotted an outcropping of significant area and decided to make his stand there. He bolted for the outcrop, and as he got there, he charged up an intense ball of lightning. Ryn ground to a halt at the ledge and fired the lightning back into the oncoming army. The electricity hit the front line of his pursuers and toasted three of them. Ryn unloaded another ball of lightning that fell two more, and then the warriors came upon him.

The outcrop reduced how many warriors could attack him at once, and generally, it was two. This made killing them much easier and the battle less threatening. Ryn fought off warriors as they came at him, sometimes slicing them and sometimes knocking them over the ledge.

As he fought them off, they got clever, and the ones in the rear pushed forward to knock him off the cliff, using their comrades as body shields. Ryn caught on to their intent before it happened and sprang into action with a highly complex combination of techniques possible for masters of multiple arts alone. Alternating these techniques, he first struck with *aryacynai*. A high-density beam of light slashed out from his blade, slicing through the front line. Then on the immediate back-swing, he cleared the stricken from the rock with a technique called *arajkaf*.

He'd cleared almost two dozen before the warriors at the back realized they were sabotaging the hardness of their comrades' auras by pushing them forward. They effectively made it easier for Ryn to slice through them with his weapon. A commander stopped them and controlled the mob. They backed up, and Ryn was secretly thankful for their intelligence as the masterful use of both high-energy techniques had drained him immensely.

One came at him with his weapons together and swung them in unison. Ryn ducked a horizontal swing and came out roundhouse-kicking the Nephilim off the cliff's left side. Ryn blocked the stabs of another and sent the warrior spinning to the ground with a simple rotation of the shaft of the Arvaita. He buried the blade into the warrior. He blocked another on-comer, spinning fully clockwise, and launching him back with a swing of his weapon.

More came, and Ryn grew tired, expending so much energy defeating excellent warriors. They had caged him with no way out. His rage grew, and he became furious with them: so many creatures trying to kill him for riches, throwing away their lives for riches. It was madness. It was Aryfaran. But unlike the madman he'd encountered, these had the disease deep within their hearts. Was *yfara* that important to them that they would sacrifice their lives for it? Face certain death? End someone's life? Over and over again, as they witnessed their comrades fall like ants, they still flung themselves forward. To go to war and help exterminate an already subdued nation? They did not see that Zeus would enslave them and that despite how vital Ryn was to resisting Zeus, they wanted to kill him. They were destroying their own future. All for the sake of the immediate payoff of something as useless as yfara!

Ryn's anger built up immensely, and although a voice inside him kept pressing him to control his energy, Ryn refused to listen. Eventually, he became reckless and clumsy, collecting a few wounds. Finally, he listened, and the voice inside him spoke assuringly of his victory and his role in defeating Zeus. His anger was not needed to survive. But it was certainly valid in fulfilling the mission and passing judgment.

And that was it. There was a place for his anger, there always was, and he had a lot of it. He channeled it towards the evil and not the persons fighting him. He felt a swell of potential external energy. He came back swinging and moving fiercer than ever, and as they closed on him, Ryn unleashed fire through the Arvaita into an arajkaf, throwing six of them off the cliff.

Ryn spun around and unloaded a set of lightning balls that cleared the outcrop and pushed the crowd back. He stopped and planted his feet; finding it difficult to move. The rage against the evil spirit behind the warriors was overpowering him, screaming to get out. Ryn stood horse-stance and sheathed the Arvaita. His fists out in front of him, Ryn's arms began to collect blue and purple light. Suddenly, wind came up from underneath him, and his eyes also turned blue.

The En Ar Mujan were slightly afraid of this spectacular show of rage and power and began to back off slowly. The light in Ryn's arms continued to grow as he pumped his rage into them. It was becoming cold on the cliff, and snowy mist began to fall, but Ryn was undeterred. Entirely focused, Ryn continued to pump rage into his arms, loading them as though they were cannons. Soon the snow became ice, and the magic of the wizards acting on Ryn was overpowered by the coldness that came from Ryn's aura. The Crovan was soaking up every wave of energy on the outcrop, and the air became freezing to the touch.

One of the generals suddenly realized that an explosion of power was imminent and roused himself to charge Ryn, hoping to knock him off the cliff before he got it off. He had taken two steps when a burst of thunder came out from Ryn. It was followed by flashes of blue and purple that shot out from him like arrows. The energy began in his gut and went through his arms.

Soon a rapid spray of light was coming out of Ryn's hands and cutting down the En Ar Mujan. The light pounded into them and seemed to blast the spirit right out of their bodies. Continuing to glow with blue light, Ryn fired continuously at the crowd as it began to disperse and retreat. He did not stop but poured everything out of him like a pitcher of water. Then after some minutes of flurry, he was empty, sparing perhaps just enough to keep his blood flowing. Ryn's arms and eyes returned to normal, and all the blue energy had left him.

The monk stood there, in a daze, not fully aware of what was happening next, feeling weightless and immobile. He seemed to just exist in that space as though he were a ray of light, weightless, un-influential, and perfectly motionless.

Cognitively, Ryn became aware of figures moving around ahead of him. He had no energy left to fight, and thinking they were warriors come to take advantage of him, he decided to escape the only way he could, whether it meant life or death.

With what he had left, he turned around and leapt off the face of the cliff. He felt so weightless. He figured he would float to the bottom. And in spirit, he did just that. Ryn's body floated smoothly towards the forest floor below him in a supernatural way. As he did, he lost consciousness.

9 MYRAIA

It was dark and cloudy. Gray storm clouds covered the sky, and piercing rain drifted across Ryn's plane of vision. He was running up a mountain along a winding rocky staircase. At the top, a small temple covered the peak. There were no walls but only a roof surrounded by gray columns. As he neared it, he looked down into his left hand and found a short staff with a golden bull atop it, and it had a sharp silver hilt. It was shiny, and on closer inspection, he saw that it was a calf. The stairs raced underneath his feet, barely noticed as he gazed at an inscription bore upon the shaft.

He tried to read it, but the air was dark, and he seemed to be lacking the cognitive ability to decipher the inscription. It was in an ancient script, one taught by the stars when they had fallen. Rarely used, Ryn resorted to his scholarship to read the characters. As he approached the top, he made out some of it, which said,

For Death to reach a key is -----

A --- of golden purity ------- -- is.
Be ------ --- ----- inside a silver template.
When ---- -- ----- --- -- - gatekeeper will ---
----- absence --- doors of death --- -- -------- at last.

He could not translate the rest, and as he tried, he saw himself step into the temple and between two columns. Looking up just in time, he saw a lamb with a single long horn laying on the ground as though it were injured and struggling for breath. The lamb was white, a brilliant white, and as its eyes looked to him, he realized that it was pure, the way he knew he wanted to be. He saw himself walk forward, and not knowing why he reached for his weapon as he approached it.

And then, just as suddenly as this world descended upon him, it floated away, fading out of his vision. Light began to pour into Ryn's eyes as he became aware of his body lying heavy on the forest floor. It felt heavy, like a pile of rocks. He slowly lifted his head and saw that he was surrounded by tall trees, lying in a patch of clovers. He began to wonder how he had survived the fall without being conscious of slowing his momentum. He got his answer shortly thereafter.

To his left, seated upon a fallen tree, was a glorious and beautiful being. She captured his vision, and he could not help but gaze upon her. A beautiful being with snowy skin and a slender sculpted form was looking at him. It was definitely feminine, though Ryn saw right away that it was a star and not sexual in any sense.

She was dressed in brilliant white silk that flowed like a river in the slightest breeze that came through the forest. A single silk gown covered her, and several sashes or belts of bright yellow silk swam in the wind anchored to her figure. Her eyes were deep pools of blue, and they were the brightest and most vivid blue he had ever seen.

In her right hand was a white staff with a crystal planted in striking gold on the top. It was lying over her right leg propped on the ground next to her. Her hair was a splash of colors in varying streaks of blond, brunette, red, black, and auburn.

She smiled at Ryn and spoke in a voice as smooth as the current of a soft stream. "Are you feeling better?"

Ryn had to divert his attention towards self-examination and came back with a grunt after a second or so. "I feel all right, but I feel feeble. It's been a while since I've eaten anything. I probably need to eat something."

She looked over his head and pointed back into the forest, "There are some fruit trees a little way behind you into the forest. You'll find them as you leave here today." She looked back at Ryn, and he sat up to talk to her. She continued, "You gave birth to a new ability back there. I saw the whole thing."

Ryn gazed up with suspicious surprise and grinned, "So you were watching out for me? Did you break my fall?" She smiled back at him caringly and nodded her head.

Ryn looked ahead at the lake and then looked up to see the massive cliff where he had fallen from some two or three alans down to his current location. It must have been some epic battle of the stars way back that had even created such an anomaly.

"What will you call it?" She asked.

"I haven't even thought of a name for the sphere of fire I defeated that dragon with. I don't really know."

She continued to look at him as she spoke, "The fire was full of passion. It was a manifestation of your heart's burning for more than what you experience. Because of the rebellion, you do not experience pleasure, and life, and love the way you know deep down you should. When you thought your wife was gone, your passion for her ignited this deep understanding and fueled the fire."

Ryn thought about this and realized just how important what she said was. "I will call it Passion Fire. For it is the fire straight from my heart."

She smiled and spoke again, "The energy you released up on the cliff was a manifestation of your rage against the rebellion and the awful things it has done. The energy you shot out was essentially controlled coldness. Your spirit desired very strongly to destroy that which is perverse."

Again Ryn thought. This time he chuckled. Her remarks were like waves of wise insight. "I will call it Righteous Fury." She smiled warmly at him, and Ryn appreciated it.

That was good. It described what he felt at that moment. The love of yfara was the reason for so much bloodshed. He couldn't help but think this Star had to look at all of them with disdain for how they treated it, how their eyes were so constantly on it. A being of her beauty seemed to be wasted on a place such as this.

The image of her beauty was too much. He began to feel like his very thoughts of her corrupted her. He redirected his thoughts to Juya. That was his beauty.

That was an inspiration meant for him.

He became ill. His anxious worry for her turned to wonder as he saw the Star standing in front of him. But before he could even ask her, she answered.

"It is admirable and strong of you to keep your love for your wife, even in the face of uncertainty. She loves you very much, and I place peace on both of you. I came here to see that you were nurtured back to health and send you in the appropriate direction."

Ryn looked at her for a few moments, gathering what she said, then got to his feet. As he did, she rose as well.

Reaching around, Ryn felt where the Arvaita should be. She pointed to the ground behind him. He saw it, picked it up, and sheathed it. As he touched it, it felt lighter, purer, and more fluid than he had remembered. She was quick to explain this.

"Being in this world and being used by fallen creatures diminishes the light of the Arvaita. I cleaned it for you by burning the decay from it."

He nodded and took no offense. He saw it. Surely, over time the Arvaita had indeed become heavier and less vibrant. He simply had not noticed it until it had been cleaned.

She looked back over Ryn's right shoulder and began to talk, "Alvyn is not even a hundred alans from where you stand. But you must ascend the mountains west of here in order to get there. Do not follow the river valley, for there are many willing to fight you. Do not go anywhere else but straight to Alvyn. Then proceed high into the mountains of Ystrafe. There you will find friends."

Ryn looked at her and thanked her. He almost didn't do it, but he had to. It was right to, he believed.

"Can you tell me anything about the fate of my wife?"

To this, she seemed to be happy and smiling back, said, "I only know that she loves you, and whatever happens, remember that."

Ryn lowered his head a bit in disappointment but did not take her words for granted. He asked her the next thing on his mind, "What of my vision, my dream I had, does it bear any significance?"

To this, she seemed thoughtful but responded, "The dream is significant, but I have no knowledge to give you as to its precise purpose or meaning. Perhaps it is not time, or perhaps it is a question you must answer yourself."

He pondered a moment, then straightened up and started to go. As he did, he moved to thank her one more time, but this time he wanted a name, so before he spoke, she gave it to him.

"My name, to your people, is Taliana, and whenever you need refreshing, I will be around to watch out for you."

"I am humbled," He said. "Thank you for your service Taliana. I thank Teoti for sending you to watch over me." With that, she gave him a slight grin, and in an instant, Ryn could no longer sense her presence.

As he thought briefly, he was tempted to sit down in bewilderment. Only his mission kept him on his feet. The opportunity to meet Taliana was far rarer than meeting Amaras. Taliana had been witnessed by only three Crovans in all its history. Once by Traijyn, when Taliana and Amaras appeared to him together, and once to Crova and Nova as the two women were grieving over the loss of their husband. On a third occasion, it is said that she gave king Alvyn a drink of water while he was alone in the Najyn Desert. According to the tale, she imparted a pearl of incredible wisdom that he held close to him. This was in a time before Ryn was known.

Her visiting and serving him was an occurrence of mythological proportions. He felt it an essential response to pray and meditate. What did it mean that Teoti had them coming to him now? Perhaps it was important to Teoti that Ryn get just that much more affirmation considering the dire state of his people.

After consuming some pear-like fruit from the trees, Ryn climbed up the western mountain range and followed its ridge through the north side of The Rugged Place until the mountains encircle a vivid blue lake. The lake was surrounded by thick evergreen forests that reached up the sides of the mountain range. The lake was called Shasaji Yata, Jasmine Lake, and its northern shores were considered part of the Crovan Empire. So Ryn circled the lake in the mountains, and when he had passed into his home country, he descended into the thick forests. As he did, he felt the land rejoice in him, as though he were its long-absent steward. In those moments, he silenced his thoughts and felt the words of the forest and the earth.

He took a break to sit down on a rock covered by the forest and watched the refreshing body of water through the thicket. A destroyed Crovan fishing town was on the shore. Though it was completely leveled and an unfortunate site, it was a good place for him to s and consider his dream. There was not a soul around.

"For Death to reach a key is... the key is to Death. The Doors of Death...the staff looked like it could be a key..." Ryn thought about the word ioy, which lay in the sentence, "An ioy of golden purity..."

This word may well signify the calf on top of the staff, made of gold. Ryn would have to find out what it meant. But the vision seemed to be a guide, a way for him to enter Hades. If this were so, then Ryn might be given the opportunity to save Juya.

This made his heart jump. "Teoti, thank you for this vision. I only hope it means what I think it does. Of course, direct me differently if it does not." Ryn focused on the imagery of the temple and the key. The temple was easy. If the vision was what he thought it was, then the temple was that of Aides on a mountaintop not far from Mount Olympus. There the gates of Hades resided, and sacrifices were made there as well. The key was unfamiliar to him. He would have to keep his eyes and ears open for any indication as to an opportunity to acquire it.

Ryn stood up from his rock and gazed at the lake one last time. Then he walked on through the woods, only stopping to drink from a brook.

The forest continued into shallow hills clothed in deciduous and evergreen trees. The hills led him deeper into Crova towards the coast of the Dark Sea. Traveling northward, he moved through the tall forests until he came to the final hill atop which he could view the city of Alvyn.

When he looked at it, though, he saw that it was a conglomeration of rubble and half standing buildings. The temple, on the north hill in town, was damaged but structurally still stood. It was the most preserved building in the city. The temple had four stone walls surrounding it, but an elevated wooden ceiling made of logs coved the top. The logs were elevated by columns outside, four to five cubits above the rock wall to allow open-air circulation. They rose over the hall at a thirty-five-degree angle until they met the logs on the other side. The structure was around twenty-five strides wide and forty deep. It faced the east, and when the sun came up, it blasted through carvings in the door that made a silhouette on the ground for the character "Patience."

Ryn looked over the city and saw movement. To the east, a colonnade of trees extended from the city over the road from that direction. Out of it came a large battalion of humans. He also saw that occasional human soldiers were scouting out the rest of the city and that some activity seemed to be going on inside the temple.

Ryn perched and watched eagerly to see what they were doing. The battalion moved past the temple and into the city. They were regimented for a few seconds in the town center, then dispersed chaotically in every direction. After watching them for some time, Ryn concluded that they were plundering the city's ruins.

What interested Ryn more was the activity going on around the temple. Ryn saw a group of soldiers that had followed the battalion carrying a cut-down tree. They moved it into the temple, and Ryn had a distinct thought that they were trying to break down some doors. If a door was barricaded in the temple, it could only mean that someone was inside, for there is no way to get into a temple room and exit another way. The person responsible for the barricade was still inside the room.

Ryn moved like a shadow down the hill and into the city. Dodging behind ruined houses to keep from being seen, he caught sight of the troops in the town. They were Arovynians, soldiers of the mostly human nation to Crova's southwest whose border upon which Ryn had been imprisoned. It was their alliance with Zeus that sprung the doors open for an invasion of the southern half of the country. Ryn concluded that he very well might be able to defeat the entire battalion, some two or three hundred, but he was still bent on minimizing his activities. From the En Ar Mujan, Zeus would already know that a renegade Crovan was plowing through the mountains. More reports would mean he could be followed.

Ryn traveled along the edge of town until he reached the temple. Seeing that all of the action was inside, he figured he could slip into the building without being seen from the front. Once inside, he would dispatch of whoever was in there. Stealthily he slipped behind the building to the north wall and came around from the back. He stopped to peer around the corner to see if anyone was in the front, and, the way being clear, he made his move.

The Arovynian troops were inside. There were a dozen trying to open a wooden door on the temple's south side, to Ryn's left as he came in. Judging by their intent, they figured a native was inside. There was another dozen watching and at least a dozen more searching rooms everywhere else. There were four columns on each side of the center hall, and there were four rooms, two on each wall. The red carpet leading up the short stairs in the back was gone, and the lampstands, which accompanied it to each side, were missing as well. The curtain that isolated the offering chamber in the back from the rest of the hall had been torn down and the altar exposed. Ornaments and weapons that he had seen hung on the wall the last time he was here were all gone.

The sight of it offended him greatly, despite the fact that he'd seen a temple plundered plenty of times in the past. Looking around, he saw that all of the troops were preoccupied, and it was not hard for Ryn to walk in unnoticed. At least just long enough so he could close the doors.

From the entrance suddenly came a slam, and the Arovynians turned to see Ryn standing in front of it with the massive wood closed behind him. There was a moment of silence and awkwardness; the troops did not know what to do, so they stared at Ryn. They were not quite sure who or what he was. The covering he wore was beyond the concealment he needed around humans. The mymtai was more than enough.

The commander of the troops turned and called out to him in a husky voice, "You! Who are you? What do you want?"

They could see his strength, and fear was beginning to strike them.

As they gazed at him cautiously, Ryn stretched out his left hand, and a flame came out of his palm. This made the men fidget. By this time, all forty to fifty men were in the center hall looking at Ryn. The leaders, whom all had some Nephilian blood, were not frightened; however and Ryn saw that they were gathering confidence in their superior numbers.

Ryn gazed at the flame for a few seconds and then opened his hand more, and it became a ball of fire about hand's breadth across. He hurled it up towards the roof, and it struck a long metal trough suspended from the ceiling. The thing lit up like a single long lantern that ran from the front of the hall to the rear.

The commander turned to his men, "Don't be scared by his tricks; we are immune to them."

Some looked at him leary of trusting those words.

Again, he addressed Ryn, "Look stranger, we are not appreciative of your presence. Unless you have something important to tell me from my commanders, you have no business here."

Ryn reached back and unsheathed the Arvaita. At this, the tree was dropped, and every sword in the hall was brandished. The Arovynians had short swords; each was empowered by a single rune. Their armor was also short and light but also carried runic protection. Ryn did not want to think that the Arvaita gave him the power to penetrate their armor, but it probably did.

He moved forward, and a wave of men ran at him.

Ryn short sliced the first attacker, and he promptly spun to the ground. The next two, he took out in a single spin with the Arvaita about chest high, underneath their outstretched swords. He transferred the Arvaita to his left hand behind his back and brought it upwards in a hitch motion that launched another off the ground. Having to block the next one's sword, he parried it to his left and countered by quickly severing his head. Then quickly, he caught the next troop charging his left with the hilt and sent him flying backward. Finally, he dropped the last three chargers twirling the weapon forward like a baton, catching each one in a downward slice as he approached, not even getting warm from the little exertion he'd done.

But in the midst of the fighting, to his utter shock,

the final troop had thrown his sword at Ryn upon approach. After Ryn had cut him, it came through the swing of the Arvaita and caught the left side of his hood while he dodged it. This was enough to knock the hood off, which revealed the Crovan features. Not only this, the surprise of being caught by such a feeble attempt foiled Ryn's presence of mind, and for a brief moment, his mymtai fell.

Ryn stood the Arvaita on its hilt as he held it and looked back at the astonished troops. They were frightened now. They all saw that Ryn was a powerful Crovan, and judging by his reaction, the leader may have recognized his royal spirit. They knew he was someone important to Zeus. Despite their fear, given the nature of whom they faced, they did not stand down.

Before they were determined to slay whoever was behind that door, or worse, and now were determined to subdue him at all cost. That could not be allowed. His will collided with theirs. Now at an impasse, a fully lethal confrontation was inevitable. The doors were locked, but all of this battling would soon attract the attention of the others outside. This had to be done quickly.

Spinning the Arvaita in his hand, Ryn closed his eyes. The troops encroached upon him very slowly as he seemed in thought. But no sooner had they begun did Ryn's eyes open, and he immediately sprung to the right and began slicing at troops along the right wall. He was like a ghost.

He would land in one spot, dispatch several opponents, and then flash into another. His movements were so smooth and uninterrupted that his attacks seemed like one long combination of techniques oblivious to the splash of metal swinging at him. In eight to ten seconds, Ryn had dispatched at least a quarter of them and moved his way across the hall towards the commander and the barricaded door.

The troops scrambled and ran in different directions. Many tried for the entrance but were cut down by the spinning and somersaulting ghost who disposed of them smoothly and moved on to the next one. Some troops tried to climb the walls, but they were as smooth as glass, covered in a substance not known to any of them.

The commander raced into the southeast corner and tried to propel himself up the wall by hopping between surfaces. The wall seemed to be about ten men high, and he could get up just over halfway but could not make the extra distance he needed to grab the top.

Ryn had worked his way through most of them and had come up against some more worthy opponents when engaging the officers. With few left, he'd finally turned his attention to those on the south wall.

A very agile officer came at Ryn from the barricaded door and seemed to be one of only a couple left. With two swords armed, he front-flipped and landed in a tornado swing Ryn had to block. He proceeded to block Ryn's short swing to his right ear and began unloading a long series of thrusts and swings with both swords in quick combination.

Ryn backed while defending, awaiting the right moment. The man took time to prepare his right arm with more power and Ryn sliced inside the swing catching his right bicep.

Undeterred, the man thrust with the left and

brought the right inside to block the chest. Ryn quickly parried the left sword down and brought the Arvaita back up to catch the left forearm. Right as this happened, the man moved in with his right to catch Ryn's now close and thrusting head, but Ryn instantly ducked it as he made the cut on the forearm. Then spinning around clockwise, he unloaded a spinning backswing that flung the warrior back with a spark of lightning. So powerful was it that he flew across the room and glanced off a pillar. That was the last real test in that temple.

The commander fell down from his last attempt, which was closer than any of the others, and felt a warm metallic blade in his belly. Facing the corner, he looked down and saw the crystal clear point of the Arvaita protruding out the front of his abdomen.

Ryn came up behind him and held him up in order to speak to him. "For the sake of all of your troop's commander... I am truly sorry." Ryn spoke right into the man's ear as he shook with fear. "Perhaps one day, the law, do not kill, and the spirit of life will be never cross. But it is not now. Be at peace now, son of men."

The words he spoke shocked the commander beyond the pain of his encroaching demise. In his last moments, he spoke to the Nephilim behind him. "You are Ryn, are you not?"

The Crovan said nothing.

"You kill, yet you have compassion... how?"

As the man's life began to wane, Ryn spoke back with a reluctant voice, "It is what must be done, to secure what is better. I am sorry."

Ryn ripped the Arvaita from his back, and the man fell to the ground with blood pouring out of his belly.

He was jolted. Compassionate? He had to admit that he'd not thought twice about killing them all. He'd been offended, had his pride threatened, and then he'd been encouraged to treat them mercilessly even more by a sense of urgency. What was so startling now was not that he'd been called compassionate when he'd been merciless, but rather, that he expected compassion from himself, and how was it that just because he was in a state of war, he could not show it here also?

He suddenly became overwhelmed with regret and sorrow. The commander's complement of him with his dying breath had stunned him. Looking around, he saw the bodies of slain men with families, wives, and children. Little boys and girls loved them and trusted them. So ignorant these men of families were, yet manipulated by more responsible powers. Was it because they were sons of men? He had not felt this way when slaying Nephilim. He assumed a higher level of accountability with them. But with mankind, he felt differently. He kept seeing images of them, people from Molnak in particular. How could anyone destroy something so wonderful?

It wasn't about this one man, no. It was about all humanity and the savage rule of the "gods." What would come of the sons and daughters of man in a world ruled by Nephilim? It was an intense revelation that became very heavy. His spirit began to ache because of the shedding of innocent blood. It was almost unbearable.

The blood: that was the only way to explain why he'd never seen this before. Until now, he'd had a nation. He'd had a people. He'd had spilt blood to avenge, a bloodlust to entertain, and a bloodline to protect. Somehow, over this time of loss, that had left his mind. He would expect to have lost something valuable, but here and now was a place in his mind for new wisdom.

Standing in that temple, or at least what used to be one, he was reminded to be a good monk. His mind sought to begin reconciliation while he attempted to address what was ahead of him. Taking a deep breath, he shut his eyes and began to focus. He needed to find out who was inside that room and had to get that person out of there before a larger confrontation erupted. A larger confrontation at this juncture only meant slaying more humans, and he did not wish to do that, at least not in light of this surpassing revelation.

Gathering his spirit, he walked across the room and over the bodies to the wooden door. Not wanting to spook anyone, he needed to know that a live person was in their first. Walking up to the door, he began to speak softly.

"Hello," He said in Crovan. "Are you all right?" Some rustling came from inside the room, and Ryn heard someone moving around. There was a long pause as he waited for a response.

After minutes it became deafly silent, and he spoke again. "Are you injured?"

There was no response, and Ryn picked up on the soldiers outside with his acute hearing. They were beginning to congregate at the temple. The awkward noise from the building was being investigated.

The entity was now right behind the door, and Ryn could tell that they were afraid to open it. These doors were made to stifle the flow of ryaj. The person could not tell him from Zeus right now. Ryn thought to slowly rip the door off, just enough to remove it but softly so as not to spook them. But a seal was on the door, which meant that if he wanted to get in, he would have to blast it. And that was not an option.

"It is all right...by the grace of Teoti...I have destroyed this battalion. It is all right for you to come out."

The entity still did not embody trust in Ryn, and he wondered what he could do to convince them this was no deception.

Ryn put his hand on the door and began to reach out with his spirit. Through the door, he pushed something through and touched the air inside. This person was a monk. They were also very young. Ryn could not sense much more because the entity was concealing itself, and the seal befuddled his efforts significantly.

Ryn spoke caringly through the door, "Listen, young monk, I know that you are afraid, but please know that I am your friend. I destroyed this entire group, and an army divided against itself will not stand. I hope you can trust that I am not in league with your enemy." Some silence past, "I know you can sense the bloodshed out here. You are trained to do so."

Ryn stopped for a second, trying to plan how to convince them, and quickly. They were coming. They would soon run out of time. "Surely, you know that this blood is more innocent than our greatest enemies. Perhaps you realize that this should not be. And if you can feel that, then you can trust me."

The tragedy struck him even deeper all of a sudden as the Wind seemed to whisper it into his inner being. A solid tear broke over his cheek. The remorse was overwhelming him like an over boiling pot. At first, it was frustrating, but his mind began to see that it was the very power of this ryaj that could breach the seal of the door. Perhaps there was a reason the wind was pressing this within him.

Pressing on the wood, he shared that powerful ryaj through the door, so whoever was on the other side might feel it also. Who could not trust such pure and convicted ryaj?

On the other side of the door, a figure sat still, waiting out the visitor. It was taking too long to secure an escape this time. This was not what she wanted, cornered like this again. She'd resourcefully escaped before, but ironically, the room that secured her was also a prison. She hadn't wanted it to end here. What did she want now? She wanted whoever was speaking in Crovan, the one they had brought to lure her out, to leave. They could just come for her properly. The games they would play with the heart and mind were offensive.

"That's what they did in Myomybyrn to those twelve daughters of Vajyn." She spoke to herself. They were often cunning in fooling those in hiding into coming out because they would never find them or access them otherwise. But not her. She was a monkess. She was trained; she knew better.

What he said was striking, though. Had he really killed everyone in the hall? He was wrong about her being able to sense it. There was no way anyone could sense that through these doors. They blocked any and all ryaj. Not even blood was smelt through these walls and doors. It was a sanction room, a room for inner quiet. That's why she chose it. Still, the words were very convincing, alluring even. Almost as if they had reached into her inner heart and pulled out an image of someone she desired greatly but never felt really existed. She shook it off. She only had to wait it out.

Then she actually began to feel something. Shocked, she slowly eyed the door and then stood up. She slid over and pressed against it. She did not know who this person was on the other side, but their ryaj somehow was bleeding through the seal.

She felt all of it. It was glorious. She'd never felt that type of purity in someone. It was captivating, like the time from her adolescence when she'd heard all her life about the wonder of the capital city of Traijyn, only to finally lay eyes on it in all of its splendor. She actually began to cry.

While resting his weight on it, his arm gave way, and the door was open. He looked up and, at first, saw a brilliant whiteness like that of a garment of incredible purity with a single point of light toward the top. He didn't know what to make of it, and something resisted seeing it further, so his eyes soon adjusted and what he actually saw was more normal.

He was a bit astonished to see a young Crovan monkess. She had a happily shocked look on her face, as though she'd found a friend she once thought dead. To his surprise, she jumped at him and embraced him with warm fervor.

He didn't stop her. He just listened to her spirit talk. She breathed heavily and held on to him for a couple of minutes. Ryn formulated her story. She'd served at this temple before the war. She was not even a hundred years old, yet a student of stature and had traveled a long way under pursuit to come here. She was accomplished and respected in her order. She was skilled and resourceful. She'd already formulated an escape and was prepared to die fighting before being captured.

What she felt slowly began to bewilder her. Reverence, authority, power, boundless wisdom, a leader of leaders...surely not. A general, no, it had to be him. Here? She saw herself as a little girl again, standing in the presence of an icon, a man of wonder. The hardened soldier seemed to leave her, and she became overcome with a sense of being covered and comforted by greatness.

She clung to him, and he felt an amazing level of awe and trust coming from her. He wondered if she'd ever let go. But she was working through it. In the meantime, he noted her appearance. The woman had light brunette hair in two long braids, and her skin was a fairer yellow than most. She wore a leather breastplate that did not cover her belly or her collarbone. A Brown and light leather jacket that looked more like a cape and acted like a shawl was thrown over her shoulders and was lined with white fur. Her skirt also was brown leather lined with white fur. And her boots were the same. Only the scarlet sash of a monkess around her waist stood out from the color pattern. Sheathed on her left hip was a medium length double-edged sword.

"Monkess," he began. "Do you know who I am?"

She opened her eyes and looked up with a factual and more reserved face. She backed up and wiped a tear away, though, giving away the emotions she'd just felt. "You are Ryn. You are the king. You are the greatest of our order."

Ryn nodded. "Though I'd hardly call myself the

greatest."

She smiled, underneath clearly believing that to be senseless self-depreciation. She'd never felt a greater person in her life.

He returned the smile and read what her eyes told him. Despite her sudden rush to embrace him, this was a reserved woman, an independent woman, living in an unusual solitude. She'd formulated the life of a soldier quickly. It seemed to somehow suit her without spoiling her wind any. That was curious. He'd hardly known any maidens like that, save for one, of course. Her spirit was evident, and seeing it all together, he grasped her name, "Myraia."

She nodded with a smile, confirming his perception was correct.

"I am glad that you are unharmed." He said, turning toward the door. "There is much to talk about, but right now, our enemies are approaching outside, and we must hurry out of this town."

The monkess nodded her head and went quickly back into the room as though commanded by a general. Grabbing a round metal shield and a leather supply bag, she came out and walked towards the exit.

Ryn followed her and came to the massive wooden doors just as she did. Pulling up his cloak, he concealed himself with the mymtai. She reached into her bag and pulled out a parka, following suit, so as to keep her knowledge of his identity a secret.

The voices were all around the temple now, and they were surrounded in every direction. The conflict was now unavoidable. Ryn hoped that he could get on the road and sprint out of town with little trouble and the shedding of very little blood. Myraia looked up at Ryn and saw the remorse on his face for all the blood spilt that day. His love for life overcame everything, even war. His heart was unique. She had never seen anything like it. She remembered it. It was seared on her heart now, like the image of the sun on one's eye. It was on her very soul. She'd never forget it.

Ryn turned and smiled at her, "It is good not to be alone anymore."

She returned the smile.

Then Ryn turned forward and pushed open the massive doors.

10 AN UNLIKELY BARGAIN

Along the road in front of them were some two or three hundred soldiers, standing in unformatted groups. Ryn moved out to the edge of the platform and looked out on them from the top of the temple steps. Myraia stood just behind him to his right with her shield equipped but with her sword sheathed. Ryn turned to her, "My goal is to blast through the crowd of them while killing as few as possible. Stay right behind me and follow me out."

She nodded her head, and Ryn looked back at the crowd of onlookers. The leader of the battalion approached the stairs and tried to look Ryn in the eyes if he could see them under the shade of the hood.

He turned back to his troops and told them to regiment into lines. This commander was wise enough to know that freelance charging against Crovans was a mistake. Being inferior soldiers, they would need to charge in regiments to be effective. Ryn was not willing to wait for them to organize; neither was he willing to kill many more men. Ryn bolted north toward the town fork in the road.

Myraia saw him break and followed. The king kept his weapon sheathed, but she felt she could not follow his example and drew her sword. She saw the sun sparkling through his blade that was pure like water. She felt a serene purity come through its material, unlike anything she'd seen. What weapon was he wielding?

Ryn ducked the first swing at him and punched the man in the ribs sending him off the ground and in reverse. He caught the next charger and threw him over his hip, grabbing the sword hand. Once the man hit the ground, he intercepted another attacker with his left foot, smashing the man in the chest to send him into a crowd. He was much faster than they were and a step ahead.

As he caught the blade hand of a man to his left, Myraia approached and swung forcefully at a wave of on-comers, parrying their blades to her left with strength they did not expect. Then bringing her blade back upwards, she knocked a couple in the center off balance and then spun clockwise, slashing two, thrusting them back.

This display of skill impressed Ryn. For a young monkess, she showed good swordplay. He glanced only for a second before his attention was demanded. He caught a soldier's swing and shoulder-blocked him hard to the ground before turning in time to evade a thrusting weapon. Taking hold of the sword arm, he slung the man off his shoulder in spin and sent him into the crowd, leveling half a dozen others. His efforts were strong, but he aimed to be less than lethal.

The crowd separated them, and Myraia fenced a few off before being lunged at aggressively. She countered with equally aggressive force and jammed him with her shield. Charging her shoulder into it, she powered through the man's blade and sent him flying, forcing the soldiers ahead of her into hesitation. With amazing grace, she suddenly reversed and slipped between two blades from behind. Springing into a tornado spin, she swung into their backs, launching them into her already reluctant opponents. She smirked, a little impressed with herself as well. But her celebration was interrupted.

A rather large man with a strong presence approached her from the circle with a longsword and heavy shield. He had a very narrow face with oddly pale yet rough skin. Myraia sensed Nephilian blood in him, perhaps Sensebone or Ad Dan Skinesh.

Ryn continued to down attackers, swiftly moving from group to group, not allowing them to congregate or close the gap on him. Taking on a crowd this size without resorting to large displays of power meant getting ahead of their organization and keeping their ranks broken.

Dashing under an attack and behind a man, he launched him away with a swift elbow. Fluidly Ryn brought his body low and came up with a skyscraper sidekick that lifted another man ten cubits off the ground. This stalled a portion of the crowd, but as he turned, a left-handed attacker to his left-back swung and appeared to catch Ryn where he could not dodge it. But to the man's astonishment, Ryn arose swiftly and bafflingly caught the blade in between the two palms of his hands. Ryn's move was followed by a powerful sidekick that threw the man back into the crowd.

The sudden catching of the blade stunned the

crowd as they hesitated with caution.

The larger man had been creating problems for Myraia; he was quick enough and had enough support on his flanks to cause her to back into a house wall. Tension began to build up in her as she was forced back, and her spirit became irritated. When she felt the energy in her body crest, she made her move and burst out with confidence.

Swinging high, she deflected several attacks then leapt shortly into the air. She leapt just enough to amass a ferocious amount of power and a burst of wind behind her sword. She came down with it vertically, and with hurricane force, blasted the man back through the crowd. The wind knocked over a score of them, clearing the flanks and creating a path. It led straight as an arrow back toward Ryn, and she promptly sprinted through it.

Ryn noticed Myraia's special attack and the opportunity it left behind. He intercepted another attacker with a left roundhouse kick. Quickly unsheathing the Arvaita, he performed a single long-reaching hurricane swing endowed with water. Like a powerful wave, it threw a ring of them back. This cleared a circle around him about twenty strides in diameter.

"Come," he shouted to Myraia.

She parried one more strike and countered with a slash to his face on her way to Ryn and his clearing.

She looked up as the groups closed in around her and suddenly saw Ryn leap at her. Ryn launched his body over the crowd like a spinning arrow. She was caught under the placket-trim at the bottom of her breastplate and lifted. Soaring through the air, he landed just beyond the mass of soldiers as they condensed. With grace, he threw Myraia ahead of him and came down, immediately bolting northward along the road. She gained her footing in stride and followed.

They quickly raced into the hills and reached the top of the tall one overlooking the town. Disappearing over the peak, Ryn grabbed Myraia while they were running and jerked into a direction change. They veered right and entered into a small depression that ran jagged between the hills.

When the first soldier reached the top of the hill and looked out over the waves of earth in front of him, he did not see them. The commander pushed his men over the rise, but none of them saw any activity. The commander was not satisfied and ordered a spread of the hills. He also sent men down into the gorge.

After a few minutes, the men on the hilltops reported seeing nothing. Only a dozen men remained running down the depressions of the landscape. Following the gorge, for some time, they eventually dispersed into the maze of hills and valleys, quickly becoming spread out. Calling them all back, the commander returned with them to the town.

As he got back to the temple, his men reluctantly showed him the grizzly scene within.

"Who were they? Crovans are strong, but he took out 50 men on his own." His captain said, stunned.

Seeing that carnage, he was fearful yet relieved. Those two could have wiped them out had they wanted to. He was lucky to be alive.

"Call off the pursuit," he said. "And send two men back west. Bring them here so I can tell them what to say."

Two scouts were sent along the road west to Coston. There a messenger would carry the events back to Olympus. Looking back over the hills, the commander of the Arovynians reflected on the battle. "He should have killed us. Now, there will be a search. A Crovan this powerful cannot be allowed to wander around."

Ryn and Myraia swam between hills for the rest of the day and eventually got to the point where Ryn felt they were not in any danger. They stuck to the high country, not saying much until they came to a sparsely wooded mountain country inland from the coast. They had been traveling east for some time. Myraia presumed they had done this to avoid the coast. She did not know at this time that Ryn had planned this course before coming under pursuit. Eventually, she caught on to this because of the way his spirit traveled, with purpose. All this time, they had said nothing to one another. Myraia was observing his spirit to try and catch on to the plan in action. He was going somewhere; he had something to do.

Where are you going, my lord? She wondered. She asked herself if it mattered and responded with a strong no. It took some time, but they finally relaxed. They stopped to rest at a high wooded mountain brook, and here they finally began to exchange words.

There was a fallen log and some soft grass. "We can rest here," he said.

She complied and sat down, briefly catching her breath. She saw him look around, observantly. He appeared to have a good idea where they were and was satisfied that they were in the clear.

As he came over, he saw her reach down and feel

under her plate where he'd grabbed her. She stared in a daze ahead as she breathed.

"Sorry," he said to her. "I didn't have your hand available."

She shook herself from her distant thoughts and removed the hand. "It is fine. I am unharmed."

Ryn thought to himself that harm was not his concern but decided to leave it at that. He sat down on the grass next to the brook and began to talk. "So tell me…how did you get to Alvyn and where from?"

She was a little amazed that he'd recovered so quickly. He seemed no more out of breath than if they'd been sitting all day. Their pace had been strong too. Lowering her head, she smiled and nearly thought to draw informal attention to her own curiosities, but naturally deferred to the king and answered his question. "The battle at Rystai was my last engagement."

"What happened at Rystai?"

"About three-and-a-half-thousand of us came out of the mountains to meet a large army attempting to advance up the roads at Rystai. Sergeant Jytsai of Mynomybyrn led the counter. He thought it would be disastrous for the resistance if the enemy gained access to these roads."

"Sergeant Jytsai did the right thing," Ryn added.

"They tried to attack from the air first. We had just enough monks and those competent in windscaping to fight them off. They made charges up the mountainside four times, and each time we beat them back. With the high ground. We had them outmatched. Even though there must have been around twenty to thirty thousand."

She paused a moment and observed that he sat

still and thoughtful as though he were being briefed by a minister or general. It was an honor to be doing this, but she was nervous. She had to forgive herself. It was the king, a myth as well as a hero, a dream, and an icon. Not only that, she had already felt his very pure and compassionate spirit; it was unmatched by anyone she'd met in her life. The sure measure of greatness she felt was distracting and intimidating at the same time. She focused.

"After the fifth assault, they deduced how to consolidate their attack to break our pattern of defense. They began to push on us, and we lost ground, having to fall back toward the road. Jytsai organized a brave counter to push them back down the slope, but they were readier for the counter than we anticipated."

He moaned with the anticipated disappointment that was coming. His eyes still locked on her image, reading her delivery as though he were watching the account through her first hand.

She felt remorseful that all she had was bad news. Still, he was not phased at all, and his spirit was confident as well as resolute. At least he wasn't angry, far from it. He had reserve and character, that was for sure.

Reconciling her concentration, she continued. "The counter seemed to be working when a massive being was dropped onto the mountain by a high flyer. We knew that it was a god, but there was great fear when it was clear who it was. It was Ares."

Ryn quiered, "in carnal form?"

"Yes," She replid. "He was not the only one, swift Hermes came up the mountain as well, and Artemis was there too, firing arrows from a distant mountain."

Ryn was shocked, "Hermes, Artemis, and Ares all at the same battle?"

Myraia nodded her head, "Apparently, Zeus is determined to destroy the resistance. Seeing as how strong it is." She said this with a smile but did not take time to really acknowledge it as humorous.

"There were one eyed men there. I had not seen them before. I thought they were legends of the past by now."

Ryn looked out over the brook, "No, they're still around. We fought some of them at Raijyn."

She was curious, "What happened at Raijyn?"

He motioned for her to continue with her account first. "Go on, please," he said.

"Ares swung a huge ax back and forth over the battlefield and made it difficult to fight off the next wave of attack. No one could strike Hermes. He was too fast. He didn't seem to do much but make light of us. Sporadically he would strike someone with a stone or something else…for fun, I think. Artemis, we had no idea where she was. Her arrows would just fall out of the sky and strike someone. She was on the mountain west of our position for sure, but that was more than ten alans from us. We could not spot her."

Ryn looked down at the trickling water. Up that point, the regular gods that campaigned with the army were Ares, Athena, and Helios. Artemis was new to this picture. And he had never heard of Hermes engaging in a campaign. He was well known for his dirty work assassinating rangers or picking off survivors. Zeus had held back a great deal of the pantheon for some time. This was possibly another escalation. But at the point of victory? After 50 years?

Myraia continued, as he seemed in thought. "The

army charged again, and we could not hold our ground, though now that I look back, I think we did considerable damage to their force. Before the gods stepped in, we had destroyed well over two-thirds of their numbers. When our position was compromised, the rebels scattered in all directions. I fled west and did not stop running until I came to the west coast. It was there that I was spotted by a century of Gullukans. I ran from them, knowing I was faster, but they sent a message ahead of me by some quick means. When I got to Alvyn, that battalion of Arovynians was waiting in ambush. So I ran into the temple and sealed myself in. I could not defeat them all. I guess the idea was to preoccupy them with the door while I burrowed out and escaped." She looked up with a short smile, "I made considerable progress. I had removed the stone foundation by the time you arrived."

Ryn glanced at her curiously. "When did you arrive at the temple, and how long were they trying to break the door?"

She looked up at his eyes but quickly diverted her attention to her feet again, which began to fidget. "The same day you came, only hours before."

Ryn leaned back and thought. Had he not been instructed to go west into Arvadia, he would have likely arrived around the time of the battle, or even sooner. Why then, would he be sent west fruitlessly, unless it was to ensure he came by this encounter while missing the battle? Yet, had he been at the battle, he would have been discovered alive by the Olympians. He had arrived at the exact time needed to miss that battle and save this monkess. He smirked.

"What is it?" She asked.

Ryn looked back at the brook, "Nothing, just that I see how our meeting each other was not a mistake."

She looked into his face and could not help but ask him questions, "Where have you been, Kyfka?"

Ryn watched the water trickle over rocks peacefully in the brook, "You do not have to call me Kyfka," he said. "Just call me, Ryn."

A broad grin broke her face, and flattered that he would let her call him by his name, she humbly looked down at her feet. "It will be done, Ryn."

Ryn spoke as he watched the brook, "The southern resistance became bottled up in Aryn. Zeus brought his army up the river valley and was coming onto the plains at Raijyn. That's where our remaining numbers met him. We would have had more, but we lost considerable forces in the valley. A great number." He said with regret.

Ryn then paused. A look of deep remorse and frustration was on his face. She watched him, wondering and feeling. His exterior wasn't so cold after all. It affected him.

"So we lost," she said, trying to move the conversation past the details.

Ryn continued his stare out over the brook. "We were overpowered by their numbers. I tried to attack Zeus himself, but I had abandoned my army. I came back to them, but they had been overpowered. I fought on. I killed countless others until I was finally subdued. By Herakles, at that."

He paused, and his eyes began to moisten. "That is a fight I look forward to repeating." He looked her in the eye and what he spoke was too much for her to take in. "The sheer..." He began to speak when his lip pursed and he stopped, perhaps thinking better of it.

Myraia looked at him with obvious compassion and could see immense trouble on his face. "You do not have to say anymore," she said.

"Come now," he said. "Am I some young sapling that my spirit should be dealt with delicately? Come monkess, what do you think?"

She tensed, a bit worried.

"No, I need to tell you. It is good to give you this account."

She sighed silently.

In all reality, he was more than grateful to finally have someone to talk to after all this time alone, especially someone trained for this. It was someone he could share some of his losses with, some of his losses.

His rage against the inexplainable came back, but this time about Juya. Somewhere inside was still the shattering question of how it made sense. But he had no answer other than it was within his grasp, and he'd failed to protect her. There was no escaping that reality and no reconciliation yet, no matter how hard he tried. Only an impending tear, should he let it fall.

He brushed his eyes before the tear formed. What had he possibly done to her? What was she enduring? Perhaps it was best to think forward and narrow his vision. He continued the story.

"I became a prisoner and was sealed in the tombs of Molnak. Zeus must not have believed Teoti would come to my rescue, but he did. Amaras burned a tunnel deep through the underworld of the mountain," he said, mustering pride. "And I escaped." He ended with a barely noticeable smile.

It was silent for a bit. He could tell she was

turning the thoughts over in her head. The King, a prisoner? Amaras burned a hole in the mountain? He escaped?

Eventually, her heart grasped and came to terms. Then words formed from her surprised and stunned expression, "That's... amazing." She started to get excited.

"I know," he replied. "It is something that sounds like a tall tale." He laughed a bit.

She laughed with him and simply meditated on that truth. "That..." She began. "That must mean something..."

He nodded. "It does." He turned to the side, a bit too depreciative of it. "It doesn't bring back the lost, but...it does."

That sparked another question from her. "Were there any other survivors?"

Ryn came out of his own deep thoughts and tilted his head a bit. "I'm sure there were," he said, standing up. "But I don't..." He chose his words carefully. "...Have anything to say on that now."

She stood with him and nodded, recognizing that he was ready to move on from the conversation for reasons that were his own. "Fair enough. What now?"

He looked east. "We go east. You are good?"

She nodded.

"Then let's be off. We've got an army at our backs, and I can tell you more on the way."

She smiled, agreeing to that and they set out.

*   *   *

He'd been traveling for some time. He'd lost his horse a while back. They happened upon it while he was gathering food, and when he returned, he had enough training to know they were waiting for the rider to ambush him. He fled, and he'd not stop running for even a moment. He was alive by the grace of Teoti.

Happening into the rocks of the Ystrafe, he didn't know where he was anymore. He presumed this was the way to go, for all the others had gone this direction. Still, there was no guarantee he'd make it. Keeping his head down, willfully ignorant of his hunger and thirst, he slid between rocks, only hoping he would not be seen.

In his weariness, he repeated his most intense thought to himself that he had had ever since that night he'd fled the Isryn River Valley. This is not my story anymore. I have neither the power...not the power...I am too small. This is not my story anymore.

He asked the Wind what would come of him. How much longer would he be allowed to wander in this state, hungry and covered in rags? His life was a side note, a small script in a book of a thousand parchments. How would it end, and would it be noticed? Whether or not it mattered, he supposed he at least had to see it through.

Stepping over cold stones, he realized the temperature had dropped. Such an uncomfortable way to die; freezing. Mechanically moving, he stumbled once and hit a rock with his chest. Wheezing, he recovered his breath but didn't get up. Should he stop here? He lay there for a moment before a footstep was heard ahead of him. It appeared they had found him. He supposed it was about time for this to end.

"What house are you from?" Came the hoarsely cat-like voice above him.

He worked for an answer that hopefully redeemed his family. "I am only a servant in the house of Traijyn, the house of Crova." Laying his head down, he awaited his execution.

The figure leaned over and set a soft and slightly furry hand on the man's head. It was gentle, not aggressive, yet calculating. "This one's a tracker and a survivor."

The other with him seemed to move slightly and speak in response. "Let's get him healthy. We'll put him to good use."

A brown cat-like face bent down and looked into his eyes. It spoke rather softly. "If we take you to a warm fire and some good food, would you reward us by offering your skills to Traijyn's house?"

The man hesitated, and for a moment, they thought he didn't understand. Then he smiled and began to laugh. It got louder, and perhaps it appeared he was a bit mad, but then again, after what he'd been through, perhaps he was.

"I will. Point me in the direction, and I will go."

The cat-like man smiled. Then he and his companion lifted him up, each carrying a shoulder. "So then tell us, son of man, what is your name? Or should we call you the one who laughs like a madman?"

The man laughed again and hobbled with them. "It's Uruvaphaz...Uruvaphaz."

They carried him between the crags and to a path. As they went, the one on his right praised him. "You are quite skilled to get through this way. Olympian patrols must have been a dash to either your left or right the entire time."

*   *   *

They traveled on through the night and into the next day. He told her all the details of what transpired after the arrival of Amaras. He told her about En Ju Mogon and the king of Molnak. He told her about Arvadia and the En Ar Mujan. As they continued their journey up into the highlands of Crova, she listened intently to everything he said, committing it to memory and marveling at the heroic journey he had undertaken. Sometimes he would take a break, and they would just walk beside each other. Then after a few hours, he would pick back up with the story again. About the end of the next day, he had come to a finish. They had come to the plains of central Crova that divided the north from the south. While in a deciduous forest covered in blue fluorescent vines, they stopped that night to sleep for the first time in days.

Ryn cut a small cave out of a short hill in the woods for them to sleep. Myraia pulled out her parka and took off her jacket. The wool around the edges made for a comfortable pillow. She had two cups in her bag, and they used them to brew an herbal tea for themselves. They sat across from one another, and he finally began to inquire of her.

"You're a daughter of Zanyr, aren't you?" he said.

"How did you know that?"

"I can sense his skill and purity in you. You take after him."

She looked over at him, "Thank you. I admired my father very much."

Ryn settled his bedding and lay to his side so as to recline while he conversed. "He was a good teacher. I worked with him at Alvyn. He always talked about his family. He was despondent over his oldest daughter, though. She died young, tragically, he said, and he missed her dearly. Did you know her?"

Myraia paused shortly and shifted onto her back. Ryn sensed a barrier within her almost go up, but it did not. "My sister Akya. Yes, she was a lot older than me. She was fifty-six, I was twelve, but she cared a lot about me. Her death…affected me greatly."

"I'm sure it would have," He said.

He saw her reluctance to share. He found in her a strange conflict of thought. He supposed he should move on to another topic. He gave it a pause and went on.

"What rank of monkess were you, Myraia?"

She hesitated, still in thought but responded, "I was a third-class *Aiket*. I was also the *Afyrat* at Alvyn. So I was given my share of responsibility and authority."

He could have guessed as much, "Third class, that's awful high for someone so young."

She smirked and looked back at him, "I was older when I got that class than you were when you became a national hero."

Ryn smiled and turned to lie on his back, setting his empty cup down. "So it seems you know a thing or two about me."

She nodded. "Yes, of course. What monk is not instructed in the wisdom of Ryn?"

Ryn scoffed. "Wisdom of Ryn," He laughed.

She glanced over, "You find that odd?"

He shook his head. "Yes, because I know your

teacher was twice my age."

She nodded. "But there is no comparison to Ryn. And after having met him personally, I am actually certain he deserves more praise than what he has received." She looked at the sky outside in silence for a moment while sipping what was left in her cup. "That is my humbly reconciled deduction."

Ryn began to speak but didn't. Staring at the ceiling, he just contemplated that.

Myraia didn't speak but wasn't resting either. Perhaps she was waiting for something. Waiting for him to say something, respond to something, ask something. She didn't feel like talking, but her engagement level was extremely high. She wondered.

"What happened to your family, your husband, your children? Do you have any? Who am I returning you to?" He finally asked.

He heard her hum with intrigue and put down her cup. She pulled the cape over her shoulders and followed his example, laying back to retire.

She didn't respond for a moment. She had nothing to hide. She just didn't know what to think of it. She found his inquiry amusing, was all.

"I am not married," she said with a hint of laughter.

Ryn sat up and looked at her. "I don't believe you."

She looked back, "Are you surprised?"

He looked at her some more before finally realizing that all the signs were apparent. He just had not admitted it yet. He had been choosing to see her spirit of solitude as either detachment or widowhood. Perhaps because the alternative was something far more intense, perhaps even a little intimidating should it come to be what he pondered.

Laying back down, he gazed back at the ceiling, "I am done prodding. You can go to sleep now."

She smirked a little and then snuggled into her coverings, "All right, Kyfka, as you wish." With that, she closed her eyes and began to lose consciousness.

Ryn couldn't make sense of her. She was a very beautiful woman. Perhaps lonesome and independent on the surface, but already he was beginning to see a soft and gentle side come out from her heart. Her body and heart were attractive, pure as glass at that. He wondered how she had not been taken into marriage. He wondered what kind of resistance she would have to have maintained to keep the boys from her. Girls like her, even a fraction of what she was, were noticed quickly. It didn't make sense.

He had to remember that not everything had deep reasoning behind it. Perhaps there was still some trauma connected to her aura of solitude; but then again, perhaps not. Perhaps it was even simpler. He himself had married rather late, and so did Juya. It might have been priorities. Or it may not have been at all anything that he pondered. He had to concede that if there were two oddities in this world, there were likely more. He supposed there were stories of goddesses, some over a thousand years alive, that remained celibate. Of course, there were other reasons for those cases, he was sure. He looked back up at the ceiling before shutting his eyes.

He hadn't been asleep long when he started to see something. He began to see the landscape unfold underneath him. He was headed in the air to Mount Molnak. But he was shocked to see he was headed to the south side, where he'd been imprisoned. What was out there? Was it someone he needed to see? It didn't matter. He felt repulsed by the entrance to the prison. There was no need to revisit it. He denied his dream, and it passed. It changed.

He saw frost, a terribly cold frost, coming over the land. As he did, he passed over village after village of Crovans. Humans and kinsman, slowly frozen in place attempting to flee, only to be torn down helplessly by monsters of Zeus. Children, women, none were spared. He panicked. Why was this happening? Why was there no one to save them? Why?

He did not realize it, but he had been breathing heavily and sweating. Suddenly he awoke when a soft and warm hand was around his left wrist. He jerked and opened his eyes.

"Hey," she said, obviously with concern on her face. "You are having a nightmare. It's not real. What is the point of dreams?" She said it with precision as though she'd been trained what to do for many years.

He felt her question and felt the warmth from her hand. The lovingkindness from it that sought him out to comfort him. He nodded and restored his thoughts.

"We walk into them with confidence monkess, as a chance to reconcile and grow."

She smiled softly. Then she held a compassionate gaze again.

Sensing that the next step would be for her to hold him if he needed it, he recovered. "I am fine. Thank you."

She nodded confidently and returned her hand. As she lay back in her spot, she spoke prayers for him, and he appreciated it. He had to face his dreams, even if they went back to the underworld. He could not spend his time being afraid, even if he feared that terrifying dream, the one where he plunged into darkness. He laid back down and accepted his heart. It quickly took him back to the first dream.

He went to the south side of the mount, but he didn't go to the prison, but into the tent, where he last saw Juya. It was like he was there again, revisiting the scene. He knew there was something outside the tent that he was supposed to see, but his rage at that moment prevented him. He wanted to burst from the tent and tear to pieces everything out there, but the dream didn't let him. Instead, he was suddenly in Alvyn. He saw the Arovyians at the temple. He saw their wives and their children. He saw them sad, at a loss. Eyes darkened enough not to realize the tragedy of the loss, yet real enough to suffer greatly. He wanted to weep.

It was a strange vision. He tried to put it out of his mind and return to normal sleep. But next, he saw En Ju Mogon, the lithy bear-god, a being who'd built a reputation for cruelty and fearsomeness. Yet he was understanding and reasonable and also caring and considerate with the sons and daughters of man. He suddenly worried about him and became regretful he'd tried to kill him. In hindsight, he couldn't believe he'd come within a moment of destroying such a noble being. A being that, by all rights, could become an ally and even a friend.

Then he saw others. He saw the golem, a sad spirit trapped in a life that was like a wakeless dream. Unable to grasp the flesh with all its sensations, passions, and emotions, living but not living. Who was that wandering soul? How honorable that even in second-life, it served a noble purpose in being En Ju Mogon's first line of defense against the underworld. He was saddened he'd attacked it.

Then he saw the young monkess next to him. Myraia. Despite the fact that she was a beautiful monkess and could be an icon of several things for a man who grew up a monk, she was still a fragile sentient being — trying to survive, seeking hope and meaning, striving to reconcile all things in the world. How many had mistaken her innocent life and targeted it for indiscriminate destruction? He felt the tragedy even more.

Surely there were actual enemies? He thought of the Olympians. Zeus, Athena, Ares, Hermes, Artemis. He envisioned them, according to Myraia's account, committing atrocities and slaughter. But his dream turned on him here too. He went back to Mount Molnak and flew over the tent to a road past it, back west. It showed him a figure wandering in a cloak. Forgotten and stepped on. But it was Olympian, and perhaps even a god. He didn't like that. He roused the images of the gods again and all their heinous acts. But it betrayed him again.

It took him to the mountain south of the engagement. There on it was Artemis. Though he'd never seen her with his own eyes, he knew it was her and saw, even in her, a familiar gleam in her eyes. It was the gleam of one uncertain and insecure.

But surely not Artemis, a member of the Olympian pantheon, a daughter of that horrid house of evil; the house of Zeus, the offspring of Samyasa himself. How dreadful. And yet he saw, very briefly, the emptiness of a god. Forever believing they could never be reconciled with The Source, forced into a state of godhood or death. For a brief moment, he felt it, the terrible trembling fear she must shove to the back of her mind when she wakes up in the morning and decides to be a god. He never wanted to feel it again.

The dreams were terrible on his heart, but they were taking him somewhere. War could not be made as it always had. They could not go to war as the Stars had taught them to. Where he had no knowledge before, he now knew. He knew better. No one's enemy is faceless. It is sentient, just as much as him. This was something he knew all along, and yet had never felt before, as though a veil were over his heart.

What did it mean? How was this possible? He didn't have the strength inside to answer all the questions, but he knew it was from the Great Wind, and he knew it was taking him somewhere and where the Great Wind took him, he would follow.

*   *   *

Zeus' iron-studded feet stood atop blades of grass that begged him to move on. Images of the blaze danced in his eyes, and squeals and shrieks filled his ears. A cloud of smoke rose into the night air blocking out the magnificent stars in the night sky. Grinning with satisfaction, he smelt the aroma of the sacrifice, a sacrifice to honor him and his great power. It was finished, now no nation on earth could say they were greater than him. His hand was the mightiest, and the shameless offspring of Traijyn had finally been all but purged. All would know that he was the one to do it. Not Osiris, Not Enki, or even their fathers. It was Zeus. Visions of what would come next swam in his head.

A tall and muscular dunatas approached from the left and bowed reverently. "Ah, you are from the north… what have you?"

The dunatas stood. "The passage in the north that you ordered taken has been taken. And your messenger Lord Hermes, he sends your victory over Crova back to Olympus."

Zeus nodded, "Good. But you have something else to tell me."

The dunatas hesitated. Sighing deeply, he answered, "Yes. Your servants Ares and Artemis have left the northern army. They are returning to celebrate." He nearly trembled at what Zeus might do to him. To his shock, he laughed.

"Ha, ha, ha, ha! Celebrate, eh? Fine. They can do what they want. I have new plans for the northern army anyway."

His mind saw Sumeria in all its' bloated splendor. Enki, claiming to be the oldest, claiming to be the first, always feeling superior. Egypt had risen up centuries back and knocked Enki off his high horse. Now they both lay dormant, always afraid of what the Crovans would do if they sought to expand. But in no time at all, it seemed Enki's pride had come right back. Now there was someone else to fear, a god who would wipe the traitorous infidels who bowed to the Source from the earth and simultaneously demand the respect of all others with the sword. He would be god above all gods.

Walking calmly down the hill, he dismissed the final sacrifice, the last city of Crova. See, he told himself. See what comes of those who do not respect a true god. The Source? What idiots! What deluded half-wits! Summoning the thunders of the sky, he prepared to ride them back to Olympus. If everyone was in the spirit to head back and celebrate, then he could entertain them in his mercy. Why not? It would motivate the people to gear up for the new campaigns to come and show his rivals his strength. A victorious return, a parade, and a holiday.

*　　　*　　　*

The next morning, they picked up and zigzagged through the forests on the plains as much as possible. Occasionally small dispatches of soldiers would appear traveling, and they would avoid moving while they were around. Myraia followed him meticulously and spoke nothing of the night before. Ryn got the idea that she didn't expect anything from it. Her comfort was a gift. He just needed to accept it, and that was all. There were no strings attached. That was good. He appreciated that, even if he felt like he owed her something for what she'd done for him.

Eventually, they arrived at the other side and began a slow descent up the same mountains where Myraia had fought her last battle. They traveled on the west side of the Rystai Mountain Range, where a thick deciduous forest covered the slopes and streams trickled down from the top.

Over a forested rise, she finally asked him, "So what are we doing now?"

He spoke without reluctance, "My commission is to gather allies. I am headed into the Ystrafe because I was told to. From there, the way will be made apparent."

She nodded. The Ystrafe was the right way to go.

"All right then. May I come with you? I am quite skilled."

He paused. He found it distressing suddenly to think she would go somewhere else. And here he was, the night before, asking her where he was returning her. He supposed she might not have anyone to return to. Before he could explore where she'd better serve the effort, his heart told him he couldn't let her go. There was no other option. He gave her a soft smile. "That would be fine. I could use the company. And," he followed. "You kind of are my responsibility."

She grinned.

He turned and continued his purposeful march. They spent the next few alans in silence.

Walking with him, Myraia embarrassingly admitted something to herself. She was falling for Ryn. Oh, this was so unlike her. She had never done this. Ever. She tried to figure out why. Was it because he had dashingly rescued her? Was it because he was the king? She did not know. But one thing was for sure, that ryaj, the purity behind him, was something she found mesmerizing, and she cherished it. What surprised her was her willingness to let him inside so easily. That moment she comforted him in his nightmare. She wanted that forever. Just to be there, to be his...

She took a breath. It had really changed her, and like a chain reaction, there was a hope inside her that was not there before. She hated it and loved it at the same time. What the other ladies bumbled about, that she'd always shook her head at, was absolutely the case. The experience was intoxicating.

But no, how could this man, the king of the

nation, even think of such things at a time like this, especially with someone, like her, a common girl of the people? Besides, King Ryn had notoriously remained wed to a single woman. What could she add when he had his Queen, the glorious Queen Juya.

Suddenly it was like a curtain was pulled back, and she saw for the first time that he was alone. He had no one until her. It was so shocking that she nearly alerted him with her spirit.

Queen Juya! She thought. Where was his queen? Why was she not with him in such a horrid time and during such an important task? How had she not thought of it beforehand? How embarrassing. Was the Queen on an important mission? Was she separated from him by the conflict? Would the King be better served by Myraia seeking her out? Was she...no more? All at once, her curiosity was beaming, and she had to find out.

While traveling over a forested hill high on the slopes of Mount Rystai, she found the right question to ask him. "Ryn," she began curiously. "Why is no one else with you?"

He seemed to balk at that a moment. "It is how it happened. I told you the tale."

She disappointed herself, even with that one. "What I mean to say is...your family, companions, and your loved ones... are they safe?"

Ryn started the pace back up again, looking back briefly with hidden thoughts.

"My children are all in exile. They traveled northeast into Omoka. The rest of my nearest relatives are dead or unheard from. I'm sure you know how Zeus targeted my father's house mercilessly. Many have passed on. Including my father and mother. My father, Amyn, was a peaceful monk, but he did not pass submissively."

He stopped a moment to consider the story. "He died most honorably, and I could not be prouder. A caravan of refugees joined them late on their way north into exile. By that time, Zeus had surrounded the city on the plains. He tried to get the exiles through the mountains, and partially succeeded but lost his life in the process."

"Your father's sacrifice is surely the fruit of a man of great courage and heart." She said respectfully.

He nodded.

Myraia asked on. "What are your children's names? I know the oldest prince is Farankyn, and he is about sixty. Other than that, I do not know of the rest."

Ryn smiled. He was happy to talk about his children. "Farankyn is knowledgeable and a skilled fighter. He is very responsible and would make a good general or leading monk. Yes, he was angered by it, but I sent him north. But he knew why I did it and accepted it. My next is Rysa, she is fifty-two, and she is wise, especially with people. She has great discernment and..." he smiled as he spoke. "You can't look into her eyes and mislead her. She will always be able to tell. She is precious. After her is Aijyn, who is a clever architect, and then there is Syra, a fair and gentle girl. Then Ykaira, she is skilled and agile in combat like her mother."

He gave Myraia a look of perplexity, "I do not know why, and sometimes it concerns me. I think she may be trying to mimic her mother. She is only twenty. Perhaps it is part of her maturing. If Juya and I were not away so often, they would have more direction, but as it is, they've been largely raised by my sister Nysala, who is slow to direct them. Then there is Syryntai, a brave and trustworthy boy, and then Anora. Anora was given a Novan name because there is no Crovan word for 'breaker of wood.' We would say Ykun Ryake, but it's a mouthful and has a distinctly masculine tone. Juya called her that because at the age of five, she split a branch and used it as a weapon to save some of our sheep from a snake. She proceeded to carry that stick around for the next two years." He laughed and smiled as he recounted this.

She laughed with him. She was worried underneath, though. Something told her it wasn't good. But she had to ask. She had to get right to the point. She had to know. "That is most pleasant. And what of the Queen?" She said it with fear for how forward it seemed. But it was the only way. Crovans didn't dance around words. She was being silly. She asked, and he would answer.

Ryn slowed his steps and came to a stop in the path. A heavy sigh came out of his mouth. Ryn felt her begin to assume the worst, so he answered shortly, "She survived the battle at Raijyn…I am unsure of anything else. What I have been told I do not wish to tell, so we will leave it at that."

What Myraia prepared for was sadness. What she felt shocked her. More than sad, she felt excited that he might have room in the future for someone like her. Reeling back from such thoughts, she uncharacteristically beat the emotion down mercilessly, quickly begging forgiveness of the Wind. It was terribly unlike her. In the next few moments, she frantically recovered.

"I am sorry. I will not ask you about it anymore."

Ryn turned to her peacefully, "When the time is right, I will tell you all that I know." He turned back around and continued to walk.

For the moment, Myraia battled what she felt inside with careful thought. He was hiding something, but he was admitting it. What did a monkess do now? He was her king. He said no. That was it. She really didn't deserve to know. Not if she was going to have thoughts like that. But how could she let him keep something unreconciled? Or was it? Was she even pure enough to ask? There was a lot to process before her next word was even spoken.

The two were approaching a brook, and Myraia stopped behind Ryn, so he turned to see what she wanted. "Ryn, I'd like some time alone. If that is acceptable."

He saw inner turmoil. He'd really done it. Not telling her had set her on edge. Who wouldn't be on edge after hearing that? But he couldn't tell her. He didn't even want to think of it himself. And who knew what the consequences could be? Ryn nodded his head and began walking ahead slowly to distance himself from her. Continuing a short way down, he made his way to the brook ahead.

Myraia mentally hovered over her footsteps until she was clear from Ryn. Then as soon as she was far enough away to ensure he could not sense her spiritual turmoil, she relinquished her form. "What is wrong with me!?"

Grunting through her breath, she looked down at her hands as though they had betrayed her. They were still a monkesses hands, right? She was a model of self-control, stillness, a shadow on the wall, and a statue of discipline. That was who she was her whole life. She had figured out who she was and gladly walked it. Everything she got, attention and praise included, she gave to others to enjoy. She had done it so proficiently for so many years that she thought for sure this was done. This discussion and dream were over. It was settled.

Yet dropping her hands, she released thoughts heavenward. "I thought we had this figured out. I thought we had an agreement." She spoke to the Wind near tears. In reality, she had no certainty that this was who she was supposed to be despite how it had affected every decision in her life. This was not a call but a commitment — her choice to be a monkess, her decision never to marry, her moving away from her family, and choosing to be a professional stranger to everyone. But no matter how it came about, in essence, this was Myraia. The woman that came out around Ryn was someone she had never dealt with before. It was as if a comfortable structure that she had built for 70 years was bursting at the seams, and these childhood fantasies were screaming to get out.

Panting and burying her head in her hands, she tried to collect herself. "Reconcile it, Myraia. You are still a monkess. Reconcile it." Only reconciling it meant embracing it. Whimpering and feeling betrayed by the Wind again, she shook her head. "Is that what is going on here? After 70 years of being alone, you will choose now to force me to someone?"

Looking at the ground in front of her, she sighed. "It's certainly an easy one. I expected a less grandiose man to be the one to tear my heart from this lifestyle." But was it even right? I couldn't be. No, it felt right. But she couldn't imagine it. She sighed long and rested against a tree hopelessly.

She had learned so much about him in so little time. It was as though he'd let her see years of his life. She thought about him. The man had been through so much. He had so much on his mind, so much on his shoulders. She at least knew what a lifetime of burdens was like even if she knew nothing of his incredible burdens.

Hanging her head back, she took a deep breath. "Teoti, I cannot do this. I don't know what's happening to me, but you are in control. Help me control this. I have never felt this way before, and it's so insanely sudden I don't even know where it is coming from. Please help me. I don't know how to deal with this." With that, she took another deep breath and settling it in her mind. She turned around and went back to join Ryn.

Ryn had gone a ways ahead of her. He twisted around the last thick tree and was startled at what he saw. An illustrious figure bent over the brook in the middle of the clearing. He stopped as soon as he saw it about ten strides away. He saw that it was a Nephilim, a woman with her back turned. She splashed water over her hair and wrung it out. The figure was very fair-skinned and had brunette hair. She wore a hunting garb with vivid green skins over a vest and a short tunic. Her sandals were laced with silver and weaved up her shins. She had a powerful presence, and the hair on the back of his neck began to rise. In a moment, he was sure it was a goddess. He looked closely at the quiver of arrows on her back and its design and realized quickly who it was.

She finlly noticed, and as quick as lightning turned, drew an arrow, loaded it, and fired it at Ryn endowed with water. At the exact moment she turned,

Ryn reacted and had just enough time to jerk his head out of the way. The woman instantly loaded another arrow as the first wisped by and Ryn, just as quickly, unsheathed the Arvaita holding it out in front.

The goddess eyed him ferociously, and he could see her calculating his strength behind her eyes, which were a splash of blue and green, an iris at least three layers deep. The two stood there, staring each other down. For some reason, Artemis did not fire. She apparently saw an unusual strength in Ryn that she was reluctant to draw into combat.

After some time, she addressed him. "Your tricks are not working very well with me, hooded stranger. If I did not know that you were Crovan, I might suspect you were a god, for I see much power behind you."

Ryn lowered the Arvaita slightly and strafed to his right over to the brook.

She did not follow him with the arrow but disarmed it and watched him with curiosity. Ryn lowered the weapon to his side and finally noticed eyes peering out at them from the forest ahead of them. They were her escorts. They were also likely armed. Would they attack?

She glanced him over again with calculation. "That is an impressive weapon, stranger. Stolen from a god?"

He thought about Myraia. She might return, or they could find her separately. He knew she knew he was Crovan. That might not be good enough to keep her horde from attacking, so he played up the real power of the Arvaita, hoping to intimidate her. "It is a gift, from Teoti himself," Ryn responded.

"Teoti doesn't make weapons." She replied.

"Amaras, the star, personally brought it to me." He countered.

She tilted her head with surprise, then smiled at him. "Amaras; subsidiary to Crovan kings." She almost laughed as she dropped her weapon and held it at her side. "Such ignorance, Ryn! Mistakes like that are a mark of your high concentration of human blood."

Ryn pulled down his hood, slightly disappointed in himself for making such an error. It couldn't be helped. He changed his plans.

She seemed to breathe him in and get a feel for him. "You are very handsome for a Touka, though." She said with a bit of amusement. "You are fortunate. I am finished bathing. I do not like to be walked in on. I might have killed you."

Ryn did not respond but continued to stare at her blankly.

She relaxed slightly and faced him, "You are confident for a Touka." She took a step and looked him over once more. "Your weapon…it makes you confident." She deduced.

"I am confident in the wind behind me," Ryn said.

She lifted her eyelids with apathy. Then she put away her arrow and threw her bow over her shoulder as though she were getting ready to leave.

Ryn spoke directly, "Where are you going, huntress?"

She calmly looked over the forest and spoke half-interested; "I am looking for a good hunt right now. I need to wind down a bit."

She looked at Ryn, and he leaned on the Arvaita as he propped it in the grass. "Funny, I was thinking the same thing, perhaps." He gazed directly at her.

Astonished, she read his spirit more carefully. It was no romantic innuendo. He wasn't that foolish. He was actually saying that he wasn't going to let her leave. How interesting.

Artemis took a strong look at Ryn and tried to gaze deep into his spirit. Surprisingly he let her and was transparent as far as it was prudent. In doing so, he let her see the types of trials that he had endured up to this point. But he also let her see all the power that resided within him. Again, to a point. The great thing about being in the presence of a god was their ability to see through the mymtai through the eyes, but it was unclear enough for them that she only saw what he wanted her to see. It was a great advantage.

Her expression changed. He could see her react with caution. Was she afraid? That was good.

Just then, Myraia came bursting through the clearing and stopped in shock at what she saw.

Artemis looked burningly at the young woman who, at the sight of the goddess, shook.

Myraia quickly caught on to what had transpired and calculated. She did not want to tempt fate by drawing her sword, so she stood shakily and watched what was transpiring.

Artemis looked back at Ryn, "A companion of yours?"

"Yes."

Artemis looked at her and gave her body a scan. Then turned her head back to Ryn, "Far too inferior for you, Ryn. Neither fit for wife or concubine."

That hurt. She didn't expect that. She'd never felt that. It confused her. Myraia quickly threw her gaze at the ground, knowing her eyes would betray her. The gods had such penetrating words too. They could pierce any exterior of thought and confidence. Artemis' insult crushed her spirit as if she had rolled a wagon over her soft heart.

The goddess was amused at first but refrained from laughing as she became mindful of Ryn again.

He did not take his eyes off the goddess, "So what is it, huntress? Are we hunting or parting on terms?"

The goddess looked into the forest at her attendants and back at Ryn. She did not have to think about it. Her mind was already made up.

"I will not report this incident to my father." She yelled back into the forest, "AND NEITHER WILL ANY OF YOU!"

She turned back towards Ryn and met his eyes. "I consider this a favor, Ryn. I could have made leaving this place very difficult for you. I will return at some point and expect one in return."

Ryn smirked, "I acknowledge you, on one condition."

She stooped down and gathered up some clothing, "And what is that?"

"That I am asked to do nothing unrighteous by my terms."

She thought about this agreement and then smiled, "Alright…we have a deal. Besides, my father has…changed his goals. Perhaps I am willing to play a game."

She spoke casually, but Ryn knew she had a wealth of thought brimming behind her smile. That was fine. So did he.

Artemis reached up to her neck and pulled a small golden arrow from her necklace, which was laced with them.

Ryn reached down to his belt and pulled from it a small silver ring, which was surrounded by them.

The two held the trinkets out in front of them, and Myraia watched as their hands glowed brightly with energy. She was enamored by the process. She had yet to witness an exchange of cartouches like this. Of course, she had witnessed them used many times. She even had her own. The cartouche was the basis of rune casting. Most runes needed the emblem engraved into an ovular circle that balanced its power even to begin the creation of the rune. But this was something entirely different.

They both concentrated significantly on the trinkets before satisfaction was reached. Rather confidently, Ryn held his out for her to take and very carefully synchronized his movement to grasp hers at the exact moment she took his. When they were traded, Myraia sighed and released her tension. The cartouches now made Ryn and Artemis accessible to one another. Should one falter on their bargain, that one could be punished through the possession of their cartouche, no matter how far away they were.

Myraia pondered the moment. How powerful Ryn must be to force a deal like this with a goddess of such prestige. Artemis turned and called her companions to follow her. She glanced back only once as she went, a look that showed intrigue. She was interested to see what came of this, and her thoughts were already turning over in her mind. The pale green-colored humanoids came out of the thicket behind her, armed, but in no way showing they were able to protect her from him. In only a few short moments, the group was out of sight.

Ryn carefully bonded the golden arrow to his belt

and sheathed the Arvaita. Myraia stood still, not knowing how to react. Ryn came over to her and grabbed her shoulders, "It will be all right. There is nothing to fear from this." He started to turn but paused and came to face her once more. "And you are a very beautiful woman. Do not be downtrodden by her spiteful remarks." Ryn turned back around and began walking.

Her heart lifted as quickly as it had fallen. Everything Artemis said had become refuse. She started to feel light-headed even. "What in…" She shook herself. That was an odd experience. Catching her breath, she wondered if she would have many more of those.

Once they had gone a ways, she had a moment to reflect. "Ryn, far be it from me to question you, so help me understand why you did what you did. Promising a favor to Artemis, is that not unwise?"

Ryn walked on and spoke to her, "It was either that or start a fight."

Myraia paused and spoke again, "Wouldn't fighting the enemy and killing them be better than bargaining with them? The consequences of her knowledge could be disastrous? And know that I mean no disrespect, I simply wish to understand and felt that you were open to…"

Ryn glanced back and took a breath, "Artemis is very skilled and very powerful in spirit. She would not die even if I killed her. She would simply resurrect in a weaker form."

Myraia sighed a sigh of revelation. She saw what he did now. Even if he killed her, she would come back with a vengeance. Not to mention that their contest would be very noticeable. Zeus would be on them in days.

"Besides, it is likely that her cooperation with us will be beneficial when the time comes. As for the act of righteousness, Artemis knows my fulfillment is predicated on the desires of the Wind. This destines her to think of a way to make the Wind work for her goals, but only her selfish ones. The idea that my aim is Zeus' destruction is not lost on her, and she knows this has to work toward that end. Thus, she will choose a self-serving purpose at the expense of Zeus. So in this way, I have positioned her to fight against her own kin on our behalf."

As he smirked, she had to admit that she was impressed.

"Wow," she said. "That's clever."

He nodded, "And believe me, I know that she is counting on gaining something from me as well. She just doesn't realize the threat I pose. She took the trade at face value. So yes, for that reason, I did it. It was a good trade."

He paused and finally admitted something that had been weighing on him. "And maybe…if I am willing to admit to such a thing…I just felt like avoiding conflict with such a beauty."

She reacted interestedly.

"Do not worry," he qualified. "I will not think twice when encountering any one of the goddesses of Olympia in battle, but for now, I can afford to do what I did to another end. I do not feel wrong about what I did." In truth, the image of his dream and its uncanny prophetic voice had garnered his attention. There was not a way in all heaven and earth he could have slain Artemis after having the dream he'd had the night before. There was no way it wasn't intentional to have that dream, only to meet her the next day. There was a reason.

Myraia settled for his explanation. She understood his desire to avoid striking against beauty. It was a fact of pride that Crovan men still went to great lengths to avoid striking a woman or damaging the land itself, any entity that embodied beauty. She could only respect that desire.

11 CATUMYN

They continued up into the mountains of Ystrafe. The air grew slightly cooler, and snow began to cover the ground. Along the way, they saw fresh camps where Olympian armies had been. Zeus had appeared to call the bulk of his armies off. Instead, the snow and ice that began to cover the slopes proved he was taking a defensive measure — using windscaping to restrict the rebels to the mountains. The evidence of his army was everywhere as roads were caved in, and high places were brought down. Their disregard for the land was disgusting and offensive. But perhaps desensitized to it, he felt his spirit moving on.

Ryn and Myraia navigated the forested folds of the mountains to remain hidden from Olympian patrols.They were well into slopes when Ryn came across a horrifying sight. Perhaps no one had sensed it, but the blood was so loud, there was no way he could not. He came to a place where broken rock was strewn up a slight incline in between trees. He scaled it and looked around a large rock to the right and saw them. There were two bodies. Both Crovan tucked slightly under a stone. They were fighters, men of years. It was apparent from looking at them that one was the son, and the other his father. They'd died together.

Myraia saw what he did and became somber. "I am sorry, Ryn. We had many battles in these mountains, and the Olympians are still about."

Ryn nodded. "We should bury them."

She watched as he dug into the earth, covered them with stones, and then set them on fire from under the ground. It was not a common way to bury the dead, but it was the stealthiest way.

When he was done, he began to feel his anger rising. Just like in his dream of the frozen villages, he found cold corpses on the ground. He sensed his rage coming to the surface. Once again, he had to reconcile it. He focused on what he had left. But that was the thing, what was left? Teoti's mission was left, but what of Crova? What of Nova? Did it really end like this for them?

As he was looking it over, she stepped next to him and looked over the scene. "They died fighting. That is honorable." She bent down and prayed over each of them.

Ryn watched her, and his anger dissipated. Not because he forgot it, but because he reconciled it. In a few moments, he began to see why and he was glad he had taken her upon himself. Good was coming out of this.

They continued to get higher, and the scenery changed from a rocky slope to a cliff-side forest. The mountainside went up at such an angle; it was almost a sheer cliff. All the soil had been washed away by some ancient torrent of the gods or nature. The beige mushroom trees here weren't anchored well and could be pulled away from the rock, so they had to climb carefully, leaping with light feet from perch to perch. Ryn eyed the lands beyond. But at least there was enough foliage to cover them by sight. With the mymtai, that was the only way they could lose their stealth. Eventually, the air grew very cold, and snow was collecting on the rocks and bluish evergreen trees.

After a couple of hours of scaling the slope, they approached the top and took a break to take in the snow-covered highlands. The highlands, usually lush with greenery, were now brown and barren in places. Evidence of warfare left shattered rock and scorched earth. There were deep fishers in the ground that could drop hundreds of cubits. At least they could verify that not another soul seemed to inhabit the place. They didn't linger for long.

A little way in, they spotted movement ahead of them and stopped to see who it was. Ryn was not surprised to see Crovanar come out from the forest of evergreens and down an embankment towards them. Ryn was surprised, however, to see Myraia begin walking calmly towards them. Looking back, she realized that she had left out a valuable piece of information.

"Ryn, the Crovanar and the Novanar, were also at Rystai. They are part of the rebellion."

Astonished, Ryn did not believe her at first. How had he, the king, not known about something like this? A new alliance? One with an estranged and bitter neighbor? Then again, how would he have heard of it? He knew nothing of Rystai or the northern resistance. Not for years. He walked cautiously towards the approaching soldiers attempting to reorganize his spirit towards them.

There were five of them, and he saw the familiar contours in their faces. These tribes had most of their descendency from the mother tribes of Traijyn's wives, Crova and Nova. Their shared national father was Mespoca, and Mespoca was, ironically enough, a son of Traijyn through his first wife and half-sister Ytmakria. The goddess gave him only six children. She left him and took Mespoca to her brother Mokrot after Traijyn flummoxed the other pantheons. She set the boy up to be a rival and vanished herself.

When Traijyn was forced out of Cainan, he had to battle them in this land to settle down. Losing handily, the Crovanar and the Novanar retreated into the Ystrafe wilderness. They did not have good relations with Crova and Nova. Their very names were derived from the relatives they were conquered by, having taken no name of their own because of their mixed heritage. Originally, they had only called each other by their hundreds of different clan names.

The Crovanar were very panther-like in appearance. They had shades of orange or brown short fur over their bodies and had panthers' heads with the exception of their eyes, which were very humanoid. They were lanky and slender but with short paws for hands with opposable thumbs. Their weaponry consisted of triple sided bronze headed spears and small shields.

Novanar were shorter but also lanky. They carried a lot of mass in their upper bodies, however, with long and powerful arms. They had wolf heads with the exception of their eyes as well and varied in fur color from blue to white. They often fought with square and flat bronze swords.

As he looked at them, those distant cousins, he was reminded of the significance of their lineage. The Crovanar and Novanar were the missing part of Traijyn's house. The only offspring of his only missing son, Mespoca, and the large sum of the tribes of his two wives, assimilated together. If one ever considered Crova and Nova together with the Crovanar and Novanar they would call that nation Traijyn. It would be the only way to have a nation called Traijyn. No one had really ever thought long about it. Why would they? The four had been at war for so long. Sometimes, family were more distant than strangers.

The wars they had fought with these two cousin tribes had been costly and tense too. The warriors of both these mountain tribes were more than formidable. They were probably the most contentious nations Crova and Nova had ever fought in terms of skill. The common blood of Traijyn was likely why they were so comparable to Crovans and Novans. Ryn often had to remember that it was Traijyn who simultaneously fought off Enki, Osiris, Onal, and Hakuna in order to demand his right to exist. If these men had that blood in their veins, it meant a lot. Even if they had not owned it, their lineage was surely blessed.

Myraia approached the leading Crovanar and exchanged bows with him. He seemed happy to see her, and they were very happy to see Ryn as well.

The leader bowed to Ryn and then spoke, "Crovan, it is good to have you with us. The more we have, the better. Might we know who you are so we may report to our chief?"

He quickly gauged the air and decided to be upfront. He removed his hood and cloak for them, revealing his identity. They responded with shock, and he heard their short gasps of amazement. Ryn had become used to astonishing people with his presence. "I am Ryn, king of Crova, and I would very much like to speak with chief Revazel. I am sure we have much to discuss."

Myraia looked gleefully back and forth as Ryn introduced himself to Nephilim that months ago could be called enemies.

The soldiers bowed to him, and the leader spoke while looking down, "My king, your authority is as much over us as is our chief's. We will gladly take you to Revazel."

This astonished Ryn further. What amazing friendship and trust had developed between the two nations? Ryn had to find out how this all occurred.

One of the Novanar escorted Ryn and Myraia through the rocky country and evergreen forests. He told them about how they had been at work regrowing the forest with the evergreen and collecting running water so as to survive the cold. Olympia had held them under assault this way far longer than the two had come together. They had also moved all of their settlements and livestock into the mountains and rocks, hollowing out caves and caverns for warmth and security. Still, their provisions had a limit, and eventually, they would run out. He spoke with seriousness, but not without optimism.

With that said, there were three main settlements with several satellite communities surrounding the wilderness. There were more than 20 fortified encampments in the wilderness that protected the hunting and gathering parties. There were somewhere around 150,000 people between the Crovanar, Novanar, and the exiles of Crova and Nova.

Ryn listened intently as the wolf brought them down a path and through another checkpoint. In front of them, at this tall point in the highlands, stood a tall peak separated from the rest of the high hills by a relatively flat evergreen forest surrounding it. As they got closer, Ryn saw a large cave carved into its side and guards at the entrance.

The guards bowed as they entered the cave. A narrow stairway had been carved in the rock, and it sloped downward. Torches on the right and left lit the inside when they got twenty or thirty strides in. The stairs came to a landing at the bottom, and Ryn saw a short hall, about twelve cubits high, stretch back for fifty strides or so. To each side of the hall were hundreds of rooms. In this hall, he saw daily business and social life being carried out. There were a few Crovans and Novans. The vast majority were Crovanar and Novanar. Children were running around, and work was being done stocking and woodworking. They entered the hall and eventually turned left, passing through a series of rooms.

People looked up at them, and a curious crowd began to congregate behind them. They came to a slope that took them up a narrow hallway that seemed to open up in a brightly lit room with furniture lining the walls. The crowd behind them was a mix of all ages and sexes, and they were all curious as to whom the visitors were and where they had come from. Whispering and talking took place right up until they emptied into the bright room, and then it stopped.

There were tables with artifacts and weapons on

them everywhere, and straight in front of them was the largest one with a number of officers standing over a large map.

Ryn recognized Revazel, for he had seen him once before. A trip by Ryn to meet with the man and decipher his opinion on Olympia. That was 30 years ago. Zeus had attempted to secure the two mountain tribes' alliance several times, but Revazel informed Ryn that he was well aware that Zeus would use them and discard them. At the time, Revazel and his Novanar counterpart took a stance of neutrality, and as such, they were left alone by Zeus and his hordes. Perhaps they had learned that with Crova and Nova scattered, their neutrality was not going to be honored.

Revazel was pointing to various places on the map and suggesting actions or improvements to the officers. He was rather heavy-set for a Crovanar and had fuller fur than most. His appearance was soft and docile. But his authority was unquestioned, and his spirit was wise.

The Novanar guide walked up to the table, and the discussion stopped. "Sir, king Ryn has made his way here to see you."

Everyone at the table suddenly turned and looked at the visitors. Revazel looked surprised and started observing Ryn's appearance. Ryn himself gave them no time to decide how to react to him.

"Greetings Revazel. On my way here, I heard wonderful news, tell me that it's true."

Revazel suddenly sprung a wide smile and walked briskly from the table. It took little time to see the men at the table barely containing their excitement and wonder. The crowd behind them began making noises again as word passed from lip to lip.

Revazel stopped in front of Ryn and gazed into his eyes. There was a look of relief on his face, as though he were genuinely plagued by the thought of Crova's King vanquished. He spoke rather fast and anxious. "Yes, our nations have finally come together. I suppose the plague of a common enemy has driven us to cooperate. In the past few months, as the last of your resistance was forced into our territory, we have begun to realize our similarities. Especially in our spiritual traditions."

To say Ryn's curiosity was peaked was an understatement. How their spiritual traditions had helped in reconciling the four nations was intriguing to him. The Crovanar and Novanar, driven back by years of war and socio-political pressure, had always felt jealously indignant of the Crovans and Novans. Such animosity went all the way back to the very rivalry between Traijyn and Mokrot. And their spiritual traditions had been a world apart from one another.

Among those fractured tribes, Mespoca was the one who became their spiritual guide and was the one common figure that united the tribes. It was also he that advised the tribes to reject Traijyn and his spiritual way. He was taught differently by his mother. But that would not keep Traijyn out. His move there was inevitable when chaos developed, and he moved to save the families of his wives. Of course, the Crovanar and Novanar would not forget that conquest and hadn't. It seemed it would be forever.

In the forests of Anytara, Ryn remembered the look of a Crovanar as he gazed at one of his men fifteen years prior. The look was one of terrible anger, yet kept still by genuine fear. Comparing that face to the one before him brought him perplexity mixed with joy. It was hard to believe, but yet, here it was, true before him.

A flood of positive energy embraced the room, and everyone quickly became light and joyous. Through its thick air, Ryn spoke genuinely. "I am honored to now call you, my brother. I have known you to have a good heart from that one encounter alone."

Revazel's face mellowed slightly in question. Then chasing his thoughts away, he leaned forward with a grin. "Despite the furious discussion we had five years ago?"

Ryn had to remember, and soon he did. Somewhat embarrassed, he brought the meeting back. "Yes, I do recall; thank you."

Revazel nodded, "You spoke angrily of our 'complacent revenge' by our decision of inaction. I should say that that decision has been reconsidered."

Ryn thanked him with his eyes. "Your wisdom has guided your people to the right side, for the sake of us all."

"For the sake of us all!" Revazel said confidently.

Then Revazel made a rather unstately move and embraced him. This ambitious and cunning ruler was showing his gentleness, something Ryn had yet to see. The crowd around them suddenly erupted in cheers. The moment was so overwhelming that Myraia's heart paused before grasping it. This warm moment between two kings officially ended centuries of bitter conflict, and it was almost unbelievable.

"The Great Wind?" Ryn asked, releasing him.

"Is the Great Wind," said Revazel. "The same one

from us to you. We now recognize that Teoti is of the Great Wind. And we all see why the Great Wind chose Crova and Nova to be victorious against us." He looked around to some at the table who had mild faces of understanding.

"The Crovanar and Novanar could never have brought the peace and righteousness to this land, or the world, your two nations did. And we were far too diverse and un-united to stand against the powers of the great empires. Your people were strong enough to not only survive them but subdue them and create peace. And in this time of great war, Crova and Nova stood marvelously against Olympia. We cannot help but respect your strength against such oppression. It is your strength that has kept Zeus from obliterating our small nations."

Ryn shook his head, "You flatter us, Revazel."

The Crovanar held his hand up and begged Ryn to hold on before he responded. "During our time in this rugged land, we have been passed through the fire." He said, pacing a bit as he spoke into the air.

"Our peoples were broken, but out of that brokenness came incredible unity and righteousness. We learned to rely not on our own power but that of the Great Wind, in our own way. We have found Teoti faithful, and he has liberated us from our fractured and bickering past. What we lacked now has been built in us through hardship. And now seeing your people in their plight…"

He began to step back toward him with excited tension. "It would be wicked for us to stand idle even if the recognition of that plight has come very late. No, Ryn, there is no revenge to be had anymore." He said, narrowing genuine eyes on his counterpart.

"Because of you, we still exist. You took Zeus' hammer, so we might not have to. "

Standing up tall and proud, he motioned to the men behind him. "We are here at this time to stand with you against Zeus, to join you and fight alongside you. We have been prepared for this hour, and we now recognize our true enemy." He looked down in reflection. "It is time that has allowed us to see how the Great Wind has worked in mysterious ways."

Ryn stood confounded by Revazel. He could never have prepared words for what he was suddenly hearing. But there were good reasons Nephilian kings did not prepare words for meeting one another. When Nephilim took time to prepare, even minutes or hours, they could build their readiness so thick that the mind games, the hidden agendas, and the subtle pleasantries could get them nowhere even after a hundred years. He could only respond to the moment.

"All I have to say is…I am glad. I am glad that Teoti worked all this out for good. And for what it's worth, I'm apologetic for all your people had to endure."

Revazel shook his head and smirked, "Oh no, Ryn. How could I ask that of you? Ask you not to undo everything that has been used us strong again? No, I could do no such thing and ask nothing of you; accept this: allow us to fight with you as brothers and sisters."

Ryn nodded with a nearly astonished grin. "I welcome you. You are like brothers to us. We could hardly do without you in this fight. I believe Traijyn would have wished it so."

The man bowed his head in thoughts of their

ancestral father, whom they'd never really known. Traijyn's house was in Crova and Nova. It was hard to relate to Traijyn, but they were certainly sprung from him. It was Traijyn who had given his allegiance to the Great Wind, and it had been said that in accepting the Great Wind, they accepted their primary father, in the flesh and spirit. Perhaps it was time for them to finally be adopted into Traijyn's house as prodigal sons and daughters.

Revazel smiled at that. "Then let it be so."

He turned to the table. "Come. Join the table."

The crowd was directed back into the hall, and some began to play music, striking up celebrations as the people were joyous. King Ryn was alive and among them. It was a holiday. Many of the men at the table smiled and laughed at the festivities, perhaps wishing they could break for a good drink of wine themselves.

Revazel addressed the table, "To be clear, Ryn has as much authority as I do. This is a joined effort of resistance, and his heroic wisdom and combat prowess are most certainly welcome here." There was no disagreement. He hardly needed to say it.

The generals at the table all nodded their heads, including one Crovan, a middle-aged man named Ydrai. Though three hundred years beyond Ryn, he looked at him in admiration and exchanged a smile with him.

Revazel spoke again, this time to Ryn. "Ryn, tell us what has transpired in Crova. What is Zeus doing? I will warn you," he said with anticipation. "I was given peace while praying in the temple that a plan was being formulated in Crova. We all had no idea what that meant, but now that you have arrived, I am expecting ideas from you."

Ryn smiled. "Something burns in your voice, Revazel. You have much hope in this unseen plan, I see."

Revazel mellowed a bit and nodded in recognition of Ryn's read of him. "I would be lying if I said we are comfortable. Life here becomes harder and harder, and we are realizing slowly that the end is much closer than we wish, should the status quo be maintained."

Ryn nodded with understanding. He could sense the urgency on all of their faces. From what he saw, he had shown up just as they had broken their ymatryai, that is, their confidence and sense of dominion over their destiny and domain. They were prime to be able to move, able to flex without a fight. His arrival had perfect timing.

He eyed them confidently and began to tell them about his journey. He began with the defeat at Raijyn and told them about his angelic visitors and the ordered offensive from Teoti. When he mentioned it, they were awed, and he continued forcing them to listen to it all. He included his encounters with Molnak, Arvadia, and the En Ar Mujan. He also told them about every patrol he had crossed, including the one in Alvyn. They listened intently, hanging on his words until he finished, upon which there was already excitement among many. The tension was building, and they all could feel it.

A younger Crovanar general across the table seemed very happy. "Praise the Great Wind! An offensive!"

Some felt his energy and smiled with him. But others nodded their heads with affirmation while their eyes spoke of their lingering doubts. They had been expecting a plan to come for such a long time with such hope that they were open to it and faithful, but the sheer difficulty and aggressiveness of the plan were offsetting. It was made more daunting by the fact that they felt pressed in from every side as it was, unable to regain a foothold. A counter-offensive of a grand nature was far from their minds. For many, the idea they could even pose a threat was impossible.

One of the older Crovanar generals, Kiazet, carefully expressed his concern, "How are we going to amass enough troops to march on Olympus? Even with our allies with us, Molnak and Rueon are hardly enough."

Rueon was a tribe of winged humanoid Nephilim residing north of Nova. Upon hearing this, Ryn figured that the rebels had gained their allegiance.

Looking over at the man, he responded, "Well, I propose we send out envoys with calls to battle just as I have been doing all this time."

Another general, a Crovan with a long beard, went next. Ryn actually knew this one from days past. His name was Azkian, and he crossed his arms and spoke candidly as though he and Ryn were finishing a war meeting they started ten years prior. "Envoys will compromise our stealth in this attack. We are talking about a massive engagement, a march on Olympus. We cannot simply walk through Olympia and the Arvadian Peninsula undetected, but we need all the advantage we can get."

Ryn responded again and motioned to the table, "Look at the position of Zeus' armies. They are thousands of alans from Olympia. This is the perfect time to attack when the vast majority of his force is abroad. He has just finished a costly campaign that bled him of almost all his soldiers. He has decided not to recall them because they are already far abroad, and he feels confident no one of great strength is poised to invade him. But he will not always think such things. We need to do this before he recalls them. Look," he said, pointing to various points on the board. "There are 80,000 in *Azirat* 300,000 scattered here along Crova's southern border with Sumer. That is most of their force."

He read their pieces and made sense of them according to his own intelligence before his captivity. "Here are these three armies of 50, 70, and 90 thousand in the east along the border with the Kogana. They are far out of range. The northern army is about 50,000, and from the looks of this, is stationed in Cedentir along the Elteran border, perhaps preparing to strike at them along with their ally there. You have no Gullukan units anywhere but along its border with Gonkon. So I presume their role is still to send out units of 100-200 for plunder and intimidation alone. And indeed, my experience in Molnak would validate that."

Heads nodded, agreeing with his assessment. He went back to the table.

These two armies of 30,000 and 70,0000 are still in Crova's inner reaches. This one of 70,000 is certainly war-weary after how we dealt with them at Raijyn. If they are staying out there, it is because Zeus intends to spend them. He will push them south or east for a new campaign. You told me that the reserve presence in Arvadia is non-existent, that there are maybe 10,000 garrisoned or on patrol there. Zeus' concern is Egypt. That is why he still has a quarter-million across the Great Sea in Numera or on

Olympia's southern islands. He cannot recall them and survive Osiris. Only this army…"

He pointed to a woodblock on Nova's western coast. "This has to be Opeleon's army that traveled with Athena. Am I right?"

They nodded.

"This army is surely gathered for an operation in the north. At best, and I am pushing my estimation, it has 150,000. It alone could return for a defensive maneuver and not surrender any of Zeus' borders, and that is assuming it fails to begin its northern campaign when Zeus recalls it. It may yet decrease in strength. But even so, it is still a week out and will be more as it clears the plains to head north. That being said, despite Zeus' enormous army, there can be no more than half a million soldiers in all Olympia able to defend the homeland, and that is an overestimate. With allies, we could approach that number and certainly match that quality as Zeus' army has, as everyone knows, lost a great deal of quality over the course of its campaign against us."

He eyed them intently, grabbing at their hearts. "You see? They are spread too thin; the time is now, and it is not any other time! If we wait for him to finish new campaigns, it will be too late. From Crova and Nova, he earned no surrender and no recruits. That will not be the case when he invades these other lands. He will swallow them and feed his horde just as he has done before."

Azkian rose his eyes respectfully, but questioningly, with confidence, some of them did not have. "Should we do as our hearts are leaping to and march all Traijyn out of these mountains…where will the women and children go with no one here for them?"

Ryn pointed to the map, "This 30,000 you engaged not long ago, where do your scouts say it is now?"

Revazel motioned to a scout off in the corner who stepped forward and gave his report. "They are getting further away still. They are perhaps beyond Rystai by now."

Ryn nodded. "And their northern patrols in Nova? Are they truly garrisoned along the coast in Nasa?"

Revazel responded briskly, "The patrols are non-existent. They garrisoned when Athena returned to Olympia. In the woods, you will find scattered units of Gullukans and Cedentir, but in numbers of non-importance. The plains are as clean as the Kajate River."

Ryn smirked, "So you have a clear path to the north. They can join the rest of the exiles. The move to Omoka has already begun, so it can be finished. I would appoint a certain amount to the task. Rely on our helpful neighbors to the north, the Gonkons, or perhaps the Rueon, for hired protection just as before."

The statement of the obvious shifted the spirit around the table slightly. Still, they were in the face of incredible odds against outstanding numbers, even if they were spread thin.

A Novanar, Rodakan, spoke this time, "Zeus has many allies, what of them? We would need to counter them with our own and avoid alerting them."

Revazel responded this time, "We know our neighbors well enough. Those who have borne great oppression are prime candidates such as Elterer and

Yugon. Strong allies of Olympus are clear to us. And we can name them all; Gulluka , Cedentir , Arovynia, Ogon , Udete , about all of the Arvadian Peninsula, as well as those in truce such as Aromeon, Egypt, Sumer, Akunan, anyone in Cainan…" Revazel continued for minutes until he ended with, "did I miss anyone?" Though slightly dark, the remark was funny, and the table erupted in laughter at his nonchalant approach to their challenge.

Ryn mentioned a few prospects to them, "There is also Baria, Rukeon, and the Karfites. All in Aeoka and all very remote or pressured in one way, or another, by Zeus. And I will mention it once again, but the only reason our numbers migrated to Omoka, to begin with, was with the cooperation of the Gonkons. Do you not think there is a willing accomplice there? Especially as Zeus continues to utilize their chief rivals, the Gullukans, and now seems to be amassing forces for an assault against them?"

The table became silent and thoughtful for a minute. The young general Ailajet, who had traveled and knew the strength of many nations, broke the silence, "An army of those nations, considering they allot us substantial state armies, would probably number two hundred and fifty thousand. Is that enough muscle to overwhelm what is left in Olympia?"

Azkian replied, "Even with his main armies dispersed. He will have recruits from the Arvadian Peninsula and Northern Olympia. Granted, they will be mostly human, but they will probably be able to amass a considerable force. As you said, somewhere around three or four hundred thousand at least."

"But we will encounter them in waves. They are spread out," said Ailajet.

"But, that's not considering possible recruits from Poseidon, Aides, or Olympia's northern autonomous mountain tribes," added Ydrai.

This disturbed the men a little more and their eyes focused on the map. To the men at the table, it looked like Olympia was just too big. It could not be taken down without the help of major rivals like Egypt or Sumer.

Ryn began to trace his finger over territories. "There are more possibilities. There are Wind fearers in Emade and western Sumer. I am thinking of a man the Sumerians call Gilga with an estate in Emade. He is a descendant of Ano himself. It is possible that he may be able to refer allies to us in that region. I would also send someone East of Sumer as Zeus seems to have an eye on that region as well."

Azkian broke in, "That's further out than Zeus' armies. How would we get them to Olympia in time for this assault?"

Ryn spoke again, "If we can acquire the allies I think we can, they will be there on time."

Kiazet questioned, "are we really going to march out in attack when we have no assurance? No formal alliances made?" His words added a dose of reality to the conversation. It let them know they were dealing in conjecture, not assets.

Ryn replied, "what you see as conjecture, the Wind has set aside as assets. This is the moment of truth," he said. "This is the moment of our decision. To fight according to our own means, or grasp the means that are out there, waiting for us to grasp. What you have done until now has brought you to despair. Does a man always fish the same spot of the river because it is the only place he has caught fish? Of course not. So fish with me. Break camp and set out for what else lies ahead in faith of what has been told us."

The table stood stunned. The conversation had been driven into two realities. There was a conversation of faith and one of reason. He had beautifully brought the two together to the same ends.

Revazel spoke with a smooth tone. "The numbers may not be sufficient to our minds. But I know that there is great force in Ryn's continence, and a fierce ryaj coming from his words that speak providence to what he is suggesting."

It was a quiet table. Sensing the right moment, Myraia moved away from the wall and spoke into the crowd, "Ryn's journey is blessed with victory. I have seen this with my own eyes and experienced it in my spirit. There are some gods of Olympus itself that fear the power Teoti has given him."

This greatly surprised the generals at the table, for there was no hesitation when she spoke. They took much greater notice of how much force seemed to be billowing behind him.

Ryn looked over the table of generals; "She speaks truthfully from her heart. Indeed, there are gods who fear what Teoti has bestowed upon me. But I seek to be no *Catumyn* before you, only the knuckle upon the fist of a killer blow set in motion long ago. We will win this battle regardless of numbers. We will devastate Zeus' military. I give you my word it will be done."

All eyes were on Ryn, staring reverently at the fire behind his eyes.

Revazel started again, "I trust my friend here. I am filled with confidence. I was filled last night with peace, and I feel that peace now." He nodded and had a look that the decision was made. "I say we go ahead with this assault. Yes, feeling my heart, I can do no other."

The table looked on the two kings as they locked gazes. Revazel gave Ryn a nod and turned to the map. "My men will travel to the Elterans and Yugonites, for they are north of here. We will also send the young Ezdarmel to Emade. He covers the far reaches of the earth like the sun covers the sky. He will find this Gilga in Emade and ask for assistance. Meanwhile, Ryn, being more discerning and stronger, should go to Aeoka and approach the Barians, Rukeonites, and Karfites. We will meet in Olympia at the coastal city of Asselius in exactly sixteen days. That should give you just enough time to make that round. I imagine your armies will come down the west coast of Olympia. Ours will come over the north around Baku and through Gosilus."

Nodding his head, Ryn agreed, and Revazel officially dismissed the men. The generals anxiously began to leave.

"It will be a spectacular effort," one said.

"We shall return the payment of our suffering," said another.

Ryn stayed and spoke to Revazel while the others disbanded. Myraia was waiting by the wall and was approached by Ydrai. "What is your name, young monkess?"

She tried to refocus herself. It was hard not to think about what Ryn had done, what the Great Wind had done. She was in awe of the incredible things she was witnessing. "My name is Myraia. I was a monkess at Alvyn. I fought at Rystai, do you not remember me?"

The man shifted his eyes in thought, "I might have seen you, but for the most part, you do not strike any memories."

She glanced over at the two kings and then back again, "Ryn found me at Alvyn. He fought through a battalion of Arovynians to get me out. I owe him my life."

The man looked back at Ryn thoughtfully. "Ryn is a great king. Quite possibly the best we have ever been graced with."

"A warrior, monk, and leader all in one," said a Crovan commander named Taimajyn as he smirked and slid out behind Ydrai. He patted the man on the back as he left, and Ydrai nodded and acknowledged him.

The general paused a moment more as he looked at his king. "It is regrettable that his reign has been marred by the loss of our homeland and the sacrifice of so many kinsmen. So many have sacrificed everything for this hope." Shaking his head, he looked back at Myraia and smiled. "I am glad you are still with us. It is not time for you to make the ultimate sacrifice yet."

With that, the man turned and walked down the hall. His thoughts hung in her mind. The last sentence, in particular, discomforted her. She knew what he meant, but she could not help but feel a kinship with his words. It was something few could understand.

She stopped for a moment and listened to what Ryn was saying to Revazel. She saw that Azkian was talking with them now as well.

"Yes, subdue, not annihilate," said Ryn.

Revazel gave Ryn a look of perplexity and almost argued but then stopped as though he'd remembered the incredible authority Ryn had been attributed with little more than a few minutes ago.

Revazel sighed, "You know it will be hard convincing the generals."

Ryn nodded. "Just tell them it's from Ryn."

Azkian shook his head. "I don't understand, Ryn. We all understand mercy. We all appreciate goodness. But...the blood, kyfka, the blood is not like ours, it is theirs."

Ryn nodded his head, "Blood does not control faith and ideas. I have learned through my life, and this experience as well, that people can be united by common faith who have differing blood."

The concept struck Azkian and Revazel as odd, yet, strangely possible. Azkian had a stronger reaction against it, which he controlled marvelously. "The blood means everything, as I have seen and been taught. My apologies for disagreeing, kyfka."

"It's quite all right," said Ryn listening to his rebuttal. "That's what I liked about you, if I recall. Your confidence in disagreeing."

Azkian took the compliment and dutifully expressed the rest of his view.

"The blood means they are breathed differently. They think differently, understand differently, choose differently; they have different values and language...to be entirely descriptive. But it is so much more than that also. Is it not so that Teoti ordains the nations? He sets them up, sees to their fall, by what he has set in motion in the blood?"

Revazel turned to Ryn, "His point is valid. It will be impossible to expect the Olympian people, should you spare them, to become fearers of Teoti and end their oppression of us. It is far less likely to think they can gain freedom from the rule of Zeus."

Ryn nodded his head, "It is true that leaving a single person alive in Olympia only jeopardizes us, and I know this is a new concept, one no army has practiced. And I do think Teoti uses the blood to ordain the rise and fall of peoples. However, men will always be free to choose. And I will say this, Traijyn himself, despite the fierce enmity between his father and Hamel, took for himself Crova and Nova as wives, who were daughters of Hamel, and forged an incredible house with great peace and prosperity."

"And it was not because he asked for them. No. It was because they saw his worship of the Source and chose for themselves to leave their father's house and ask Traijyn to be their husband. They, who are family to you and me, were once separated from Traijyn by blood, yet chose his worship and to unite with him all the same."

He continued, feeling a passion that made sense out of everything he'd been seeing. What he saw at the temple of En Ju Mogon, in Aryn, and even when he met Artemis. There was no way he could back down from this wind. "Not only this, Traijyn spared Hamel's line, and when we invaded these lands, we did not remember such enmity and merely drove you back. As a result, you are here hundreds of years later to become our brothers. In light of that always being a possibility, and because of what the Great wind has taught me, I am prepared to be Teoti's hand of judgment on Olympia, but I will not assume to wipe it out unless I am told."

Azkian shook his head, "What you propose could change the way warfare is done! In fact, I'm not even sure that is war. What nation goes into another and allows it to remain?"

Ryn spoke softly, "A gracious one. One that realizes Teoti may have a purpose still for that people. As I said, if I were told by Teoti to wipe Olympia from the world, I would not hesitate, for his word is supreme and always right. But he has told me no such thing. In fact, he has ordered me to defeat Zeus, not necessarily Olympia. Now it is true we must weaken Olympia significantly to ensure Zeus' weakness, but I am not obliged, nor asked to perform warfare in the traditional manner. Aside from that, I cannot ignore the most urgent conviction in my soul regarding this campaign. Trust me; I would not have asked for it had it not been so important."

Revazel nodded, "I know you know what you're doing, Ryn, so I won't argue. It will be done. We will be tolerant of the people of Olympia. But there are many, mostly of your own, who will be heavy to have their revenge denied. I know your way and that revenge is not your virtue, but reconciliation and the righting of wrongs. So, I will see to it the towns and peoples are left. We will be like fathers disciplining their children, hoping they learn their lesson."

"I understand," said Ryn with a smile. "It is not the way we have done things. It is the way above that. What is it we aim to do? To kill Olympians, or correct a corruption? A high-minded man, a man of the heavens, corrects the corruption. The killing of Olympians is a mere part that may occur in getting there, but only if it is necessary. For they are made for a reason just as we are, and Teoti is a gracious ruler, despite our state of rebellion, sparing us and defending us. Perhaps we can't match his goodness, but the more we are able to do as he does, the better we shall become." Then the two men nodded and ceased their objections.

Ryn spoke to them for a few moments more and then came over to Myraia and motioned to her. "Come, let's get something to eat. Revazel has invited us to visit with him, and I will perform a tasan syntya. Have you heard of it?"

"I've heard of it. But I haven't seen one." She replied as they began to walk.

"It is a coronation, of sorts. When an army goes to war, the king prays a blessing over his leadership, as well as his champions."

She nodded. "That makes sense."

"Revazel has discussed a list of the current leaders and champions. I want to meet them." He had a look of severity on his face but suddenly looked at her casually with a grin. "And after that, I want to get a good night's rest."

She smiled. His confidence and warm smile put her at ease from her cascade of troubling thoughts set on by her talk earlier.

The tasan syntya was not at all what she expected. There were several generals and three champions that came by. Unfortunately, not everyone was able to come. With Ryn leaving the next morning, it was limited to who was there. But of three champions, there were two that stuck out.

The forgettable one was a Novan who was serving as a leader. Not because he was any less noble, he simply did not stick out. One of the ones she remembered vividly was Syjomaryn. A tall man with a handsome face. His weapon was the krykytyr. Ryn had a lot of good to say about him and said that he felt the man had a valuable role to play in the army's engagements. Revazel seemed hesitant on that one, but not because he disagreed. Myraia learned it was because Revazel wanted Ryn to take a guardian with him.

That brought up the subject of the third one, another Crovan champion, Balyr. A dark-haired man a bit younger than Ryn, he was serious and formal. Balyr was said to be one of the most skilled with a dycucyn. In their last battle, he'd claimed forty-seven heads.

Revazel made the case that he was the perfect person for Ryn to take on his journey, and he had, at some times, been a bit stiff and inadaptive for command, so he didn't fill too many roles with the army well. Still, he was lethal in combat and would serve as a valuable protector.

Even listening to that, Ryn was cautious for some reason, and Myraia saw his concern. Revazel asked if it was because of a vision, or his loyalty, or because of his courage. Ryn said it was none of those. He felt Balyr was a Crovan among Crovans. Loyal to the core, and plenty courageous. He simply felt there was someone better.

Myraia remembered Revazel sighing. "I will do my best to find someone more fitting. But there are few as qualified."

Ryn nodded, "I appreciate it, but I am not afraid to go without someone."

Revazel didn't seem to like that but yielded. "It will be good, whatever happens. The Wind will bless us."

That night, Ryn took Myraia with him and spent time talking with fellow countrymen and new brothers and sisters of the Crovanar and Novanar. Ryn was approached by many, including young boys, telling him how eager they were to fight. Ryn encouraged those too young to fight to stay guard over their families and siblings. He talked for a while and began amassing a crowd as he went. Many wanted to hear his stories. Others wanted him to speak wisdom. At one point, he was exhausted and, hiding; he cloaked his presence to fade in among them.

He had been given another option. Revazel would have invited him into exclusive accommodations. But they both knew he'd decline as a temporary guest, no matter his stature. That was the Crovan way. He planned to spend the night just like the least of them.

Myraia was surprised she was not approached by any of the young men. She had perfected the art of deflecting advances over the years. But this time, it seemed they backed away from her. Shortly she realized it was because she came in with Ryn, and as his traveling partner, she was, effectively, his woman, whether it was true or not. She supposed she didn't mind it. It kept down the effort she had to put into distancing herself. Also, should she admit it, she knew she entertained the notion of being Ryn's woman a bit too much for someone of discipline.

When she felt adequately disengaged from the crowd, she spent a lot of time befriending a young Novanar girl. She loved knitting, her friends, and talked about a particular boy she liked. Myraia listened intently, simply enjoying her innocence. Was it possible to return to that? If all the aggression, manipulation, and horrors stopped, it seemed like it was the way life was designed to be.

When they'd gotten away, they went deep into the springs where they could separate and take baths. She felt refreshed by it, even if being wet felt like a nuisance.

Sitting up in his bed, Ryn was wrapping his weapon and placing it beside him right next to the dividing curtain. Myraia peered around the curtain. "Ryn, is it all right for us to talk here?"

Ryn looked around at the two men and three boys lying down around him. They seemed volitionally blocking out their surroundings in favor of a good rest, so he approved.

Myraia came around, dressed in the robe she'd been given, and lay down between him and the curtain, propping her head up under her right arm. Her hair was still moist, but she didn't seem to feel intentional or guilty.

It dawned on him she wasn't aware Crovan women only came before men after their hair had dried. Coming with wet hair sent a signal. One, she surely didn't mean to send if she had any modesty, and she absolutely did, that was obvious. It showed a bit of gender awkwardness he hadn't seen before. She'd probably never been in a situation where it was necessary to be told and had accidentally toyed with a man or two in her life. Of course, that was a bit of an older tradition. After the war had matured, a lot of little cultural symbols like that had faded among the youth.

She fidgeted and took note he was amused by something. That was odd. Had she done something wrong? She got through it and spoke what was on her mind. "You said you taught with my father. When did you teach at Alvyn?"

"Before I was king, I taught on and off at the school in Alvyn and the school in Traijyn, the capital. I taught for thirty-six years until they made me king. Then I had to stop teaching."

"What year was that?"

Ryn thought a second, "It was the eleven hundredth and eighty-fifth year from the rebellion of the stars. I was seventy-seven. You're right. Not that old."

Myraia was intrigued, "oh, that's not my intent. But, that's the same year I started school. How did I not know this? I must have just missed you." She said it with disappointment, as though she had lost a great opportunity.

Ryn smiled. "So if you started that year at about eighteen or twenty, then you are about seventy-eight or eighty now, right?"

"I am seventy-eight," she said.

Ryn sighed and shook his head with a smirk.

"What?" she asked curiously.

"You're just so young to be involved in the things taking place." Before she could bring up his unusually young rise to authority, he chimed in, "I know, I was that old when I became king... and no matter what you could have heard tonight from surely many people, it is not uncommon for you to be unmarried at this age. I wasn't married until I was crowned king. You have to follow the purpose of your life. That is the most important thing."

She was intrigued by that. "Why did you wait so long?"

He hesitated a moment but went ahead. "There

were two main reasons. One was my military and educational involvement. I simply had no time to arrange for a marriage. The second was that for the longest time, I wanted to marry a monkess."

This was the obviously awkward part he was reluctant to tell her. "I had this fixation in my mind. I would marry someone of the same order. The problem was that I was never around monkesses enough." He almost laughed. "It was almost funny. After I became public, I turned down so many offers because I knew what I wanted. When I started teaching, I just expected to find someone amongst the schools. After some time, after watching the only available monkesses go by as students, I broke down and accepted I'd have to find a student. Only the very year I made that decision, the students stopped being available. It was catamyra."

She raised an eyebrow. When one heard that word, they envisioned Teoti's agents of change in this world, causing a series of events that happened to fall in the path of the person experiencing it. Like someone riding into a storm and then turning every way to get out, only the storm had predetermined to go every way the sailor ended up turning. Thus, they were stuck in the storm.

"It wasn't until the last two years of my teaching that I was able to spend adequate time at the temples as well. But in those two years, I didn't meet a single available monkess either, nor did I meet a father with a monkess to allow me courtship. Well, I suppose if I really wanted to, I could have found someone, arranged something. But I was driven with my goals and very confused about the whole thing, and of course, never told anyone why I was actually waiting.

My intent was to keep anyone from using their daughter as a political maneuver. I wanted to find my own companion." There was obviously more, but he did not share it all.

"When the council voted me in as king, I had to get married. So after doing some soul searching, I realized that I had wanted to marry Juya all along. I just never figured it was possible. I only wanted a monkess because that was what I thought was good for me and what I thought I was supposed to do. Marry someone of the order, someone I felt was apt to understand me and synchronize with me best. I never considered Juya, a soldier and a shepherd's daughter, as a prospect. I thought I was supposed to find someone with great schooling like myself. I soon saw that that wasn't the case."

"Juya was out and around as much as I was, and we rarely saw each other. We had been childhood friends, growing up in the same community together. When I was eighteen, and she was thirteen, we parted. I went to study as a monk in Myrokaijyn. As a result, she enlisted in training to be an archer. She always loved combat. She quickly became an accomplished warrior and even fought in the Sumer war." He smirked with remembrance. "It was there that I saved her life, you know."

Myraia interrupted during a brief pause, "I know about that. It launched your popularity when you killed that god."

"Yes, it did. But after the war, I did not see her again for twenty-five years. At this point, I started making trips to talk to her. As I rose in the ranks, and she did as well, we found her intuition and adaptability a great match for my strategy and innovation. We had many 'general to general' strategy meetings, each one seemingly innocent yet deeply involved. We both knew something was there and had become great friends…we just didn't cross that barrier in our minds. It wasn't like there weren't those who wondered. She wondered. Wondered if I'd ever talk about it…" He paused in deep thought, then continued.

"Anyways, when I became king, news of my singleness spread like wildfire. Juya heard the news of my kingship and knew, immediately, that I would be by to propose to her. I did not need to ask her father." Myraia thought that a little funny, knowing a father's permission was important. You couldn't just take a woman as your wife. Who knew if she had consented. He was prompted to explain.

Ryn smiled, recalling the funny memory. "Once, on my trip home to see my father and siblings, Juya's father spoke to me during a social. He said, 'Ryn, it is good to see you have made yourself into a fine gentleman. If you ever want to take Juya as your wife, do not bother with asking me. You have my permission. I would be happy just to see her married."

Myraia laughed a little and gawked at the words of Juya's father.

"I thought it was out of place, too," said Ryn. "At the time, it did not mean much to me. I thought he was just trying to get his daughter married. He did proclaim to many patriarchs that their sons simply need to convince Juya to marry, and he would be happy with it. The problem was convincing Juya to marry. In any case, I did not think it meaningful until the day I was proclaimed king. But when I was, she knew as well as I that I would be making the trip to see her. She and her army were on the southern plains. I ran from Traijyn almost a thousand alans away to meet her."

"She said yes, right?"

Ryn laughed. "Well… kind of."

Myraia looked at him, confused.

Ryn laughed again while reminiscing and continued, "Juya is very strong… a very… unique… woman with great combat skill. She wanted a man to be stronger than her, and the way she had me prove that was…unorthodox."

Myraia urged him on.

"Before I became king, she said that she would force anyone proposing to her to defeat her in hand to hand combat first. No weapons and no elements. I used to make fun of her for it. Little did I know how I would be affected by those words."

Myraia's jaw dropped.

Ryn spoke on. "When I arrived at the camp ten alans from Zanyr, her entire division encircled a space on the plains ready to watch the fight. I moved very fast to the plains, and I was bounding over the countryside. When I came upon the army, I bounded high over the crowd and landed right in the middle. She was right there, all ready to go. And we had a crowd."

Myraia laughed lightly and watched him as he paused. "Well," she finally said, "Did you win?"

Ryn looked over at her with a smirk, "She married me, didn't she?"

The monkess chuckled slightly and stared at the floor between them. The two were silent for a minute. Myraia spoke again, "Wow, what an amazing story."

She thought on it for a moment, and he

commented. "So, that's how it took so long for me to marry."

She responded genuinely. "I would not be ashamed of how long you waited. Things happened the way they did for a reason."

He agreed, "Yes. All circumstances worked to the good. She was the best choice for Crova. A military queen for a people at war constantly." In his mind, though, he suddenly had a second thought. The thought was, if Juya had never been Queen, she would not be where she was right then and there. In that regard, would a non-warrior queen, one that would have stayed out of the battle, been better? For her sake? A warrior queen had ended up captured as gehel. How was that good for the nation?

Draping her head toward the floor, she became a bit humble. "True. I have to admit, I had entertained the idea of how it would have been different if you had met me there. It was so close. But it turned out how it would have anyway."

Her thoughts went to the word of Artemis and to her old ideas. There was a good reason she hadn't been married. It had to be catamyra also. Whatever the case was, she couldn't be right for marriage. "Queen Juya was the right person for us," she finished.

Ryn knew how she was thinking and countered. "That is incorrect. It very well could have been different, and seeing into your growth, I can tell you would have been an excellent partner."

She wondered into his affirmation before it even hit her what he was saying. "You...mean that..."

She said without a filter, or rather, those words

came out without a filter. Very soon, she realized what she had allowed him to see when she spoke. Her heart bled through her words like a leaky dam. Her emotions were suddenly in the air, and everything was chaotic. Quickly she realized she was exposed, almost like feeling naked. She reached up in her heart and controlled that feeling. Everything settled again. But in doing so, she owned it. She admitted what she was feeling. It wasn't going away. It was real. One part of her jolted her, hoping he'd confess the same. The other told her to be prudent.

"Of course," he said genuinely. "You keep talking and acting as though you aren't desirable, but you are. Very much so."

Ryn meant not to lead her on but admittedly allowed a faint semblance of attraction come through his words. He recognized it and regretted it. Or did he? Did he want to distance himself from this woman, or did he not? A sudden wave of unresolved questions tugged at him from both sides. Was this circumstance also destiny? Was it a test? Was she a blessing? What was the purpose of this new companion? Was it his choice to make, and would that choice in any way affect whether or not Juya was returned to him? There were too many serious questions and not nearly enough time to answer them.

Myraia's spirit jumped inside her. Like trying to catch a poured pitcher of water with her fingers, there was no way she could stop it now, not when it felt that good. The affirmation, the hope…never in her life…

When Ryn sensed the condition of her heart, he became still and began looking for a way to wash over the thought prudently. She tried to battle her feelings, but she could not help it. She grabbed her chest with her left hand. She felt her breath soon would become short, and she quickly realized she was actually beginning to swoon at the thought of King Ryn calling her 'desirable.'

Sensing the fragments of that chain reaction, Ryn noted the poor thing was losing it. Pushing his maze of thoughts aggressively back into the cages of his mind, he acted. "Sorry, but…"

She recovered faster than he could speak and was shaken awake from an emotional dream without words or images. Conscious again and ferociously back in control, she wisely decided to call it a night. "Good night Ryn. I'll see you in the morning."

Ryn looked up at her as she rose and nodded with full agreement. She lowered her eyes and turned the corner, then disappeared.

With her gone and the cage rattled, the thoughts re-emerged. Surely, he was confused. Why had Teoti brought this beautiful young monkess into his life now? Was Juya dead? Was she here to comfort him? What? What was her role? Was she going to be his next wife? He liked her enough. She'd already blessed him immensely on his journey. She was nearly everything he thought he wanted before he became king. Honestly, he thought that he had put that fantasy behind him. In reality, he had, but having Myraia here and now just made things awkward. It had the potential to resurrect all of the old desires. What was he supposed to do?

What of his vision of Hades and the doors of death? Was it not to bring back Juya? Ryn felt himself get angry, so he decided to let it go. "Teoti will do as he pleases. I may not understand it, I may be frustrated by it, but I will not turn from my mission."

He went into prayer and after much time had passed Ryn, found peace in letting it subside. There was plenty else to think about, like their itinerary and contingency plan. But at the moment, he needed to rest.

Myraia drifted off as best she could with a feeling of heavy remorse. After hearing that story, her first reaction should have been to be in awe, to respect all of that, and in reality, she certainly did. But again, completely ignoring her very prudent structures of life, she found she had allowed it to come out again like water breaking from a dam. Where did it come from? What was happening to her? These were not normal experiences, were they? Who or what was behind this sudden ryaj? She could not think of it. Shutting down, she begged Teoti for forgiveness that should be asked of Ryn and shuttered off to sleep.

12 THE ROYAL DOCTOR'S DAUGHTER

It was dark, save for the fires of destruction that came through the air. The gods were coming down from the sky, hurling earth at him. He fired back. Myraia was injured. She was there? Not only this but as he carried her off to a cave, he saw Juya taken captive. The gods surrounded her and she was gone.

He debated. Juya was gone, that was clear in the dream. Getting her back was a suicide mission ending in death. Myraia, he could protect as they came. He feared keeping her safe. If he let her out of his sight for a moment or left a flank uncovered, he was certain a sneaky assassin would end her. He tried to grasp it, tried to understand it when he was awaken.

A reverent voice spoke to Ryn out of the darkness of his unconsciousness. Cracking his eyes, he saw a guard he had asked for a wake-up call. The Crovanar waited until Ryn made eye contact, then went out into the hall and back to his post.

Ryn breathed a moment. He thought a long while on Juya, but his heart was too heavy, and entertaining the dream made him feel hopeless. He couldn't consider it. He grunted again, knowing his thoughts were unreconciled, but there was no other way. What would the monkess say, knowing he had this struggle?

He sighed and glanced in the direction of Myraia. Something inside Ryn told him that he was pulling her into something tragic and disastrous. She was too good for this war. And yet, he could not let her go. How did he fight then? How did he go? He didn't know. He thought about her. Why was she here? Who was she? She was gentle of heart, submissive even. She couldn't be here. This was no place for her. As he'd thought the night before, a more lady-like queen would have been better to be removed from combat.

But then again, he had to realize that as a monkess, she would have been sent into combat early on. It was rare not to see the hardness on a person's face, even though the Crovan culture of reconciliation made living well in the midst of war far more palatable. But any signs of war fatigue, coarseness, brokenness, Ryn could not see in her.

This woman did not show it but had likely seen dozens of engagements and been a part of several campaigns already. Perhaps, an unseen purity and resolve kept her innocent somehow amidst all the death and chaos. If that were the case, she was hardly untested…naïve about people? Perhaps. But the real Myraia lay at the center of something, well protected and untainted. How pure was she? If that were true, how could he let her come along. Yet, he did not feel wrong in his heart. Why?

His dream had to have the answer. Her state was

a tragedy. But not for the nation. She was never made queen. Juya's state was a tragedy for the nation. But, Myraia? No, her state affected him.

Myraia woke up and saw a whole different set of women around her, fast asleep. The people seemed to sleep in shifts. She kept as quiet as possible, picking up her things. When she got up and came around the corner of the curtain, Ryn was just finishing his thoughts. "Ryn," she said softly.

He looked up at her and gave his attention.

"I want to acknowledge my regrets to you about what I said last night..." She was tense but spoke calmly and slowly. "I felt my words were careless and undermined the honor of your house." She did not look into his eyes except for occasional glances every few seconds, which she immediately withdrew.

Looking at the floor, Ryn smirked then rose to his feet. From his perspective, this was far more his fault for not being able to keep her at a distance. If Ryn was meant to get Juya back, he was doing a hard thing. It was not uncommon for Crovan men to have two or three wives. Especially after a large-scale war, when the number of men decreased to a severe degree. But after living so many years with Juya alone, it would be hard to suddenly divide himself up between her and someone she'd not known before.

Like two conflicting winds, they seemed to push him against himself. Not knowing the fate of Juya, not being told he'd retrieve her yet having a dream about the gates of Hades, versus suddenly being gifted this talented and gentle beauty to journey with him. The woman was lonely, needing a protector and comforter, something he'd love to offer. It made no sense. Why had Teoti not simply made the path clear so this conflict would not come about? Teoti had not told him to get his wife, and not one of his commands had anything to do with her. Breathing gently, he reminded himself that conflict was not conflict forever and that two winds opposing one another find their way into a dance that moves them around one another.

She waited through a long pause and started speaking again. "If...if you feel that my presence with you is unhelpful or...." He cut her off.

"Myraia... no." Ryn stopped to reorganize his thoughts the way he wanted them. What made things complicated was that she wasn't admitting her desire openly yet, only saying her words were careless.

"I am very appreciative of your company. You are a beautiful and compassionate woman. I have enjoyed your presence. Whatever things you might say that could be offensive are not. You cannot hurt me because you speak so innocently and so honestly. You know it is wise to practice prudent speech, but you will not harm me, and you have done nothing wicked. If you ever do, I will not hesitate to tell you."

Ryn caught her gaze. She looked at the floor for a second in thought and then raised her head, closing her eyes. Breathing a big sigh of relief, she let it go. "All right. Thank you."

Ryn smiled at her and turned his head away. After he had picked up his things and they began leaving, she wore some measure of peace on her face again, and this pleased him.

Passing through the hall, they came to the steps leading outside. On the way up, Myraia saw a silhouette and was certain who it was. Ryn prepared as the figure came down and met him on a landing.

"Ryn," Revazel said as he greeted him. "I trust you slept well. We are sending you with many blessings, but no fanfare, just as you requested."

Ryn nodded. "From here on out, my mission is one of secrecy."

Revazel understood. "Of last night. Did you have a revelation?"

Ryn knew he meant companions. He had none. He knew he needed someone, but he still didn't know if it was Balyr, and the Wind had not spoken anything of it. "I have no new thoughts. Whom would the other two kings select if they were here with you?"

Revazel looked at him genuinely, but not as confident as before. "They would agree with my suggestion from last night."

Myraia watched them. It was almost complex how they spoke non-verbally. It was like Revazel was admitting that Ryn was right but still felt this was the best decision. Ryn, to her surprised, seemed to feel the same.

"Then tell him to fall in with me until I no longer need his service."

Revazel turned and sent a man up to the entrance. "He is waiting at the entrance."

Ryn nodded and turned to the generals that were there, Azkian among them, and looked them in the eye. "Revazel has my authority while I am away from this army. My wind goes with him. Go with the Great Wind."

Revazel prayed a blessing over him. They all saluted him, and he turned to leave.

Once at the top of the stairs, Balyr was waiting. He wore a standard leather vest for a Crovan. His forearms were covered by bracers. His pants were of leather with no tassels. His hair was short and dark, his beard short with nothing under his nose.

"My king," Balyr said, kneeling. "King Revazel informed me I was selected to accompany you."

Ryn acknowledged him. "Stand up, Balyr."

The man stood and expertly seemed to avoid looking anywhere but at his king.

"Remember, our mission is one of secrecy. Shall I fill you in on the details?"

He shook his head, "you should not have to waste your words, kyfka. I will support you."

Ryn nodded. "Very well, let's be off."

As they neared the cave exit, a guard approached and wanted to say something, but Balyr stepped in front. "Do you have something for the king?"

Ryn interjected. "Balyr. It is fine."

Myraia looked at Ryn cautiously. This was going to be interesting. As soon as Balyr had come into his company, it was like Ryn had changed slightly. That was odd. How would he react to this, and why was it so different? Was it because he was being treated like a king, finally? Had Myraia not been doing that?

"King Ryn," the guard said.

"Yes," he responded.

"There is someone outside waiting for you. I do not know much more than that. I was only told to give you this message."

Balyr motioned. "Shall I go see?"

Myraia could tell that Ryn was already getting a bit frustrated. He had clearly become accustomed to handling his own affairs without a subordinate. That further told Myraia she'd been treating him differently.

"No. I will talk to them."

Ryn thanked the man for the information. He began to think oddly of it, though. Weren't there a thousand people here waiting for him? Or was it that by now they had all understood his objective and reverently removed themselves. Of course, so. So how was it that someone up there was still special enough to be 'waiting for him'? In a moment, the three ascended the stairs leading out of the caves.

The wind had picked up from the day before, blowing blankets of snow over the white ground. But this was only so for the open-walled-in flat ground at the cave's entrance. The evergreen forests around them minimized the harshness of the weather everywhere else, especially down the path that descended slowly towards the highland ridges.

Ryn stepped outside into the snow and began looking around to see if anyone was watching for him. There were two Crovanar guards on each side of the entrance and a couple of conversing woodworkers. Two more men, a Crovanar and a Novanar carrying a cut-down tree, passed them and went inside. Finding no one, Ryn scanned the area one more time, and this time saw a figure wrapped in a blue blanket walking slowly towards him. The person had a single leather bag over their right shoulder. The guest also carried a bow. Ryn turned as they approached.

The mystery person stopped a little over a stride in front of Ryn and looked up from the ground through the wisping streams of snow. Seeing her face, Ryn saw that she was a Novan, a very young-looking one at that. She had pale skin and green eyes surrounded by typical Novan features. She had pitch-black hair and a black button nose. Her cheekbones were high, and Ryn could see her doggish ears on top of her head, poking through her hair. She gave off a very vibrant spirit, and Ryn felt the life coming out of her. He thought that she must be some sort of healer or doctor.

"King Ryn," she yelled over the howl of the wind while she showed reverence.

"Yes," he responded. "I heard you were looking for me. Why don't we step just inside so we can talk?"

She nodded and went in after Myraia.

As Ryn turned, Balyr was there. "Kyfka," he said softly. "I know of this one. She has been somewhat of a loaner. And she is Novan."

Ryn gave him a curious look a moment before covering it. "It will be fine. Stay here and wait." Balyn nodded, loyally, and stood attentive outside.

Ryn turned and walked back into the entrance. Stepping inside, he brought his hood down and stood next to Myraia against the wall. The Novan leaned against the other wall in the passage. Balyr waited at the top of the steps and pulled over his cloak because of the chill.

Ryn and Myraia looked at her as she put her hands together and shivered as though she had been in the cold for a long time. As she removed her hood, she revealed her hair, which was braided into hundreds of dreads reaching down to her shoulders. They also saw that she was indeed very young, much younger than Myraia.

"Were you waiting for us outside?" Myraia asked her briskly.

The girl hesitated with a rather innocent-looking expression of thought. "Yes. I stand in the cold to remember ice." She looked up at them and thought they might have no idea what she meant. "Forgive me; combat skills are new to me. I have learned them through the harsh elements. Meditating outside reminds me how to use them."

Ryn stopped her with a gentle expression of the hand, "No need to explain. We understand these things."

She settled it, and a slight measure of nervousness came through her aura. "My name is Jana, daughter of Zomoan," she said a little fast. "I am from Vona and have been serving as a healer in the resistance." Ryn was suddenly more interested than before.

"You're a daughter of the Zomoan. The Royal Doctor of Nova?"

"That's right," she said, happy to hear they were familiar with her father. "I am his third-born daughter, and his apprentice... or... was his apprentice."

Ryn looked over at Myraia. "This is Myraia, daughter of Zanyr from Alvyn. She is accompanying me on my journey."

The two women exchanged greetings.

"The man up there is Balyr, son of Yfarys."

She nodded, "oh, yes. I met him earlier. He kept leering at me, so I had to vanish on him."

That humored Myraia, and she could tell that Ryn was trying not to find it funny.

Jana got serious again and turned back to Ryn. "Last night, I heard from the guards about your mission and the dangers you face. Back when there were many battles, I was put to good use here before a brief hiatus. But now, there is little to do. I am very skilled as a healer and..." She paused, shaking slightly with anxiety. "And a combatant... and I wanted to join you on your journey. It would be a great honor to me."

Quickly a slew of thoughts worked out in Ryn's mind. "I have already declined the offer of several because I am compelled to keep my party light."

She showed no resignation, only hope. Her eyes gleamed, and her heart held fast. Where most would have taken the sentence as a rejection, her heart neatly stepped over it with hope, awaiting a solid answer. Her spirit impressed him so greatly he immediately went back into deliberation. In an instant, he liked this girl. Now he had to decide if it were wise to take her along.

He was already worried about letting Myraia join him, and having another young woman come along such a perilous journey was, at best, reckless. He did have Balyr, but that didn't necessarily mean much. Balyr's intent was to cover Ryn, not the girls.

He thought for a little bit, and Myraia watched with anticipation as he did. "How old are you, Jana?"

She responded eagerly, gazing into their expressions, "I am forty-seven."

Ryn's lips tightened. If it were not for the peace and life coming off of her, he would have seriously doubted her abilities. She was also an apprentice of her father's. This did much to give her credibility.

Jana's eyes flipped back and forth between the gazes of the two Crovans, and she became well aware of their lack of confidence in her. Looking at their expression, she spoke again, "Do not be discouraged by my youth. My father and my brothers trained me well, and if any of them were still alive, I might as well just refer you to them, but since I am the only one left in my father's house, I have only myself to offer."

She realized letting it be known she was the last of

her father's house was not helping her. "But their learning and wisdom are with me. I know I will be an asset to you. I humbly ask that I be allowed to use those gifts for the King's needs."

Ryn's resolve to take her along deteriorated slowly. The only thing that brought it back was his remembrance of the previous night's dream. Like it or not, Myraia was his responsibility now, and he could see himself in that cave with no way to recover Myraia's wounds and no one to look after her so he could pursue Juya. The alternative was to leave them both behind, but he knew by now that Myraia's wind was taking her where he went. That was settled.

But in that light, he became suddenly aware of a need for her. Someone with the resolve to follow through and the meekness to stay behind and nurture or remain safe when asked. She seemed to have no pre-arranged idea of what this should be, and the ryaj she put off, when he paid attention, was very impressive. A healer of that ability greatly boosted the strength of his party. No matter what form or perhaps, "blood" that came in, she fit the role, and he knew it.

"All right," he said. "You may devote your skills to our journey."

Jana hopped slightly with excitement. "Thank you so much. You will not regret this; I know it," she said gleefully with a broad smile.

Ryn smiled at her and moved towards the exit. Putting his hood back on, the two ladies followed behind him. As he was leaving the narrow passage, he turned his head. "No, I do not think that I will. If I had a second thought within me right now, I do not believe I would have let you come."

With that, Ryn turned and walked into the sheets of snow. Jana gave Myraia a smile of excitement and followed him out. Balyr fell in behind them and began looking around intently, as though it were his duty to call out anything suspicious.

Jana passed near Balyr for a moment, and he seemed to deal with her in passing. "You're a healer?" He asked.

She gave him a look, "if I was a healer at Raz Elen, wouldn't I still be one now?"

Realizing he'd been called out for somehow missing that they'd been at a battle together, Balyr turned away and seemed to put his attention back to the forest surroundings.

"Ryn, may I go out ahead and scout?" He asked.

"Please do."

He went out quickly.

Jana gave Ryn a satisfied look, and he looked back as though he had done it on purpose. That almost made her laugh.

Myraia stood for a second and battled down her possessive feelings. The girl innocently assumed nothing. That was good. It wouldn't affect things as long as she could stay under control. She sighed. Ryn was not hers to feel this way towards anyhow, and she needed to remember that. She needed to devote herself to the cause first, and him second. That was paramount. The fact there were two more people now on this journey helped her reel the emotion back in. "This should do it. I'll be fine now," she said to herself. "It will be fine."

EPIC OF RYN

EPIC OF RYN

Glossary of Terms

Alans - An alan is about 1.15 miles or 1.84 kilometers.

Ad Cubit - An Ad cubit is generally 1.35 feet.

Afyrat - The afyrat is a student placed over the other students as a mentor.

Aiket – A designation for students that indicates they are 'catechized' and can be commissioned for service, social or military. There are 4 classes; 4 being highest. Not all classes will be achieved by every student. Even class 1 is considered a 'graduate' designation.

Arajkaf - "Air Palm". A technique sending concentrated gusts of wind from a weapon over a wide area like a sweeping palm, rather than a punching fist.

Arya - Ary (Permanent), -far (earthly, non-divine) Aryfar – a permanent, non-divine substance. Since Arya is "Light" and is seen as permanent, there is a correlation between aryfar and light. In that wind/ryaj may cause something to move, but it is not seen or visible without light. Light, then, is simultaneously the revealer and co-creator of substance with wind.

Aryacynai - "Sword of Light." A technique concentrating all ryaj into raw penetrating power.

Aryfaran - Materialism; the loss of faith in oneself for funtion, and replacing it with the faith in other materials.

Azirat – A mountain in Southern Arovynia

Catumyn - In the acts of God, it is the agent of his first cause in a series of intercessory or revelatory acts.

Comtyr - Basically a steel shaft with a heavy cast-iron rock on the end.

Daicome - Sacred skill taught by a god, for the worship of a god. To use it for oneself was profane.

Dunataso - Mighty men; personal guard; highly trained soldiers of strength, skill, loyalty, and ethics from a school of learning that once sourced all the officers for the Olympian army. Their role was reduced to the personal guard of Zeus and the gods as the long war with Crova changed the values of the army.

Dycucyn - Dycucyns are double-ended Yncucyns

Felycar - A cat with horse characteristics bearing outstanding riding speed (an alan in 16-20 seconds in full stride) and feline agility.

Gehel - The common image of gehel is the rotting head on a pike of a great leader or scores of people. Gehel is anything of the defeated party or nation that is spoiled as a warning not to oppose the victor.

Gullukans – A race of lizard men with smooth green to brown hides standing 5-7 feet tall.

Herkon Fall - The Fall at Herkon was created and is maintained by Herkon's magic, which actually creates a smooth canal falling into the Dark Sea, and another flowing up to the Olympian Sea. The canal, not deep enough for ships, requires the assistance of the god in his water-form to sail up and down; at least safely.

Kyfka – Kyfka is the Crovan word for an earthly ruler or king as opposed to the true ruler, Teoti.

Mayaje Tantajai Yantaj Aya – Darkness Before Him Scatter.

Mina - The Sumerian mina is equal to about 1.25 pounds(0.45kg), or 60 shekels

Ryajakapai/Windscaping - The practice or art of seizing Wind: life-force, energy; and changing its structure. Ryaj/wind is in all things and is the force that creates all life and movement.

Sasyrat - A seminar to teach a particular skill requiring a specific spiritual lesson. Often each lesson is associated with the specific teacher known to advance it.

Semaltars - Among the most beautiful Nephilim. Looking horse-like with glistening fur, sculpted muscles, and flowing hair with the form of a man. They are among the most elitist Nephilim; hateful of inferior humans and disdainful of inferior Nephilim, any chance to "Cleanse" the earth of inferior blood, they take.

Touka - Name given to Nephilim with not enough celestial blood to be called gods. It is typically derogatory.

Tyrakuma - A term used for when it is impossible to enforce the bond between a nation/tenant, and its land.

Uressines - The term 'pig-dragon' would be fitting. The same rule applies to all animal descriptions of the Nephilim.

Yfara - "Things that come from, or are made from, material (non-divine) stuff." This includes money, weapons, clothing, etc.

Yncucyn - 10-12 feet in length; a weapon resembling a couse, lance, or halberd, with a large spade-shaped blade on the end.

Yshalyr - Ishaleer – Unveil; a command to remove a barrier. The same word is used for intellectual enlightenment.

ABOUT THE AUTHOR

Stephen L. Burkhart, MA, graduated from Nazarene Theological Seminary with certifications in Church History and Christian Thought. He is a student of religion and anthropology and has a passion for bringing ancient lessons of the human and divine experience to modern readers and language.

Made in the USA
Monee, IL
25 January 2022